Some other books by Gillian Cross

THE DEMON HEADMASTER
THE PRIME MINISTER'S BRAIN
THE REVENGE OF THE DEMON HEADMASTER
THE DEMON HEADMASTER STRIKES AGAIN

THE GREAT ELEPHANT CHASE
NEW WORLD
ON THE EDGE
PICTURES IN THE DARK
ROSCOE'S LEAP
TWIN AND SUPER-TWIN
WOLF

For older readers

CHARTBREAK

For younger readers

RENT-A-GENIUS
THE ROMAN BEANFEAST

GILLIAN CROSS

THE
DEMON HEADMASTER
TAKES OVER

Illustrated by Maureen Bradley

PUFFIN BOOKS
in association with OXFORD UNIVERSITY PRESS

PUFFIN BOOKS

Published by the Penguin Group
Penguin Books Ltd, 27 Wrights Lane, London W8 5TZ, England
Penguin Putnam Inc., 375 Hudson Street, New York, New York 10014, USA
Penguin Books Australia Ltd, Ringwood, Victoria, Australia
Penguin Books Canada Ltd, 10 Alcorn Avenue, Toronto, Ontario, Canada M4V 3B2
Penguin Books (NZ) Ltd, 182–190 Wairau Road, Auckland 10, New Zealand

Penguin Books Ltd, Registered Offices: Harmondsworth, Middlesex, England

First published by Oxford University Press, 1997
Published in Puffin Books 1998
3 5 7 9 10 8 6 4

Puffin Film and TV Tie-in edition first published 1998

Text copyright © Gillian Cross, 1997
Illustrations copyright © Maureen Bradley, 1997
All rights reserved

Made and printed in England by Clays Ltd, St Ives plc

British Library Cataloguing in Publication Data
A CIP catalogue record for this book is available from the British Library

ISBN 0–141–30024–8

Contents

Chapter 1

Switched on Again

'It's the army!'

'What?' Dinah Hunter blinked and rubbed her eyes. Her younger brother, Harvey, was standing in the doorway. 'Are you mad?' she said. 'It's the middle of the night.'

'But the army's here!' Harvey ran across the room. He was holding a pair of binoculars, and he pushed them at her. 'They're opening up the Research Centre!'

'*What?*' Dinah sat up. 'Don't be silly, Harvey.'

'I'm not being silly. You can see them clearing the doorways. And look at the lights!'

'The lights? You mean they've turned the electricity on?' Dinah grabbed the binoculars and jumped out of bed.

The Research Centre was on the other side of the village, but she could see it over the roofs of the houses. For months it had been closed and sealed up, a dark, silent building gradually disappearing under layers of creeper.

Now the windows were blazing with light. Through the binoculars, Dinah could see vehicles pulled up all round the building. There were shadowy figures too, hacking at the creeper with machetes. One of the figures walked through a spotlight beam and she saw his army uniform.

'What are they up to?' she muttered.

'They're trying to get in,' Harvey whispered. 'Maybe they know—'

He was speaking softly, but not softly enough. Suddenly, their mother shouted up the stairs.

'Harvey? Dinah? Are you *talking*?'

'Sorry, Mum,' Dinah called. 'We're just—'

'I don't care what you're doing.' Mrs Hunter sounded tired. 'Go to sleep. The removal men are coming at half-past eight tomorrow and they'll expect us to be up.'

'That's right.' Their father joined in. 'Whatever you're discussing, it can wait until tomorrow.'

Dinah shrugged and handed the binoculars back to Harvey. 'He's right,' she whispered. 'We can't do anything tonight. Go back to sleep.'

Harvey hesitated for a second, frowning at the Research Centre. Then he padded back to his room. Dinah sighed and climbed back into bed, snuggling under her duvet. In a few moments, she was asleep.

But it wasn't a peaceful sleep . . .

She dreamt she was inside the Research Centre again, standing in front of a huge, humming computer. Lights flashed on the control panels and words flicked on and off the screen, but she hardly noticed them. Her eyes were fixed on the black hole that gaped below the screen like a great, greedy mouth.

Something moved inside the hole. Something long and pale, that scrabbled at the sides, hunting for a place to grip.

A hand.

Its fingers closed round the rim of the hole, clamping tight, and another hand began struggling out of the darkness.

On the screen above, there were bright red letters flashing on the screen.

EVOLUTION ACCELERATOR ACTIVATED
DNA REPRODUCED

The hands tightened, pulling on the edges of the hole, and slowly a head emerged. A man's head, with a stern, pale face and strange, sea-green eyes . . .

'No!' Dinah shouted. 'No!'

The thin lips opened soundlessly, mouthing words that hung in the air. *You are feeling very sleepy* . . .

'No!'

Dinah woke with a jolt. Slowly she sat up and looked across the room.

Now that it was light, she could see the Research Centre even more clearly. The soldiers must have been working all night. Yesterday, its walls had been green with creeper. Now they were half bare.

Sliding out of bed, Dinah went to take a closer look. There was still creeper growing over the top of the building,

and snaking out from inside, but the soldiers had cleared a huge amount. There was a big stack of broken stems in the car park.

As she watched, one of the men picked up a flame-thrower and aimed it at the stack. A jet of fire shot out and the huge green heap shrivelled into a little pile of smoking ash.

One flame. That was all it took.

The scientists at the Research Centre had used all their skill and knowledge to produce that creeper. They had studied the structure of DNA. They'd learnt how to manipulate it. They'd designed a machine that could reproduce the new DNA. *And the army's going to wipe it all out in a single day*, Dinah thought.

She couldn't just stand by and see it all vanish.

Picking up her jeans, she felt in the pockets and found her little notebook. She leafed through the pages, until she came to the name and address she wanted.

Professor Claudia Rowe
Biological Sciences Department
University of Wessex.

Underneath was the telephone number. She hadn't thought she would ever need that, but maybe she did now. The soldiers were destroying the creeper very fast.

'They're doing *what*?' Professor Rowe shrieked down the phone.

Dinah had to shout too. The removal men had arrived, and it was very noisy. 'They've already cut quite a lot.' She stepped out of the way as two men came past with her bed. 'They're burning it.'

4

'But it's unique!' Professor Rowe sounded horrified. 'There's nothing like it, anywhere else in the world. *You* know that, Dinah.'

Dinah knew all right. She knew more than Professor Rowe. She'd been in the lab where the creeper was made —and seen the Evolution Accelerator that had made it. 'But what can I do?' she said.

Professor Rowe was thinking out loud. 'We must get hold of some samples, before it's too late. You'll have to go down there and talk to them, Dinah.'

'Me?'

'There's no one else. I'll set out straight away, but it'll take me at least an hour. You've got to stall them until I get there. Plead. Threaten them with a scandal. Do whatever it takes—but don't let them destroy that creeper!'

'But—'

But we're moving, Dinah was going to say. Professor Rowe didn't give her a chance.

'Once they destroy that creeper, we've lost it for ever!' she said fiercely. 'They're destroying *knowledge*, and knowledge is precious. Go and fight for it, Dinah! I'll be there as soon as I can.'

She rang off, and Dinah put down the phone and took a deep breath. She'd have to go. She hated the sight of the creeper, but Professor Rowe was right. Knowledge was precious.

She called down the hall. 'I'm just going out for a bit.'

'Are you mad?' Lloyd, her other brother, stuck his head out of the kitchen. 'You can't go out now.'

'I've got to,' Dinah said stubbornly. 'I'm going to the Research Centre.'

'To see the army?' Eagerly, Harvey came rattling down the stairs. 'I'll come too!'

Mrs Hunter ran out of her bedroom with an armful of bedding. 'Dinah, you can't—'

'It's important,' Dinah said quietly.

'To go and look at a lot of soldiers?' Lloyd looked scornful. 'You're like a couple of two year olds.'

But Mrs Hunter was watching Dinah's face. 'Really important?' she said.

Dinah nodded.

'All right. You can go. But don't be long.'

'Thanks, Mum.' Dinah snatched up her coat and headed out of the house. Lloyd turned away in disgust, but Harvey was right behind her.

The road outside the Research Centre was crowded with villagers. Three soldiers were stationed at the gate, to keep people away from the building. Dinah looked at them and then wriggled through the crowd to Mrs Pritchett from the Post Office. She always knew what was going on.

'What's up, Mrs Pritchett?'

'They're destroying that creeper,' Mrs Pritchett said. 'About time, too. It'll be all over the village next.'

'It's slowed down,' Harvey said. 'It used to grow much faster than that.'

Mrs Pritchett sniffed. 'That's only the season. If they leave it till next spring, it'll be twice as bad. Got to get rid of it now.'

'There's lots inside the building,' Dinah said. She could see it pressing against the windows. 'Are they going to burn that too?'

6

Mrs Pritchett shrugged. 'Suppose so. But no one's gone in yet. Except one little fellow in a brown anorak.'

'Perhaps he's in charge,' muttered Harvey.

'Him?' Mrs Pritchett looked scornful. 'No, *that's* the commanding officer. The tall man, by the gate.'

That was the man they needed to speak to, then! Dinah grabbed Harvey's arm.

'Come on.'

Harvey went pale. 'But we can't—'

'Yes we can!' Dinah started pulling him towards the tall soldier. 'You can't burn that creeper!' she shouted. 'You're destroying knowledge!'

Back at the Hunters' house, Mrs Hunter was getting impatient.

'Aren't Dinah and Harvey back yet?'

Lloyd was watching the removal men shut the lorry. He turned round and shrugged. 'Not unless they're hiding.'

Mrs Hunter frowned. 'How can they be so thoughtless!'

Mr Hunter put a hand on her shoulder. 'No problem,' he said. 'Lloyd can go and fetch them back. He's not doing anything useful. Off you go, Lloyd!'

Typical! Why was it always him who had to sort things out? Lloyd sighed and set off, grumbling under his breath.

He was half-way through the village when a white sports car came screeching past. It stopped abruptly and the driver jumped out and called back to him.

'How do I get to the Biogenetic Research Centre?' She was a fairly young woman, in jeans, and she looked fierce and anxious.

'Turn left at the top.' Lloyd pointed. 'You can't miss it—'

Before he could finish, she had jumped back into the car and driven off.

What was the big hurry? Why was everyone obsessed with the Research Centre? The place had been shut down for months and nothing was going to happen there.

By the time he reached the Centre himself, the woman was talking to the soldiers. She was waving her hands about and shouting.

'I'm a biologist, Major Pearce! That creeper is unique! It's already given me crucial ideas for the work I'm doing! If you destroy it, you'll be setting scientific development back for years!'

Dinah was there too. Lloyd couldn't hear what she said, but her cheeks were pink and she was nodding fiercely. Harvey was just behind her, looking embarrassed.

Major Pearce was obviously trying to be polite. 'I appreciate your concern, but there's important equipment in that building. It must be rescued before the creeper destroys it.'

'What sort of equipment?' the woman said scornfully.

The major avoided her eyes. 'I'm not at liberty to say.'

Lloyd decided it was time he took Harvey and Dinah away. He went marching up to them. 'Come on, you two. We're leaving. Now!'

'Not yet!' Dinah said impatiently. 'Professor Rowe needs me.'

'Professor who?' Lloyd looked round. He was imagining an old man with a mop of white hair.

It was the young woman from the sports car who answered. She stopped shouting at Major Pearce and held out her hand.

9

'*I'm* Professor Rowe. Call me Claudia.'

'I . . . er . . . hallo.' Lloyd let his hand be shaken. 'I'm Lloyd. Dinah's brother.'

'Come to get her?' Claudia said briskly. 'Well, she won't be long. We just need some samples of this creeper. Come on, Dinah!'

Catching hold of Dinah's hand, she side-stepped neatly round the soldiers and began striding towards the Research Centre.

Harvey looked frantically at Lloyd. 'They'll get shot!'

Major Pearce's hand was already sliding inside his jacket, but it wasn't a gun he pulled out. It was a mobile phone. He tapped in a number, very quickly, and began to talk in a low, urgent voice.

'Mr Smith? Major Pearce here. Sorry to trouble you, sir, but we may have a problem.'

Lloyd couldn't make out the answer, but it sounded irritable. Whoever Mr Smith was, he didn't like being disturbed. His voice went on and on and Major Pearce rolled his eyes up to the sky.

'Intelligence!' he muttered, under his breath.

But his voice was polite when he spoke into the phone.

'Yes, sir, I realize you're doing something important in there. Yes, sir. And confidential. But a professor's turned up. She says we can't torch the creeper because it's unique. And she's on her way into the building.'

There was another burst of irritable words.

Major Pearce sighed. 'Yes, I could have stopped her. But she would have caused a lot of trouble. It's Professor Rowe, sir. From Wessex University. Claudia Rowe.'

There was a silence, and then something that sounded like an order. Major Pearce switched off the phone hastily. Without even glancing at Lloyd and Harvey, he set off after Dinah and Claudia, almost running across the forecourt.

'He's going to arrest them!' Harvey hissed.

But he was wrong. Major Pearce caught up with Claudia and Dinah, said something to them, and led the way towards the doorway the soldiers had cleared. Lloyd watched the three of them disappear inside the building. *Oh great*, he thought crossly. *How am I going to get Dinah now?*

Harvey was watching too. 'Do you think they'll be all right?'

'Of course they'll be all right,' Lloyd snapped. 'Why shouldn't they be?'

'Well, there's . . . there's the Evolution Accelerator,' Harvey mumbled, staring down at his feet. 'You know it can copy people, from their DNA. You don't suppose—?'

Lloyd knew what he was thinking. 'Oh, stop worrying! He's gone. He's never coming back. We all saw him disappear into that hole. The Evolution Accelerator swallowed him up.'

'But what if—?'

'He's *gone*, Harvey.'

Chapter 2

Who Stole Mr Smith?

Dinah shivered as she walked into the Research Centre again. It felt like going back into a dragon's mouth.

But everything had changed. Last time, the place had been bustling with people, all working hard. Now it was empty, and the corridors were full of creeper.

Claudia was staring round in amazement. 'It's like the Sleeping Beauty's palace in here.'

'Maybe that's what's happened to Mr Smith,' Major Pearce said crossly. 'Perhaps he's turned into the Sleeping Beauty.' He punched at the buttons of his mobile phone again. 'Why isn't he answering?'

'He's not far away,' Dinah said. 'Listen.'

Very faintly, from the far end of the long corridor, they heard another mobile phone ringing.

'What's the point of phoning if he's that close?' Claudia said. 'We can go and see him.'

She began to walk down the corridor, stepping over tangles of creeper and brushing aside the strands that hung down from the ceiling. Major Pearce followed her, but he didn't stop dialling. Dinah could see that he wanted to warn Mr Smith that they were coming.

When they were half-way down the corridor, the distant ringing stopped.

'Hang on a minute, Professor,' Major Pearce called. He spoke into the phone. 'Mr Smith?'

His voice echoed down the corridor—and back towards them from the other phone.

Mr Smith?

There was no answer.

Major Pearce hesitated, and then tried again. 'Sir? I'm on my way to the lab with Professor Rowe, from the University of Wessex.'

His unanswered voice echoed forlornly in the silence. *. . . on my way to the lab with Professor Rowe. From the University of Wessex.*

Claudia was starting to get impatient. 'What's going on? Who is this Mr Smith, anyway?'

Major Pearce looked evasive. 'He's . . . well, it's a little delicate . . . I can't exactly spell out—'

'Oh, he's from Intelligence, is he?' Claudia looked scornful. 'They get everywhere.' Her voice rose, irritably. 'It makes me sick the way Intelligence has all the power. It takes over everything!'

She spoke so loudly that the major's phone picked up her voice. Dinah heard the words coming back from the far end of the corridor.

Intelligence has all the power. It takes over everything!

The major glared at her. 'That's nonsense. I'm the one in charge. I'm just wondering what's become of him.'

'Maybe he's been kidnapped by aliens,' Claudia said drily. 'Let's hope there's a security camera. Then we can watch it all on the video.'

The ghost of her voice echoed from the other phone. *We can watch it all on the video.* The major switched off his own phone and pushed it into his pocket.

'All right,' he said. 'Let's go and see.'

He walked briskly down the corridor ahead of them and pushed at the lab door.

'Hallo?'

It took him a few moments to get the door open properly, because there was a thick tangle of creepers behind it. He put his shoulder against the top panel and shoved. Then he waded over the creeper stalks, with Claudia close behind.

As she followed, Dinah glanced up at the ceiling. She spotted the security camera straight away. It was mounted high in one corner, where it would catch the face of everyone who walked into the lab.

It must have filmed her face, last time she was there. And the video had probably not been changed. The past was still there, in pictures.

The idea made her shudder. She stepped further into the lab, feeling as if she'd walked into her dream. She half-expected to hear the Evolution Accelerator humming and clicking, and see that tall, terrible figure facing her across the room. Staring at her with his sea-green eyes . . .

But the lab was empty.

Someone had obviously been there recently, because the creeper that grew across the floor was trampled and bruised, but there was no sign of anyone now. Everything was switched off.

Claudia walked into the middle of the room and stared around. 'There's some pretty strange equipment here. What's *that*, for example?' She nodded at the Evolution Accelerator.

'It's for analysing DNA,' Dinah said. 'And altering it. That's how the creeper was produced.'

'Fascinating!' Claudia's eyes gleamed. 'I suppose the

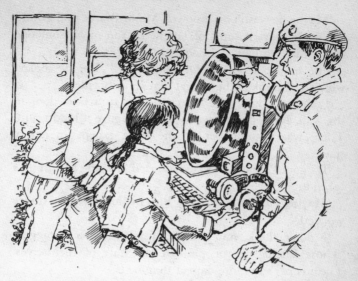

samples went into that hole under the screen.' She walked across and peered into it. Then she glanced sideways. 'What about those headphones?'

'There's some kind of concentrated learning system, I think.' Dinah reached out to pick up the headphones.

'Leave those alone!' the major snapped. 'All this equipment is highly secret.' He looked round the room. 'Is there another way out? What's that door over there?'

'It leads down to the old cellars,' Dinah said. 'And out through the ice house.'

Major Pearce strode across to the door and wrenched it open. The three of them stared at the brick steps that led down into the darkness.

'Mr Smith *could* have gone that way,' Claudia said. 'But why would he bother?'

'Maybe he wasn't on his own,' Major Pearce said grimly.

Claudia gave a snort of laughter. 'You mean someone else got in? With all those soldiers outside?'

The major frowned. 'Of course not!' But he looked worried. 'I think I'd better get that security video.'

Taking out a key, he marched over to a little door in the wall. But when it swung open, he gave a loud grunt. There was nothing behind the door, except an empty space.

'It's gone?' Claudia looked amused. 'Maybe Mr Smith's taken it.'

'Maybe,' the major said. But he looked even more worried.

'I don't think you need to fret.' Claudia shrugged. 'Those Intelligence people can take care of themselves. The creeper's in more danger than he is.'

'Oh yes. The creeper.' The major glanced round absent-mindedly. 'You want to take some samples?'

'Lots,' Claudia said briskly. 'With seed pods if possible.'

'There are some lovely seed pods in the corridor,' said Dinah. 'I'll show you.'

She turned to lead the way and caught her foot in the tangled creeper on the floor. Staggering sideways, she put out a hand to steady herself against the Evolution Accelerator.

It was warm!

Dinah was so startled that she couldn't speak. And before she could collect her thoughts, Major Pearce began to hustle her. He was obviously anxious to get the two of them out of the building.

'Come along. I can't give you very long.'

Claudia was already out in the corridor. With a last backward glance at the Evolution Accelerator, Dinah followed, rubbing her fingers together.

Had she imagined that strange, warm tingle? Or had the Evolution Accelerator been running?

Outside, Lloyd was fuming.

'It's ridiculous! Dinah can't stay in there for ever. We'd better go and get her out!'

'I don't think—' Harvey began timidly.

Lloyd ignored him. Squaring his shoulders, he marched up to the main gate of the Research Centre, as if he were going to walk straight through. But he didn't get very far. The moment he got near, a soldier barred his way.

'Sorry, laddie. It's top secret in there.'

Laddie! Lloyd tried not to look sick. 'I've got to get my sister out. We're leaving here any minute. Moving away.'

The soldier shrugged helplessly. 'Not my fault. I don't make the decisions around here.'

'What's the matter?' Mrs Pritchett called from the other side of the road. She came bustling across to Lloyd. 'Do you need any help, dear?'

Dear! Lloyd forced himself to smile politely. 'We need to get into the Research Centre. To fetch Dinah.'

Mrs Pritchett glared at the soldier. 'Where's the harm in that? You can let the boy in for a moment, can't you?'

'I haven't got the authority,' the soldier said patiently. 'No one except the major or Mr Smith can give permission for people to go in there.'

Lloyd glanced round at the other soldiers. 'OK, then. Which one's Mr Smith? I'll ask him.'

'Oh, he's not in uniform.' The soldier looked amused. 'Wears a sort of shabby brown anorak.'

'The little fellow who went inside earlier on?' Mrs Pritchett said. 'Well, they can't ask him. He drove off about five minutes ago. Though he wasn't fit to be in charge of a car, if you ask me. He looked half asleep.'

'He drove off?' The soldier looked startled. 'But—I thought he was inside.'

'Came out the back way and went off in a car.' Mrs Pritchett looked pleased with herself for knowing more than the army. 'That man who used to run the Research Centre was with him. Seemed to be ordering him about.'

Harvey caught his breath. '*What* man who used to run the Research Centre?'

'*You* know,' Mrs Pritchett said. 'That tall man in dark glasses. I haven't seen him around for a while.'

'He's come back?' Harvey said. He went pale and looked at Lloyd.

'It must have been someone else,' Lloyd said quickly. 'Come on, Harvey. We're not going to get into the building. Mum and Dad will have to come and get Dinah out.'

He pulled Harvey away, before he could start talking nonsense. Keeping hold of his arm, he started marching him down the road.

'But it's *him*,' Harvey whispered. 'You heard what she said. He's come back!'

Lloyd sighed. 'Rubbish!' he said.

Their friend Ingrid said the same thing. Harvey telephoned her when they got back to the house, and she shouted with laughter.

'Come back? That's crazy! We saw him vanish.'

'But the Evolution Accelerator had a record of his DNA—'

'So?' Ingrid was scornful. 'It's been switched off for six months. Forget about him, Harvey. Now you're coming to live round here again, we're going to have *fun*. Mandy's cooked you a Welcome Back cake, and Ian's discovered a fabulous new computer café.'

'Yes, but—'

'Stop butting. When are you getting here?'

Harvey gave up. 'In a couple of hours. We're setting out as soon as Mum and Dad get back with Dinah.'

'Great! I'll be there!' Ingrid said. 'And so will Ian and Mandy. SPLAT for ever!'

'SPLAT for ever!'

Harvey put the phone down and turned round. Lloyd was standing in the kitchen doorway, watching him.

'You see?' he said. 'Ingrid thinks it's rubbish too.'

'But we're still SPLAT,' Harvey muttered. 'The Society for the Protection of Our Lives Against Them. We ought to be ready—'

'There's nothing to be ready *for*!' Lloyd said.

Chapter 3

Michael

They reached the new house an hour later than Harvey had predicted, because their parents hung around at the Research Centre talking to Claudia.

'*Such* a nice woman!' Mrs Hunter said when they came back. 'You'd never think she was a professor!'

'That's right,' Mr Hunter agreed. 'And she and Dinah get on like old friends.'

They went on talking about her most of the way to the new house, until Harvey was wriggling with impatience. He didn't care about Claudia Rowe. He wanted to arrive before Ingrid and the others got bored and went home.

He should have known better. Even though they were an hour late, Ingrid, Mandy, and Ian were sitting in a row on the front garden wall, chatting to the removal men.

'Here we are!' Ingrid shouted cheerfully. 'SPLAT support!'

'We've come to help you with the unpacking,' said Mandy.

Mrs Hunter jumped out of the car and gave them all a hug. 'It's lovely to see you! But you don't have to help.'

'Of course we do!' Ian said. 'It'll be great. Like a party. We'll come every day, until you're straight.'

They were as good as their promise. For three days, they all worked flat out. After three days, Mr Hunter started his new job and had to go off to California, but there was no let-up for the rest of them. They went on for another two days, until everything was unpacked.

And they'd all told so many jokes that Dinah felt weak from laughing.

'I don't think I've ever heard so many silly riddles in my whole life.'

'So?' Ingrid said. She was standing on Dinah's bed, balancing a book on her nose. 'What d'you want? *Solemn* riddles? *Sensible* jokes?'

Dinah grinned. 'No one tells sensible jokes. Not even a computer.'

She was just trying to think what a sensible joke would be like, when the phone rang, and Mrs Hunter called up the stairs.

'Dinah! It's for you!'

Clambering over three piles of books, Dinah ran downstairs and picked up the phone. 'Hallo?'

'Hallo!' said Claudia's voice. 'How's the new house? Got any good creepers growing in the garden?'

Dinah laughed. 'Haven't you got enough creeper?' Claudia had driven off from the Biogenetic Research Centre with her boot crammed full of samples.

'Don't!' Claudia groaned. 'It's making my office into a jungle.'

'Is it any use?'

'Oh yes. That's why I'm phoning. I've made a breakthrough in my research, and I wondered if you'd like to come and take a look. How about tomorrow?'

'Tomorrow?' Dinah hesitated. 'I'd love to, but I don't know if I can come then. We're still unpacking—'

'Rubbish!' said her mother. She was standing right behind Dinah. 'It's that nice Professor Rowe, isn't it? If she's inviting you to visit her, you go. You've done your share of the unpacking.'

Dinah smiled over her shoulder. 'Thanks, Mum.' Then she spoke down the phone. 'Yes, please. I'd love to come tomorrow.'

'I don't know exactly where your house is, but it should only take you about twenty minutes on the bus,' Claudia said. 'Go to the main entrance and ask for my office. About eleven. Bring your brothers too, if they want to come.'

Dinah put the phone down and raced up the stairs.

'Lloyd! Harvey! I'm going to the university tomorrow, to see Claudia! Do you want to come?'

There was a wail and Ingrid came out of the bedroom pulling a face. 'You *can't* go to the university tomorrow! Don't be such a boff, Di. We want to take you to the cybercafé.'

'To the . . . what?' Dinah said.

Mandy stuck her head out of the bathroom. 'The cybercafé. Ian found it. They've got computers and an Internet link and—'

Dinah hesitated. It sounded great, but she did want to go and see Claudia.

'Why can't you do both?' Ian said helpfully. He was coming upstairs with his arms full of coat hangers. 'You can go to the university and meet us for lunch at the café afterwards.'

'Spot on!' Ingrid beamed. 'And we'll all go surfing the Net together. We'll show you how to explore!'

There's more than one way of exploring, Dinah thought, the next morning. She had just got off the bus, and she was walking down the slope, on to the university campus.

22

All round her, people were exploring ideas. Studying different kinds of knowledge, in the different buildings. She read the names of the departments as she passed. English and American Studies. Engineering. Law. Social Sciences.

Beyond them all, at the far end of the campus, was the university library. Dinah's mind spun at the thought of all the knowledge in there, packed into books and magazines and disks.

She was so busy daydreaming that she stumbled into the carved stone outside the next building and fell over. Rubbing her shins, she sat up and read the words on the stone. Artificial Intelligence Unit.

Well, it wasn't a very intelligent place to put a stone! Brushing the grass off her jeans, she scrambled up and looked round for the Biological Sciences building where Claudia worked.

It was opposite. A tall, greenish block with a front wall made entirely of glass. Claudia's room was right at the top and Dinah went up in the lift. That was glass too, and as she went up she stared out at the rest of the campus.

There was a man coming out of the Artificial Intelligence Unit. He was small and thin and he looked oddly out of place. His brown anorak didn't look like something a student or a lecturer would wear. Dinah wondered who he was.

The lift stopped at the top of the building. As the doors slid open, Dinah heard a boy's voice from the room across the corridor. He sounded angry and upset.

'He was horrible! He said, *Curiosity is the curse of the human brain!*'

23

'Oh come *on*, Michael!' That was Claudia. She sounded kind, but disbelieving. 'You must have misunderstood. No scientist would say that. Science is *about* curiosity.'

'He did say it!' The boy's voice was shrill and insistent.

'Well . . . maybe it was a joke.'

'It wasn't a joke!'

Dinah stood outside the door, not quite sure what to do. She didn't want to eavesdrop, but there didn't seem to be any way to avoid it.

On the other side of the door, Claudia made a soothing noise. 'He's under a lot of stress, you know. This Hyperbrain Conference he's planning is very big.'

'I know!' There was a defiant note in the boy's voice. 'He's told me all about it. He *always* tells me about his work. That's why it was so peculiar this morning. Don't you understand?'

He didn't wait for a reply. Flinging the door open, he raced out of the room, pushing Dinah to one side and jumping into the lift. Dinah had a brief glimpse of a

24

round, freckled face with grubby glasses and uncombed hair. Then the lift doors closed and the boy slid out of sight.

Claudia came to the door and called after him. 'Michael! Wait!' But it was no use. She sighed, and beckoned Dinah into the room. 'I'm sorry. That wasn't a very nice welcome.'

'It doesn't matter,' Dinah said. 'But he did sound upset.'

Claudia sighed again and shut the door. 'I wish he'd stayed to meet you. You're just the sort of friend he needs. He finds it hard to get on with most people, because he's so wrapped up in his father's research.'

'His father's a scientist?'

Claudia nodded. 'He's Tim Dexter.'

'The one who wrote that fantastic book about artificial intelligence?' Dinah's mouth dropped open.

'You *are* well-informed!' Claudia said. She smiled. 'Yes, that's him. He's a really nice guy, but he's up to his eyes in work at the moment, organizing a conference about artificial intelligence. I think Michael's feeling neglected.'

'Is it a big conference?'

Claudia nodded. '*Everyone* will be there. That's pretty frightening, because I'm giving the first paper.'

'But you're a biologist,' Dinah said. 'What's that got to do with computer intelligence?'

'Aha! That's what I want to tell you about. Artificial intelligence needs a phenomenal amount of memory, and I've cracked the information storage problem. Using molecular structures.'

'Using . . . what?'

'I'll show you.' Claudia looked pleased with herself. 'I've been working on it for years, but it was your creeper that helped me crack the problem. The DNA structure is really intriguing. Come and look at what I've made.'

She led Dinah across to her desk and handed her a dull, heavy cylinder, about the size of a coffee jar.

'There you are. The world's first Molecular Storage Unit.'

Dinah turned it over in her hands. 'But . . . what's it made of? How does it work?'

'*That's* the interesting part. Take a look at these calculations . . .'

By the time she left Claudia, Dinah's head was buzzing with new ideas. She wouldn't have given Michael another thought, if she hadn't bumped into him again. Literally. He came charging out of the Artificial Intelligence Unit, and ran straight into her.

'Hey!' Dinah said crossly. 'Don't you ever walk? You ought to—'

Then she recognized him. And she remembered what Claudia had said. *You're just the sort of friend he needs.* She stopped glaring and grinned.

'Claudia said your father wrote that book—*Electronic Einstein.*'

Michael blinked and looked at her suspiciously. 'So?'

'So it's brilliant! I've read it twice.'

'It's not bad,' Michael said. 'But his new project's way ahead of that stuff. It's—' He stopped.

'Secret?' Dinah said.

'Oh no. It's just—' Michael shuffled his feet. 'Well . . . people usually get bored when I start talking about it.'

Dinah laughed. 'Not me. I think artificial intelligence is fascinating.'

'Really?'

'Really. I'd like to hear all about your father's research.'

Michael looked at her as if he couldn't believe his luck. His face blossomed into a smile. 'Well, if you're sure—'

That was the moment when Dinah remembered that she'd promised to meet the others for lunch. But she couldn't walk out on Michael. Not when she'd just got him to smile.

'Look,' she said quickly. 'I'm going to the cybercafé. Why don't you come too? Then we'll have lots of time to talk.'

'That would be great, but I'm not sure—'

'Can't we go and ask your father?'

Michael glanced back at the Artificial Intelligence Unit. For a second, Dinah thought he was going to say no. Then he grinned.

'OK. Want to come in and meet him?'

'Of course.'

There was a security lock on the door. Dinah thought they would have to buzz to get in, but Michael tapped the number straight on to the keypad. When he saw Dinah looking surprised, he grinned.

'Dad says I help him so much that I'm part of the department.'

He led the way in. The Unit wasn't very large. A couple of offices opened off each side of the square hallway, and there was another room at the back, opposite the front door. Tim Dexter's office was the first on the right. Michael knocked and pushed the door open.

'Dad?'

'Hi, Mike.' The man at the desk looked up. He had a young, freckled face, very like Michael's, and his denim jacket was covered with badges. He noticed Dinah and smiled at her. 'Are you a friend of Michael's?'

Dinah held out her hand. 'I'm Dinah Hunter. Claudia Rowe's working on some creeper I found.'

'Oh *yes*!' Tim Dexter jumped up. 'Claudia told me all about it. You've done the Hyperbrain a big favour!'

'There's really going to be an international Hyperbrain?' Dinah said.

She couldn't stop herself sounding excited, and Tim Dexter laughed.

'There certainly is. It'll take everyone years to agree, of course, but we're on the way. I wish I had time to tell you all about it.'

Dinah seized her chance. 'Michael's going to tell me. If he can come and have lunch in the cybercafé.'

'Great idea!' Tim Dexter fished in his pocket and pulled out some money. 'There you are, Mike. Have a good time.' He was still smiling when they left the room.

Dinah grinned at Michael. 'He's really nice, isn't he? You'd never think he was such a famous man.'

'He's great,' Michael said. 'He—'

He stopped as someone came in through the front door of the Unit. It was the man in the brown anorak that Dinah had seen before. He looked them up and down, with a strange, cold stare, and then knocked on the blue door opposite Tim Dexter's office.

'Who's that?' Dinah said, as he went inside. 'He doesn't look very nice.'

Michael's smile disappeared. 'He's OK,' he said gruffly. 'It's the other one who's horrible.'

'What other one?'

'The tall one.' Michael scowled at the blue door. 'He turned up a couple of days ago and started bossing everyone round. Tried to tell my dad that he shouldn't let children into the Unit.'

'But I thought your dad was in charge.'

'He is. And he'll sort it out after the conference. When he's not so busy.' Michael pushed the door open and stepped outside. 'Don't let's talk about that. I was going to tell you about the Hyperbrain, wasn't I?'

'Great!' Dinah forgot about the man behind the blue door and they talked about the Hyperbrain, all the way to the cybercafé.

Chapter 4

The Cybercafé

The others had been at the cybercafé for hours. Lloyd thought it was a wonderful discovery.

It sold snacks, like an ordinary café, and there were plenty of tables, where people were simply drinking Coke and eating burgers. But the tables round the walls had computer terminals as well, linked into the Internet. He and Harvey had been watching Ian and Mandy and Ingrid chat to people they'd never met.

/MSG, Ingrid was tapping in. *Hey, Plum and Jelly, say hi to our newbies.*

'Plum and Jelly?' said Harvey.

'Those are their Netspeak names.' Ingrid leaned forward. 'And here's their answer.'

It didn't make sense to Lloyd. *Greetings from the Outdoor Centre. Tell them to try toenail clippings.*

'Try what?' he said.

Ingrid hooted with laughter.

'It's a silly game,' said Mandy. 'They choose something, and we have to guess how many times it appears on the Net.'

Harvey stared. 'Toenail clippings are on the Net?'

'Everything's on,' Ian said. 'But how many times?'

Lloyd hadn't got the faintest idea. 'Six?'

Ingrid grinned and shook her head, but she typed it in. The answer came back almost immediately.

:-D from Plum and Jelly.

'They're laughing at you,' Mandy said. 'I think you've got it totally wrong.'

'Got what wrong?' said a voice behind them.

It was Dinah. She was coming into the café with a boy Lloyd had never seen before. A pale, scruffy boy with glasses. He looked younger than Harvey and Ingrid. And much less fun. Lloyd felt like groaning.

'This is Michael,' Dinah said. 'His dad works at the university.'

Mandy smiled. 'Is he another biologist? Like Claudia Rowe?'

'He's Tim Dexter,' the boy said.

'So?' said Lloyd. 'Are we supposed to have heard of him?'

'He's famous,' Dinah said. She gave Lloyd a look that meant *Don't be mean.* 'He does computer research into artificial intelligence. He's setting up something called the Hyperbrain.'

'The Hyperbrain?' Ingrid gave a hoot of laughter. 'Sounds like science fiction.'

Harvey began strutting around stiffly. 'I. Am. The. Hyper. Brain. I. Will. Ex. Ter. Min. Ate. You.'

'Don't be an idiot!' Mandy said. She smiled at Michael again. 'Where's he building this Hyperbrain? At the university?'

Michael shook his head. 'It's not like that.' His voice was small and squeaky. 'It's going to be all over the world. Dad—'

Now he had started talking, he was speaking at top speed.

'—Dad's worked out a way of linking hundreds of computers, all over the world. And they'll really *think*—like a human brain! It'll be the biggest brain in the world, and—'

31

'Yuck!!' Ingrid pulled a face. 'A monster brain?' She started wobbling around. '*I am the Hyperbrain! I am the Hyperbrain!*'

'So people will be able to talk to it?' Lloyd said. 'And ask it what it thinks?'

Michael nodded.

'Weird!' said Ian. He reached over and pretended to type on the keyboard. '*What do you think about toe-nail clippings?* It's a pretty awkward way to have a conversation.'

'We won't be using keyboards,' Michael said scornfully. 'Or mice. Dad says they're "primitive interfaces". He's designing a completely new way to talk to the Hyperbrain. An advanced interface—'

Ingrid gave a last, enormous jelly-wobble and landed in Mandy's lap. 'It sounds great! When can we come and see it?'

Michael stared at her. 'See what?'

'The Hyperbrain. Can we come tomorrow?'

'You don't understand,' Michael said. 'It'll be years before it's ready.'

'You mean it doesn't exist?' Ingrid was outraged. 'So your dad hasn't really done *anything*?'

'Of course he has!' Michael went red in the face. 'He's done more for artificial intelligence than anyone in *history*! His Hyperbrain conference is going to be *huge*! There's even going to be a programme about it on *television*!'

'OK, OK.' Lloyd patted him on the shoulder. 'Don't blow a fuse.'

'You don't have to take any notice of Gerbil-Brain,' said Harvey.

32

'Gerbil-Brain?' shrieked Ingrid. 'What do you mean, Custard-Face?' She launched herself at Harvey and he dodged away between the tables.

'Oh no!' Mandy said. 'They'll get us thrown out!' She jumped up too, and ran after them.

Michael stared. He looked completely bewildered. Hadn't he ever heard of fun? Lloyd began to feel sorry for him.

'He's really lonely,' Dinah said. 'Can't we ask him round, Mum?'

She and her mother were in the garden, unpegging the washing. Mrs Hunter smiled at her round the side of a sheet.

'Of course we can. What about his parents? Should we ask them as well?'

'I think his dad's too busy at the moment. And his mum's in Australia, on a lecture tour.'

Mrs Hunter frowned. 'So who looks after him?'

'There's a person called Mrs Barnes. She's a house-keeper or something, but she doesn't sound much fun.'

'Poor little soul! Why don't you ask him round? We can have a barbecue and invite the others as well.'

'That's great!' Dinah beamed. 'Can it be next week? His father's got a big conference on Wednesday, and Michael can tell us all about it.'

Mrs Hunter smiled again. 'I don't see why not. You'll enjoy that—and the others can always talk about something else.'

'You never know,' Dinah said. 'They might even talk about the conference, if they watch it on television first.'

It looked as if she could be right. When she went back into the sitting room on Wednesday evening, to turn on the television, Lloyd and Harvey both trailed in after her.

'Are they going to show everything that happened at the conference?' Lloyd said.

Dinah shook her head. 'That would take hours. It's just highlights. The opening speeches and stuff like that.' She picked up the television magazine and flipped through. 'Oh bother, it's started already.'

She turned on, and they found themselves looking at a hall full of people.

'Bor*ing*!' Harvey said. 'Can't we watch the football instead?'

'Sssh!' Dinah said impatiently. 'Look, there's Claudia in the audience. I wonder why she looks so fed up? And there's—'

It was the man in the brown anorak. The man she had seen in the Artificial Intelligence Unit. But, before she could point him out to the others, the picture changed and she leaned forward excitedly. 'Look! That's Michael's dad up on the stage.'

Tim Dexter was standing at a lectern, making a speech.

'. . . never been a conference like this before . . . if we can agree to pool our computer resources . . .'

Harvey pulled a face. 'Sounds dull.'

'Of course it's not dull!' Dinah said impatiently. 'He's talking about the Hyperbrain. Listen!'

Harvey pulled another face, but Lloyd sat down and started watching.

'Lay off, Harvey. I want to hear what's going on.'

Tim Dexter seemed to be announcing some change of plan. '. . . a slight alteration to our programme . . . We shall not now be hearing from Claudia Rowe about her development of Molecular Storage Units.'

'What?' Dinah said. 'But Claudia's spent *months* writing that speech! No wonder she looks annoyed. She—'

35

'Sssh!' said Lloyd. He was trying to work out what was going on. The people in the audience were all turning to look at each other, and there was a buzz of whispering.

'They're surprised too,' Harvey said. He sat down on the other side of Dinah.

Michael's father was still talking. '. . . instead, we have a completely unexpected speaker, who has some exciting new developments in technology to tell us about. He—'

They couldn't hear the next words, because the screen started to fizz noisily and the picture dissolved into chaos.

Lloyd grabbed the remote control and flicked through the other channels, until he got a picture again. He switched back to the conference and they saw Tim Dexter, beaming and holding out his hand.

'I'm very proud to introduce him. Here he is!'

They had a brief, blurred glimpse of a tall figure walking on to the stage and then the picture disintegrated completely, into a pattern of tingling dots.

A moment later, letters spread themselves across the screen.

WE APOLOGIZE FOR THE LOSS OF SOUND AND PICTURES. THIS IS DUE TO CIRCUMSTANCES BEYOND OUR CONTROL.

'Oh, *brilliant*!' Harvey said. 'Why waste time talking about a Hyperbrain? They can't even invent televisions that don't break down.'

Dinah was still staring at the screen. Lloyd waved his hand in front of her face.

'Hey, square eyes, there's nothing on.'

'What?' She blinked and turned round. 'I was just thinking. It's pretty odd to change a conference speaker at the last moment. Especially at such an important conference. There were all sorts of people there—from universities and newspapers and all the media—everyone. And Claudia can't have been ill. I saw her.'

'So why didn't she give her lecture?' said Harvey.

'I don't know, but I bet she was furious. I'm going to see her again next week. I'll ask her what happened.'

'I wonder who they had instead of her,' said Lloyd. 'He must be pretty important. It's a pity the television broke down before we saw him properly.'

Chapter 5

A Shock for Dinah

There was nothing about the Hyperbrain Conference in the next day's newspaper, either. In fact, there was nothing all the week. When Dinah set off for her second visit to Claudia, she was looking forward to hearing what had happened. She jumped off the bus the moment it arrived at the university, and ran down the slope on to the campus.

She was running too fast for her own good. If she hadn't had very quick reactions, she would probably have landed up in hospital. A white van came roaring along the road at the bottom of the slope, so fast that she only just pulled herself out of the way in time.

'Crazy!' she muttered.

The van swung left, driving round to the back of the Artificial Intelligence Unit. For a second, Dinah glimpsed a green emblem painted on its side. She was peering after it, trying to make out what the emblem was, when her attention was distracted by a group of students coming through the front door of the Unit.

There was something bizarre about them. Individually, they looked like ordinary students, in jeans and trainers and baggy jumpers—but they were all wearing the same kind of jeans and trainers, and their jumpers were exactly the same shape. It was as if they were wearing a uniform.

They went past Dinah without even looking at her, and she was still glancing back at them when she reached the Biological Sciences building. As she went up in the lift, she could see them marching through the campus, side by side, without speaking to each other.

Then the lift reached the top, and she forgot all about them. The thought of finding out about the conference was much more interesting. Running out of the lift, she knocked on the door of Claudia's office.

There was no answer.

Dinah frowned and looked at her watch. She wasn't early. And Claudia had sounded really keen for them to meet again. *Come and hear all about the conference*, she'd said. *I'll enjoy telling you.* She couldn't just have forgotten. Not even if she was upset about having her speech dropped from the conference programme.

Dinah waited two or three minutes and knocked again, more loudly. This time, footsteps came across the room. The door opened and Claudia looked out at her.

'Hallo!' Dinah smiled brightly. 'How was the conference? I couldn't watch—'

Her voice died away. Claudia wasn't smiling back. She was looking at her as if she were a stranger.

'You did . . . remember I was coming?' Dinah said nervously.

'Of course I remembered.' Claudia's voice was cold and distant. 'But I'm busy.' She began to turn away.

Dinah couldn't believe her ears. 'But you asked me to come! You said you'd tell me about the conference.'

Claudia turned back. She was wearing an odd little badge on her blouse and it caught the light for a moment, making Dinah blink. 'What happened at the conference is none of your business,' she said. 'It is confidential scientific information.'

Dinah stared. 'But I thought scientists shared their knowledge. I thought that was the point of conferences.'

'Knowledge is too precious to waste on ordinary people,' Claudia said stiffly.

It didn't make sense. How could she be saying things like that? Dinah was bewildered. 'I don't want you to tell me anything secret. But I can't help being curious—'

She didn't get any further. The moment she said *curious*, Claudia's eyes glazed over. 'Curiosity is the curse of the human brain,' she said.

'What?' Dinah couldn't believe her ears. 'But that's what Michael's father said. And you told Michael no scientist would say it!'

Claudia didn't answer. She stood perfectly still, staring at Dinah. Waiting for her to go away.

It was like a nightmare. Dinah saw herself reflected in Claudia's dull, glassy eyes. Two tiny Dinahs. Puzzled and miserable. She edged away, and the little green badge on Claudia's blouse caught her reflection as well, like a third eye.

Three tiny, miserable Dinahs.

For a moment, the two of them stood facing each other, without a word. Then the phone started to ring inside Claudia's office. She turned away to answer it and Dinah hurried into the lift. The noise of the telephone echoed down the stairwell, repeating like the word that hammered in her brain: *Why? . . . Why? Why? . . . Why?*

Before the lift reached the ground, the ringing had stopped. As she pushed the front door open, Dinah heard someone calling.

'Dinah!'

It was Claudia. Glancing over her shoulder, Dinah saw her face staring down from the top floor.

'Dinah! Come back!' she shouted.

For a second, Dinah thought, *It's all right! It was all a mistake.*

Then she saw Claudia's face. It still wasn't smiling. She was leaning over the banisters and peering down with the same glazed expression as before. And when she called again, there was an odd, shrill note in her voice.

'Dinah! Wait!'

I can't, Dinah thought. *I can't.*

She ran outside and dodged away round the side of the building. Looking back nervously over her shoulder, she saw the empty lift swoop up to the top floor again. Claudia stepped into it and reached out to press a button. Still looking behind her, Dinah bumped hard into someone coming the other way.

It was Michael.

'You're getting like me,' he said cheerfully. Then he saw her face. 'What's up?'

'I—' Dinah took a deep breath. 'I've just been to see Claudia. And she was horrible.'

'*Claudia?*'

Dinah nodded miserably. 'She wasn't like herself. She—'

Claudia's voice called again, from just round the corner. 'Dinah! Where are you?'

It was even shriller than before. Dinah grabbed Michael's arm.

'I can't talk to her!' she hissed. 'I know it's silly, but . . . I can't. Where can I hide?'

Michael didn't waste time arguing. 'Come into the AIU,' he whispered. Running down the path, he punched in the security code and pushed the door open. 'We can go to Dad's office.'

But they had hardly stepped inside the building when Tim Dexter appeared. He looked much the same as he had the last time Dinah visited the Unit—the same untidy clothes, covered in badges—but this time he was obviously not pleased to see her.

'What are you doing here?' he said coldly.

Michael looked startled. 'We've just come in to see you. I was going to show Dinah—'

'This isn't a place for visitors.'

'But, Dad—'

'I'll see you at home, Michael. When I've finished work.'

Michael's mouth dropped open. Dinah could see that he was completely amazed.

'It's OK,' she said quickly. 'We can go somewhere else. Come on, Michael.'

Tim Dexter looked as if he meant to stand watching them until they left. But the phone began to ring in his

42

office. He gave them a last glance and said briskly, 'Off you go.' Then he turned and went back inside.

Miserably, Dinah pushed the front door open. 'Why is everyone suddenly being horrible?' she said.

Michael fired up. 'Dad's not horrible!'

'Oh, I'm sorry!' Dinah suddenly realized how her words must have sounded. 'I didn't mean—'

But Michael wouldn't let her finish. 'Dad's *not* horrible,' he said again. 'It's *him*. He's the one who's done it!' He glared at the blue door opposite his father's office as he followed Dinah out of the building.

Dinah looked back at it—and saw that there was a notice on it. She was sure it hadn't been there last time.

Controller, it said.

She frowned. 'If your dad's in charge—what's that?'

Michael's lips pinched together. 'It happened after the conference. *He* took over.' He nodded towards the door.

'He? You mean the man in the brown anorak?'

'Of course not,' Michael said scornfully. 'Brown Anorak just runs the errands. It's the other one who's taken over.'

A small, cold shiver ran down Dinah's back. A lot of odd things had happened that day. She found herself remembering the warm feel of the Evolution Accelerator under her fingers. She'd never mentioned it to the others, in case they laughed at her, but suddenly it seemed horribly threatening.

She took a deep breath. 'This other man. Is he—?'

But she didn't get any further. Michael suddenly grabbed at her sleeve.

'Look out! There's Claudia!'

Back at the Hunters' house, Lloyd was telephoning Ian.

Or, rather, he was *trying* to telephone Ian. The first three times he dialled, nothing happened at all. The fourth time, he got through, but the line was so bad that he could hardly make out a word.

'Is that you, Ian?'

'Hzzz there? I czzzz harzzz oossssh.'

'Ian! It's Lloyd!'

'Czzzzzzz hooosssh wozzzzoooza.'

'Can you hear me?'

Mrs Hunter put her head over the banisters and called down to him.

'Is that wretched phone still bad? I tried to phone Dinah's friend earlier on. The boy at the university. I was trying to tell him what time to come for the barbecue, but I don't suppose he understood a word.'

'I'm not surprised.' Lloyd looked at the phone in disgust. It was making noises like a storm at sea now. 'I can't even tell if this *is* Ian.' He gave up and put the receiver down.

'It's a nuisance,' Mrs Hunter said. 'You'll just have to go round to see Ian and Mandy and Ingrid. Tell them to be here at half-past six.'

Lloyd pulled a face, but he could see that she was right. 'Come on, Harvey. We'll go to Ian's first. Maybe we can phone the others from there.'

'Tell them not to bring anything,' Mrs Hunter said. 'This is a thank you barbecue, because they've helped us so much. And tell Ingrid I'll make her some really hot chilli sauce.'

44

Harvey groaned. 'Death By Chilli?'

'Is that what she calls it?' Mrs Hunter laughed. 'I don't know how she can eat the stuff, but she adores it, doesn't she? I must go and find the recipe.'

She rattled downstairs and disappeared into the kitchen. Lloyd picked up the phone for one last attempt at getting through to Ian. This time there wasn't even a dialling tone. Only a noise like aliens twittering to each other. He slammed it down and opened the front door.

'Come on then, Harvey. Let's spread the news the Stone Age way. I'll race you to Ian's.'

Chapter 6

The Green Hand

'Claudia's coming!' Michael said again.

She must have been to the bus stop, because she was coming back down the slope again. Dinah looked round wildly.

'What am I going to do?'

'Hide round at the back of the Unit.' Michael pointed. 'I'll come and tell you when she's gone.'

Dinah ran down the side of the AIU building and crouched behind a clump of bushes. From there, she could see Michael's back. And although she couldn't see Claudia, she could hear her voice clearly.

'Michael!' Claudia was calling. 'Have you seen Dinah?'

'Dinah?' Michael's voice was vague. Dinah could tell that he was playing for time. 'Do you mean—'

'I mean Dinah Hunter,' Claudia said impatiently. 'I must find Dinah Hunter.'

'Oh, *Dinah*.' Michael hesitated. 'No, I haven't really—'

Peering out of the bushes, Dinah saw him shifting from foot to foot. *Claudia's never going to believe him*, she thought. *She's going to guess—*

But it didn't happen, because, just at that moment Tim Dexter came hurrying out of the AIU.

'Michael!' he said briskly. 'Where's that friend of yours? The one you brought in just now?'

Dinah felt herself grow icy-cold. Was he looking for her as well? What was going on?

Whatever it was, it made Michael pull himself together. 'You mean Dinah? She's on her way home,' he said firmly. 'She was really upset about something.'

There was a funny little noise from Claudia, but she didn't say anything. Peering out, Dinah saw her march off to the Biological Sciences building and into the lift.

Tim Dexter sighed with impatience. 'Bring that girl to see me as soon as you can,' he said. Then he turned and went back to his office as well.

Michael walked slowly down the side of the AIU building, looking puzzled and unhappy.

'That was *weird*,' he whispered as he reached Dinah. 'Why does everyone want to talk to you all of a sudden?'

Dinah shrugged. 'Maybe it's something to do with the creeper. And those Molecular Storage things.'

'I suppose so,' Michael said doubtfully.

'Perhaps I'll phone Claudia when I get home. Before the barbecue.'

'Oh . . . the barbecue.' Michael's face cleared, as though he'd suddenly remembered something. 'That's why I came to look for you in the first place. What time shall I come?'

'Didn't Mum tell you? I thought she was going to phone this afternoon.'

Michael nodded. 'I think she did. Someone phoned anyway, but the line was so bad I couldn't understand a word.'

'Never mind. You can come back with me. It won't matter if we're early. We can go now, if the coast is clear.'

47

'I'll go and see.' Cautiously, Michael walked back to the corner of the building and peered round. Glancing back at Dinah, he started to beckon her—and then stopped, suddenly.

'What's the matter?' Dinah hissed. 'Is Claudia coming back?'

Michael shook his head. 'Nothing like that,' he muttered. 'It's just—' He was staring up the campus towards the huge university library. 'There's something peculiar happening. Come and look.'

By five o'clock, Lloyd and Harvey were setting up the barbecue. They'd just assembled it when their mother came out of the kitchen.

'My barbecue book wasn't in that box, was it?'

Lloyd picked the box up and shook it. Nothing fell out except an old paper cup.

Mrs Hunter frowned. 'I can't find my chilli sauce recipe.'

'So?' Lloyd said. 'Make something else.'

'But I promised Ingrid. And she really loves it. I can't find a recipe anywhere.'

'No problem,' Lloyd said. 'There's bound to be a barbecue book in that little library round the corner. Harvey can go down and find a recipe there.'

'Me?' Harvey looked indignant. 'Why can't you go?'

'I've got to light the barbecue, and Mum's making the salads. It has to be you.'

'But I don't know where—'

'Don't be so useless. It's the little building on the corner of Orchard Street.'

48

'It'll be shut,' Harvey said obstinately.

Mrs Hunter grinned. 'No it won't. It's open every afternoon until seven o'clock. I looked the other day. Go on, Harvey, there's a dear.'

Harvey went off, grumbling under his breath, and Mrs Hunter hurried back into the kitchen. *Thank goodness for that*, Lloyd thought. Now he could concentrate on lighting the barbecue without Harvey twittering round and telling him he was doing it all wrong.

He dragged the sack of charcoal out of the garage and filled the barbecue. Then he spent ten minutes hunting for the firelighters.

He'd only just found them when Harvey arrived back. He was red-faced and indignant.

'I told you! I said it would be shut! All that way for nothing!'

Lloyd frowned. 'But Mum said it was open every afternoon.'

'Not any more.' Harvey collapsed on to one of the patio chairs. 'It looks as if it's shut for good.'

'What are you talking about?' Lloyd forgot the barbecue and sat down too. 'Libraries don't just *shut*.'

'That one has. There's a big sign stuck on the front door. *Closed until further notice, owing to cuts*.'

'But there would be posters,' Lloyd said scornfully. 'People get up petitions about things like that. They make a terrible fuss.'

'It's shut,' Harvey said. 'There are men taking the books away in vans.'

Lloyd shook his head. 'That's very odd.'

'What's odd?' said a voice.

Lloyd looked round. Dinah and Michael were coming through the back door, and Dinah had caught his last few words.

She's going to be furious, Lloyd thought. Dinah read more library books than all of them put together. Wherever they'd lived before, she'd always visited the library at least once a week. Now she'd have to go right into town. She was going to *explode* when she heard the news.

'What's odd?' she said again, rather sharply.

'You're not going to like it,' said Harvey.

'The library's closed down.' Lloyd held his breath, waiting for the explosion—but it didn't come. Instead, Dinah turned pale. She looked over her shoulder at Michael.

'Did you hear that?'

Michael nodded. His face was strange as well. 'What do you mean—closed?' he said.

'Shut,' Harvey said. 'Finished. They're taking the books away in vans.'

'White vans?' Michael said slowly. 'With a green hand painted on the side?'

Harvey looked startled. 'That's right. How did you know?'

Dinah sat down at the table. Her face was very pale now. 'It's happening at the university library as well. There's a big sign on the front door: *Closed until further notice, owing to maintenance*. And the car park at the back is full of Green Hand vans taking the books away.'

Lloyd shrugged. 'So? Maybe the Green Hand's a firm of bookbinders. Perhaps they're repairing all the old books round here.'

Michael shook his head. 'They weren't old books. It was all the new, expensive books they were loading up.'

'And there are other things, too,' Dinah said. She had gone very quiet, the way she did when she was really worried about something.

'Like?' Lloyd said.

Michael opened his mouth to answer, but Dinah shook her head. 'It's too serious to chat about,' she said. 'I think we ought to wait till the others come. And have a proper SPLAT meeting about it.'

'OK,' Lloyd said.

But he couldn't see why she was making such a fuss.

Nor could the others, at first.

'Perhaps it's just a coincidence about the vans,' Mandy said. 'They may not be the same at all. There are lots of white vans around.'

'With green hands on them?' said Dinah.

Ian was looking down at his own hand, wriggling the fingers around. 'Maybe they weren't the *same* Green Hands.'

Michael took a piece of paper out of his pocket. 'The ones at the university were like this.'

He began to sketch a shape in tiny, neat lines. A square palm with long, clutching fingers like claws. Harvey watched him and nodded.

'The ones down the road were like that as well.'

Mandy shuddered. 'It looks horrible. Greedy. As if it wants to snatch everything away.'

'Oh, don't exaggerate!' said Ingrid. 'It's not snatching *everything*. Only books.'

51

Dinah was staring down at the little drawing as well, and her eyes were wide. 'I'm not sure it *is* only books,' she said softly. 'I've seen that hand somewhere else.'

Michael glanced up. He looked surprised. 'You have?'

Dinah nodded. 'I've just realized. Claudia had it too. On a badge.' There was an odd note in her voice. Almost scared.

'So?' Lloyd said. 'I thought you liked Claudia.'

'I did. But she was different today. Horrible.'

'And she had a Green Hand badge?' Ian said, trying to make sense of it all.

Dinah nodded. 'I didn't realize when I saw the vans, because the hand on them is so big. But seeing it little—the way Michael's drawn it—it was just the same!'

Slowly Michael picked up the pen again. He drew a small circle round the hand, to make it look like a badge. Then he gazed at it.

'My dad wears one, too,' he said, at last. 'His jacket's covered in badges, so I didn't notice it much, but I'm sure he's got one.'

Dinah leaned forward. 'Where did it come from?'

'From the Hyperbrain Conference. I think.'

Lloyd decided it was time he took charge. He sat down next to Dinah and rapped on the table. 'OK. This is a proper SPLAT meeting. Who's going to take notes?'

'I will.'

Mandy reached for Michael's piece of paper and drew a line under the picture of the Green Hand badge. Then she started to make a list of the things they'd said.

1. *Libraries are closing and Green Hand vans are taking the books away.*
2. *Michael's father came back from the Hyperbrain Conference with a Green Hand badge.*
3. *Claudia has a Green Hand badge.*

'And Claudia was at the Conference,' Michael said.

Lloyd looked down at the list. 'So it all started there?'

'Not exactly.' Michael frowned, gathering his thoughts. 'Dad started being strange before that. When those men came.' He glanced at Dinah. 'You know—Brown Anorak and the other one. That was when Dad started to say peculiar things.'

'Like this?' Dinah said. She took the pen from Mandy and added another line to the list.

4. *Curiosity is the curse of the human brain.*

Michael looked at her in amazement. 'How did you know about that?'

'I overheard you telling Claudia. She said you must have misunderstood, didn't she? But today *she said it too!*'

She looked round at the others, and Lloyd could see that there was something else in her mind.

'Go on,' he said. 'Spit it out.'

Dinah looked down at her hands. 'Michael's dad and Claudia have both gone strange. And they're both saying the same thing. *Curiosity is the curse of the human brain*. It's as if—' She lifted her head and stared at Lloyd, challenging him. '—as if they've been hypnotized.'

Chapter 7

Crazyspace

Michael didn't understand, but the others did. Dinah saw their faces change, and Lloyd erupted, just as she knew he would.

'You're as bad as Harvey! He kept going on about the Headmaster when we were at the Research Centre. That's all nonsense! We saw him disappear into the Evolution Accelerator.'

'Yes,' Dinah said. 'But it recorded his DNA, didn't it? That's all it needs, you know, to . . .' She hesitated and then forced herself to say it. '. . . to make a clone.'

'A *clone*?' Michael's mouth dropped open. 'What are you talking about? And who's the Headmaster?'

'He used to be at our school,' Lloyd said grimly. 'He hypnotizes people.'

'And he wants to take over everything.' Dinah ran her finger lightly over the Green Hand drawing. 'To grab it, like this, and make it totally efficient.'

'So?' Michael was looking more and more bewildered. 'What's wrong with efficiency? We could do with a bit more of it in our house, I can tell you.'

He grinned, but no one grinned back. Mandy shook her head.

'You don't understand. He doesn't just make things run smoothly. He makes people do exactly what *he* wants. And he doesn't care about feelings or differences between people. He'd like the whole world to be a sort of machine.'

Ingrid frowned. 'But if this Controller person is him—why is he bothering with people at a university? What's he going to take over? The rugby team?'

'It's the other teams he needs to hypnotize,' Harvey said. He gazed into Ingrid's eyes. *'You are feeling too sleepy to tackle anyone. Funny how you keep falling over . . .'*

Ingrid grinned and slumped sideways. This time it was Michael who didn't smile.

'There's other things at the university, besides the rugby team,' he said. His fingers tightened round the drawing of the Green Hand, screwing it into a little, crumpled ball.

'Like what?' said Lloyd.

Michael swallowed. 'Like something very powerful. Powerful enough to deal with all the knowledge in the world.'

Dinah felt sick. 'The Hyperbrain.'

'That's right.' Michael nodded. 'If he's taken that over, he can control all the major computers in the world.'

'But the Hyperbrain doesn't exist!' Ingrid said indignantly. 'You told us it wouldn't happen for *years*!'

'I know,' Michael said. He looked up, and his face was very pale. 'But when Dad came back from the conference he said it was ready to start. Because everyone had suddenly agreed, without any arguments at all. As if—'

'As if they'd been hypnotized,' said Mandy softly.

There was a long, unhappy silence.

Then Lloyd said, 'So you think the Headmaster's controlling all the knowledge in the world?'

Dinah nodded. 'And he's making sure no one else can get any.' She picked up the crumpled drawing of the Green Hand and smoothed it out. 'Don't you see? Books are already disappearing from libraries. And people are being told not to ask questions. Is that just round here, or is it everywhere? We've got to find out.'

'That'll be really easy!' Lloyd said sarcastically. 'Let's put an ad in the papers, shall we? *Please tell us if your library's closing. Let us know if your parents are hypnotized.* Get real, Di! We can't investigate all over the country.'

'Yes, we can,' Dinah said. She'd worked it out already. 'We can use the Internet.'

She knew exactly what she wanted to do. But they couldn't start until the next morning, when the cybercafé opened. And the next morning was a long time coming.

All night, she had nightmares. She dreamt she was back in the Biogenetic Research Centre, standing beside the Evolution Accelerator. In front of her, on the bench, was a mobile phone.

. . . on my way to the lab with Professor Rowe. From the University of Wessex.

Intelligence has all the power. It takes over everything!

We can watch it all on the video.

The words resounded with meaning, as if they were the first words she'd ever heard. As if they were telling her crucial things about the world.

Intelligence has all the power . . .

In her dream, she reached out for the mobile phone— but the hand that reached out wasn't her own. It was pale and square, with long fingers, curved to grab . . .

She woke up with a scream, and found herself sitting bolt upright in bed.

57

'Dinah? Are you all right?' Mrs Hunter came running along the landing in her nightdress. 'What's the matter?'

'I—' Dinah caught her breath and rubbed a hand across her eyes. 'I had a bad dream. That's all.'

Mrs Hunter put an arm round her shoulders and hugged her. 'Is there something wrong?'

'I—' Dinah wanted to pour the whole thing out, but she knew what would happen. Mum wouldn't believe her. Or, if she did, she would tell her to be careful. And forbid her to investigate.

Dinah swallowed and managed rather a shaky smile. 'I'm fine. Just a bit . . . unsettled.'

Mrs Hunter gave her another hug. 'Never mind. All the moving's over now. Dad's got to travel about, because of his job, but we'll stay here, where your friends are.'

'That's great,' Dinah said. And she meant it. If she was right about the Green Hand badges, she was going to need SPLAT more than ever.

Mrs Hunter smiled. 'Have you got any plans for tomorrow?'

'We're meeting at the cybercafé. At half-past nine.'

'Better get some sleep then, or you'll be snoring over the computers.'

Dinah laughed and lay down, and her mother tucked the duvet round her.

But she couldn't sleep. She wanted to be doing something.

It was harder than she expected. When she arrived at the cybercafé next morning, with Lloyd and Harvey, Mandy and Ingrid were huddled over one of the computers. They were muttering unhappily.

'What's the matter?' Dinah said. 'Something wrong with the computer?'

Mandy shook her head. 'The computer's fine. It's the phone lines that are dodgy. We're having real trouble getting on the Internet.'

'I'll try again,' Ingrid said doggedly. 'Hang on.'

She had to make three more attempts before they got a connection. When they did, she didn't waste any time.

'I'd better get chatting before we lose it again.'

How does the Green Hand grab you? she typed.

Answers began to appear immediately.

It came and grabbed us yesterday.

They took our library books away!—Plum and Jelly

Us too! It's a badge on the cadge, man! :-(—Griddlebone

That mangy mitt has sticky fingers!—Workaholic

'You see?' Dinah said. 'I knew it! It's going on everywhere! See if you can find out where they are!'

Ingrid's fingers reached for the keyboard again, but she didn't have time to type even a letter. Suddenly, the screen blacked out. There was a confused flutter of lights and then a single message spread itself across the screen:

ACCESS TO SERVER SUSPENDED
CURIOSITY IS THE CURSE OF THE HUMAN BRAIN

Ingrid groaned. 'Is it the phone line again?'

'I don't think so.' Lloyd looked round the café. 'Everyone else has lost it too.'

He was right. At all the computer tables, people were muttering angrily. And Dinah could see the same square letters spreading across every screen.

ACCESS TO SERVER SUSPENDED
CURIOSITY IS THE CURSE OF THE HUMAN BRAIN

The only person still typing was a girl on the far side of the room. They'd never spoken to her, but she always seemed to be in the cybercafé, hunched over the same machine.

The man at the next table got up to see what she was doing. He came back looking disgusted.

'She's not on the Net,' he said to the woman next to him. 'Just that kids' thing—Crazyspace or whatever it's called.'

'Typical.' Crossly, the woman picked up her briefcase. 'We can't do our work—but kids can chat as much as they like.' She stamped out and most of the other adults followed.

Kids can chat as much as they like . . .

The words echoed in Dinah's head. Maybe they weren't finished after all. She got up and walked across to the girl.

'Hi. I'm Dinah.'

'I'm Kate.' The girl looked up and blinked as she saw the café emptying. 'What's up?'

'The server's packed up.' Dinah waved a hand at the blank screens. 'How come you're still on line?'

'I'm not on the Internet,' Kate said. 'This is a separate network for kids to chat. Supposed to be *safer* than surfing the Net.' She pulled a funny face, and laughed.

Dinah didn't laugh back. She leaned forward, eagerly. 'So you can still chat? To people all over the place?'

'Only children.'

'Children will do fine.' Dinah pulled up a chair and sat down. 'Can you show us how to get in?'

Within ten minutes, Dinah had explained what was going on, and they were all huddled round Kate's screen. She obviously thought they were playing some kind of game, but she was quite happy to show them how to get into Crazyspace.

'You've got to do a bit of Crazyspeak, to show you belong.' Her fingers moved over the keys like lightning. She was twice as fast as Ingrid.

Seen a badge with a seasick mitt?

What did it grab? Was your library hit?

Mandy frowned. 'But that looks like nonsense.'

'Great!' said Ingrid. 'I bet that's why no one's closed the network down. They think it's just kids talking rubbish. Give this a go, Kate—'

Go on and tell us your place and the trouble it's in.

Is it hard to ask questions? Are the books getting thin?

The words went in almost as fast as she said them, and Ingrid reached over and added her signature— *Werewolf*.

Straight away, the first answer came flooding on to the screen:

Books and phones—we've lost them both.

GHB plague has hit Arbroath—Smoky.

Ian frowned. 'GHB?'

'Green Hand Badge, pea-brain.' Lloyd leaned closer. 'Look, here's another one.'

Badges, badges everywhere!

Get those green things out of our hair!

You should hear us moan and grouse.

We've got HUNDREDS in our house!

'Hundreds?' Ian frowned. 'What sort of house is it? The House of Commons?'

Harvey and Lloyd started laughing, but Ingrid was peering at the screen and reading the rest of the message.

'No, look. It's *them*.'

'Them?' Dinah said.

'Plum and Jelly. They live in the country. In some sort of outdoor centre near Manchester.' Ingrid pointed at the last lines of the message.

(Thought we'd lost you when the Internet crashed. Fancy you knowing about Crazyspace too! You're a network queen, Werewolf!— Plum and Jelly.)

Mandy was still looking puzzled. 'It's nice they've turned up again, but they're not making sense. Why would there be hundreds of badges in an outdoor centre?'

There was no time to work it out. The messages kept on pouring in, as if they'd unblocked a river.

No more smileys from Bettws y Coed.

Our borrowing has been destroyed.

Dinah began writing down the place names as fast as she could.

Cheltenham.

Cardiff.

Peterborough.

Arran.

Newcastle.

Truro.

There were still problems with the phone line, but the picture they were getting was clear, even though messages kept being cut off in the middle. All over the country, there were libraries closing. And all over the country people had noticed Green Hand badges.

'It's dreadful!' Kate said. She looked round at them all. 'What's going on?'

'That's what we're trying to find out,' Dinah said.

'But it's so complicated!' wailed Ingrid. 'You'd need a Hyperbrain to keep track of it.'

'There *is* a Hyperbrain keeping track of it,' Lloyd said. 'That's the point, you thicko.'

For the first time that day, Dinah thought about the Hyperbrain—and she remembered Michael. She put down her pen and looked round the café.

'Where's Michael? He said he'd be here at half-past nine, like the rest of us. It's almost eleven now.'

Lloyd shrugged. 'Must have got delayed. Maybe he forgot.'

'He wouldn't forget. He's very precise.' Dinah frowned. 'Go on writing the places down, Mandy. I'm going to phone him.'

There was a phone in the corner of the café and she spent ten minutes trying to get through, but it was no use. All she could hear was a jumbled buzzing noise. Finally, the telephone ate her money and refused to give it back.

She turned to go back to the table—and there was Michael. He was just walking into the café, and he looked dreadful. His face was pale and his eyes were red, as though he hadn't slept all night.

He spotted Dinah, and threw himself across the café towards her. 'Thank goodness you're still here!'

Dinah grabbed his shoulders and led him over to the others. 'Whatever is the matter?'

'It's my dad!'

'What do you mean? What's happened?'

Michael sat down suddenly in the nearest chair, as if his legs wouldn't hold him up.

'I can't find him anywhere. He's vanished!'

Chapter 8

Your Wildest Dreams

So it's not just books, Lloyd thought. *The Green Hand's grabbing people now!*

He sat down next to Michael. 'What do you mean he's vanished?'

Michael looked up, and his face was desperate. 'He didn't come home yesterday. I waited up till midnight, but there wasn't a message. And there wasn't one this morning, either.'

'The phones have been peculiar,' Ingrid said doubtfully. 'Maybe he tried and he couldn't get through.'

Michael shook his head. 'It's not that simple. Mrs Barnes says he's gone to Brazil. But he would never go off like that, without telling me.'

'So what makes her think he's there?' said Dinah.

'The Controller told her he was!'

'The Controller?' Harvey said. 'You mean—?'

Michael nodded. 'Him. I think he's kidnapped Dad. I think he's got him hidden away somewhere.'

'But why?' Mandy said.

'I don't know. But I've got to find out.' Michael glanced round the cybercafé to make sure no one else was listening. Then he leaned forward and whispered. 'I'm going into the AIU tonight. To search for clues.'

He looked very small, and his voice was even squeakier than ever. Lloyd thought the whole idea sounded ridiculous.

But Dinah obviously didn't. 'I'll come with you,' she said.

It took Lloyd's breath away. 'But—'

'Someone's got to help him,' Dinah said fiercely. 'And I'm the best person, because I'll be able to help him search the Hyperbrain. If there are any clues, they're probably there.'

'But you can't go!' Harvey said. 'It's too dangerous, Di. You might meet the Headmaster—and he hates you.'

'Does he?' Dinah said. She grinned suddenly, and the others blinked at her.

'Of course he does,' Harvey said.

Dinah went on grinning. 'If this man in the AIU is made from the Headmaster's DNA, he'll be exactly like the Headmaster—but he won't have the Headmaster's memory. DNA only carries things you can inherit.'

'So?' Ingrid said.

'So he may have learnt things like language and science—there was a concentrated learning system at the Research Centre—but he can't have learnt about me. Even if he does see me—*he won't recognize me!*'

Lloyd tried to imagine the Headmaster coming face to face with Dinah, staring at her with those terrible sea-green eyes—and then walking past without taking any notice. It didn't seem possible.

Dinah was happy about it, though. She was already going on with her plans. 'Has anybody got any change? I'll have a go at phoning Mum, to tell her I'm spending the night at Michael's.'

Mandy produced a couple of coins and Dinah went back to the phone. Lloyd and Harvey looked at each other.

'We can't let her go,' Harvey muttered.

Lloyd shrugged. 'We won't be able to stop her, if she's made up her mind. And I suppose she's right. Even if it is the Headmaster, he can't possibly remember her.'

Dinah was already on her way back from the phone box, looking annoyed.

'The phones are dreadful! I thought I'd really got through this time. Then the line started crackling and we were cut off. It's no use going home, because Mum's going shopping at half-past four. You'll have to tell her, Lloyd.'

'Thanks.' Lloyd pulled a face. 'What am I supposed to say? *Hallo, Mum. Dinah hasn't come home because she's going to break into the Artificial Intelligence unit tonight.*'

'You'll think of something,' Dinah said. 'Come on, Michael.'

Harvey caught at her sleeve. 'Be careful.'

'Of course I will,' Dinah said. 'Don't worry. I don't want to see the Headmaster any more than you do. But I've got to go.'

She began heading out of the café, but Michael hesitated. When she reached the door, she looked back at him.

'What's the matter? Aren't you coming?'

'I just thought . . .' he wavered. 'Are you sure you want to do this? What about Claudia?'

'I can dodge her,' Dinah said. 'Come *on.*'

She went outside and Michael started across the café after her.

'Hang on a minute,' Lloyd called. 'What did Dinah mean? Why does she have to dodge Claudia?'

'Claudia was looking for her,' Michael said. He reached the door himself and pushed it open. 'So was my dad. It was weird, really. They both got phone calls, and then—oh, sorry. There's a bus.'

Through the window, Lloyd saw Dinah beckoning, and pointing at the bus. Before any of them could stop her, she and Michael had jumped on the bus and gone.

Lloyd and Harvey looked at each other.

'We shouldn't have let her go,' Harvey said miserably.

As they went home, Harvey was still fretting.

'I hope Mum's furious,' he kept muttering. 'I hope she goes straight off to the university to fetch Dinah back. I hope—'

'Shut up!' muttered Lloyd. He wasn't looking forward to telling his mother that Dinah was away for the night.

But it turned out to be much easier than he expected.

'Look, Mum,' he began, when she came back from the shops, 'Dinah's gone off to stay the night at the university—'

And, before he could get any further, Mrs Hunter beamed. 'So *that's* what Claudia wanted!'

'I . . . I'm sorry?' Lloyd was confused.

'I couldn't make sense of her telephone call,' Mrs Hunter said. 'She phoned up at lunchtime, but the line was terrible. I thought she was saying *I want to find Dinah today*. But it must have been *I want to have Dinah to stay*.'

Lloyd and Harvey glanced at each other. 'I . . . er . . . yes,' Lloyd said. He didn't like the sound of that telephone call, but at least it saved a lot of awkward explaining.

And Mrs Hunter was delighted. 'I'm so glad Dinah's in touch with Claudia again. It sounded as if there was something wrong last time, but it's obviously been sorted out.'

From the corner of his eye, Lloyd saw Harvey get ready to speak. The idiot! He wasn't going to tell Mrs Hunter she'd made a mistake, was he? That would start all sorts of trouble.

Lloyd kicked out at Harvey's ankle. He only meant it as a warning, but he hit it rather harder than he intended.

Harvey ran off, with a snort of rage, and Mrs Hunter looked up.

'What's the matter with him?'

'Haven't got a clue,' Lloyd said innocently.

He heard Harvey go into the sitting room and turn on the television. *Good*, he thought. *Maybe that will put him in a better mood.*

But it didn't. A second later, there was another snort of rage.

'What's up?' Mrs Hunter called.

'The television's useless!' Harvey shouted back. 'It's supposed to be the news. But there's nothing on except silly game shows. *Everything's* going peculiar!'

'Oh, stop moaning!' Lloyd said. He sighed and went into the front room. 'There's bound to be news on BBC One.'

He picked up the remote control and flipped to Channel One.

But Harvey was right. There was no news on there. Instead, there were five people dressed up as penguins, trying to squeeze into a telephone box.

'Why do you want the news, anyway?' Lloyd said.

'I want to know about the football.'

Mrs Hunter heard that. She came in, pulling a face. 'That'll be in the paper tomorrow. If it's anything like today's paper. That's *all* sport.'

'Better than game shows,' Lloyd said in disgust. 'There's another one coming up now.'

The title was already spreading across the screen.

YOUR WILDEST DREAMS!!!!!

'Maybe there's something on the teletext,' Harvey said.

Picking up the remote control, he punched the button. The picture disappeared, but they could still hear the voice of the presenter on *Your Wildest Dreams*.

'In a minute, we'll find out what happened to Philip Murphy when his WILDEST DREAM came true!!! But first, let's swirl the Dream Machine to pick out the name of our next lucky person. Surname first . . .'

Lloyd barely heard it. He was staring in disbelief at the page of teletext. The whole screen was full of random characters, as if a monkey had been playing with a keyboard.

'That's hopeless!' he said.

Harvey groaned. 'Everything's falling to bits. The library's shut. The phones are wonky. We can't get on the Internet. And now—no teletext and no proper television programmes or newspapers.'

'Oh, don't exaggerate,' Mrs Hunter said. 'No one's *making* you watch the television.'

She reached out for the remote control. As she did so, the unseen presenter of *Your Wildest Dreams* became even more manic.

'So here it is, folks!! The magic moment. First we activate the left side of the Dream Machine. Ready, Gloria?'

'Let's turn the whole thing off,' Mrs Hunter said impatiently.

She flicked back to the television picture, and her finger moved towards the *standby* button. But she didn't press it because, at that very instant, the surname card came whirling down the chute of the Dream Machine. Gloria pulled it out and held it up for everyone to see.

'There it is!' screeched the presenter. *'The magic surname is—Hunter!! So if that's your name, cross all your fingers and toes, because IT COULD BE YOU. Activate the other side, Gloria!'*

Harvey grabbed at the remote control. 'You can't turn it off now, Mum! We've got to wait and see what the first name is. It might be me!'

'You wish!' Lloyd said scornfully. But he was watching too, and so was Mrs Hunter.

The Dream Machine went into action, with all its lights flashing. There was a loud fanfare, and Gloria picked up the first name card.

'*And the name is—*'

Lloyd was holding his breath. Surely it couldn't be . . .?

'*And the name is DINAH!*' squeaked Gloria.

'*Hallo, Dinah Hunter!*' bellowed the presenter. '*If that's your name, and you're under eighteen—start heading for the studio. If you get here before midday tomorrow, we'll make YOUR WILDEST DREAM come true!!!*'

Mrs Hunter began to dance round the room triumphantly. 'That's fantastic! Dinah's going to be so happy! You'll have to go and get her back, Lloyd. Her wildest dream!!'

Lloyd and Harvey looked at each other. Lloyd could see that they were both thinking the same thing.

It didn't feel right. Not in the middle of everything else that was going on.

It felt like danger.

Chapter 9

Midnight Investigation

Mrs Barnes was watching *Your Wildest Dreams* as well, when Dinah and Michael arrived at Michael's house. She was so absorbed that she just nodded absent-mindedly when Michael asked if Dinah could stay the night.

''Course she can, dear. Do you want to come and watch this with me? It's really good.'

'Er . . . no thanks,' Michael said. He started shuffling away again.

Mrs Barnes looked past him. 'What about you, Deborah? Don't you want to see it?'

'Er . . . no thanks,' said Dinah politely. 'I—'

But Mrs Barnes had turned back to the television. Michael and Dinah crept out of the room and escaped upstairs.

'She's very *nice*,' Michael said. 'But she does watch television most of the time. And I couldn't bear to sit there. Not when I don't know if Dad's OK.'

'Of course not,' Dinah said briskly. 'We can't waste time, anyway. We ought to be hunting for clues.'

'But where can we look? It's too early to go to the AIU.'

'Where does your dad work when he's at home?'

'This is his study.' Michael pushed the door open. 'But I don't know if there's anything—'

Dinah stepped into the study and looked around. She'd been picturing an untidy room full of books, with piles of paper everywhere, but she was wrong. There were books all right—arranged on long shelves, in alphabetical order—but there were no papers at all. Only a bare desk with a computer terminal.

'He keeps everything on the computer?'

'Sort of,' Michael said. 'Most of it's on the university computer—the one that's part of the Hyperbrain. This one's linked to it. Dad had a special cable laid across the campus, so he wouldn't need to worry about the phone bill.'

'You mean—we could link up to the Hyperbrain from here?'

Michael nodded. 'That's how he did all his routine work. There's only personal stuff on this computer. Like his diary and the household records.'

Dinah looked thoughtful. 'His diary might be useful. Can you get into it?'

Michael hesitated.

'I don't think it's snooping,' Dinah said gently. 'Not if we really need to find him.'

Slowly, Michael sat down at the desk and switched on. The moment he began tapping at the keys, he started to relax. Dinah could see that he knew his way around the files. *He must have spent a lot of time in here with his dad,* she thought.

'There you are!' he said, after a moment. 'That's the diary.'

It was open at the beginning of the previous month. The entries were brief, and they were all about the Hyperbrain Conference. Tim Dexter's mind had obviously been buzzing with details:

Tues   13th 10.30 —Phone Hamburg re HBC. Helmut J. to speak?
Wed   14th p.m.   —See Claudia re HBC. Display Molecular
                        Storage Units?

Fri   16th a.m. —Phone caterers. See Peter Giles
Thurs 22nd 09.30—BBC to discuss filming.

'Who are these people?' Dinah waved a hand at the screen.

Michael leaned forward to look over her shoulder. 'Helmut Jaeger's a professor at Hamburg. Peter Giles is one of Dad's research students—he's done a lot of work on the Hyperbrain—and you know who Claudia is.'

'Fine.' Dinah scrolled down. The entries went on and on, each one carefully dated. Then suddenly, about two days before the conference, the style changed. There was a single, undated entry, written across the screen.

The Controller will speak first.
Curiosity is the curse of the human brain.

The rest of that screen was blank.

Dinah shuddered. 'Scroll down again. Quickly.'

She was hoping for some information about what had happened at the Conference, but there was nothing like that. The next entries were very brief—and she couldn't understand a word of them.

Tues   2nd   —Submit report on DiBrAc to Hyperbrain
Wed   3rd   —Hyperb: more DiBrAc info by 6p.m.
Thurs 4th   —2p.m. Hyperb needs DiBrAc data.

Dinah frowned. 'What's DiBrAc?'

Michael shook his head. 'Haven't got a clue. Dad never mentioned it to me.'

'Do you think it had anything to do with the Hyper-brain?'

'It must have done. All Dad's work was linked to that. But I haven't got a clue what it means. Let me see what else I can find.'

Michael tapped away again and the screen changed, filling with notes and calculations. Dinah squinted at them, her brain whirring.

'I've never seen anything like *that* before.'

'No one has.' Michael gave her a quick grin, over his shoulder. 'This is all Dad's stuff about the new interface. The one that will let people talk directly to the Hyperbrain without a keyboard or a mouse or anything.'

'Sounds fantastic. Is there anything else about it?'

'Probably. You take a look.' Michael slid off the chair so that Dinah could sit at the desk.

She began to work her way methodically through Tim Dexter's files. Most of them seemed simple enough to understand, but the interface files baffled her.

'They don't add up. It's like trying to do a jigsaw with half the pieces missing.'

'That's because Dad had all the key bits in his head. There were some things he didn't tell anyone, not even people like Peter Giles. He said that spies could hack into the computer, but no one could steal his research without getting direct brain access.'

Dinah grinned. 'Direct access to a human brain?' she said. 'I don't suppose we'll ever—'

And then the words exploded in her mind. *Direct Brain Access*. *Direct Brain Access*.

DiBrAc.

She had to bite her lip to stop herself saying it out loud. The entries from Tim Dexter's diary were roaring through her memory.

Tues	2nd	—*Submit report on DiBrAc to Hyperbrain*
Wed	3rd	—*Hyperb: more DiBrAc info by 6p.m.*
Thurs	4th	—*2p.m. Hyperb needs DiBrAc data.*

'What's the matter?' Michael said, looking at her face.

Dinah didn't dare tell him what she was thinking. She made herself flip through a few more pages of equations before she answered. Trying to sound offhand.

'Nothing's the matter. I was just wondering—d'you think it will *ever* be possible? Direct Brain Access, I mean.'

Michael frowned. 'Dad said there *might* be a way. By diverting the electrical discharges in a person's brain. But it's too dangerous to use. No one knows what sort of damage it would cause.'

Abruptly, Dinah exited from the file she was in. 'I don't think we're going to find anything here,' she said quickly. 'Let's think about tonight. How are we going to get into the AIU?'

'You are staying?' Michael said anxiously.

'Of course.' There was no way she was letting him go in there on his own. Especially not with what she was thinking about DiBrAc. 'Can I have another go at phoning my mum?'

Michael picked up the phone from beside the desk and handed it to her. But when she dialled, there was nothing except a loud crackling noise.

*   *   *

Just before midnight, they sneaked through the campus to the AIU building. There were groups of students wandering about, talking and laughing, but no one took any notice of Dinah and Michael.

'Thank goodness for *normal* students,' Dinah muttered. 'I saw some really weird ones the other day. They were—'

But Michael wasn't listening. He had reached the back door of the AIU and he was keying in the entry code.

'Be careful,' Dinah whispered.

Michael nodded, tapped the last number and pushed at the door. Immediately, a bell started ringing inside the building.

'Burglar alarm!' he hissed.

It sounded terrifyingly loud, but he didn't hesitate. He raced through the door and across the hall, to turn off the bell. Dinah went after him. Even in the dark, she could see the notice on the closed door of the first office. *Controller.*

'Are you sure there's no one here?' she whispered.

Michael put a finger to his lips and they stood dead still, holding their breath. The alarm hadn't sounded for more than a split second, but anyone in the building would have heard it.

No one came.

After three or four minutes, Dinah relaxed. 'All right. Where are we going to look?'

'Everywhere,' Michael said. 'Let's start with the offices.'

He pushed open the door of the Controller's office. Cautiously, Dinah stepped in after him as he flicked on the light.

It was very tidy and almost bare, except for a filing cabinet in one corner and a computer terminal on the desk. Michael raced across to look in the filing cabinet and snorted with disgust.

'There's nothing in here except a video.'

'A *video*?' Dinah went to look over his shoulder. Why would the Headmaster be watching a video?

It was impossible to tell what it was. There was no label on the black plastic of the cassette, or on its box. Impatiently, Michael dropped it back in and pushed the drawer shut.

'There's nothing here. Let's look in the others.'

But the other offices were the same. Tim Dexter's had a bookshelf on one wall and a filing tray full of letters waiting to be answered, but otherwise it was as bare as the Controller's room.

'How about the lab?' Dinah said.

Michael marched over and threw the door open. The lab was bigger than the offices, but it was almost as empty.

On the right hand wall was a row of shelves crowded with small pieces of equipment. The rest of the room was bare except for the big computer that dominated the room. The screen on the far wall was dull and blank, but Dinah could hear a low, continuous hum.

'Is that it?' she whispered. 'The Hyperbrain?'

'The bit that's here,' Michael said. 'But there are bits all over the world, of course.'

Dinah walked further into the room. There was a small video camera mounted in one corner, and it swivelled disconcertingly as she moved. She glanced up at it, thinking of the one she had seen in the Biogenetic Research Centre.

'Is that a security camera?'

Michael shook his head. 'Not exactly. It's part of the Hyperbrain Input System.'

'You mean . . . the Hyperbrain's watching us?'

Michael shrugged. 'I suppose so. But it's got information pouring in from all over the world. It's not likely to notice us.'

'I suppose not.' But Dinah didn't like it. She wandered over to the shelves. On the bottom shelf was a stack of dull grey cylinders. 'Oh look. These are the things Claudia invented, aren't they? Molecular Storage Units.'

Michael nodded and came to join her. 'Dad was really excited about those. He said they could store as much information as a human brain. He thought—' Suddenly he frowned and leaned forward. Moving the top Storage Unit, he took out the one underneath.

It wasn't dull grey like the others. It was translucent and glittering, as though it had been lit up from inside.

'What's happened to that?' Dinah said.

'I don't know. Unless it's been used.' Michael's frown deepened, and he began turning over the other things on the shelf. 'Someone's done something to this headband too.' He picked it up. 'This is what Dad used for brain mapping. He studied how people's brains worked, when he was designing the Hyperbrain.'

'And the headband's been altered?' Dinah said.

Michael nodded uneasily. 'I don't like it. I don't understand what's been going on in here.'

Dinah was horribly afraid that she did understand, but she didn't say so. She wasn't going to frighten Michael unless she had to.

'Could we . . . find out?' she said. 'Whatever the Headmaster's done, he'll have used the Hyperbrain, won't he? Can we get into it?'

'Maybe,' Michael said cautiously. 'But would you know what to ask?'

I hope not, Dinah thought. But she knew she had to try. 'I'll have a go,' she said. 'If you show me how to log on.'

'Sure.' Michael went across to the keyboard and tapped in some entry codes. He was answered not by a display on the screen, but by a computer voice.

'*What is your name?*'

He beckoned Dinah across. 'You answer,' he whispered. 'Just say your name.'

She was a bit startled, but she gave her name, in a clear, precise voice. 'Dinah Hunter.'

There was a noise above her head. Glancing up, she saw the camera on the ceiling swivelling towards her.

'*Wait for face identification,*' said the computer voice.

She blinked. 'What's going on?'

'It's the security check. Hyperbrain won't let you in until it's recognized you.'

'*Recognized* me?' But it's never seen me before.'

'It's not a person,' Michael said impatiently. 'Think of all the information it can get at—passport photos, newspaper files, all sorts of stuff. It's bound to have a picture of you somewhere, even if it's only a school photo.'

'Oh, great.' Dinah groaned. 'And it'll find that?'

'Now it's got your name. It's standard security procedure.'

He was still speaking when a grey, grainy picture began moving across the screen. He waved his hand at it.

'There you are. It hasn't just got a picture of you. It's got a video.'

Dinah stared. 'But how? What is it?'

Then another person stepped into the picture, and she knew what she was looking at.

'It's the Headmaster!' She whisked round to Michael. 'This must be the security video from where he was before. The place where Claudia got the creeper. Someone from the army took us in to get samples, and he was really worried because that video had disappeared. The Headmaster must have taken it.'

'And brought it here,' Michael said softly. 'You were right, Dinah. That *is* the Controller.'

'And if he's seen that video—he knows who I am.' Dinah took a long, deep breath. 'I think I ought to get out of here.'

But before she could even turn round, a voice spoke from behind them. A voice as smooth as syrup.

'What are you doing in here?'

For one, sick second, Dinah thought it was the Headmaster. Then she realized that it was a woman's voice.

There was a strange woman standing on the far side of the lab. She was tall and slim, with dark hair pulled into a heavy bun. Her hands were pushed into the pockets of her dark green lab coat. There was something disturbing about her stillness and the steadiness of her eyes.

Taking one hand out of her pocket, she pointed at them with a long, pale finger. 'This is no place for children.'

'Who are you?' Michael said. 'What are *you* doing here?'

In the silence, the computer behind Dinah hummed more loudly for a moment. The woman said, 'I am connected to the Hyperbrain. I work here.'

Michael's eyes brightened, and he took a step forward. 'Do you know where my dad is, then?'

'He is not here,' the woman said. 'He has not been here for two days.' There was no trace of sympathy in her voice—and no trace of curiosity.

Dinah shuddered. 'Come on, Michael. We're not going to find anything here.'

She thought they would be shepherded out of the building, but the woman didn't move. She stood in her corner, watching them go. And, on the ceiling, the video camera swivelled, watching them too.

'How did she get in?' Dinah hissed, as they went out.

'Haven't got a clue. Never seen her before.'

'But she knew you.'

Michael stopped and stared. 'What do you mean?'

'When you asked about your father, she knew who you meant.'

Michael didn't answer, but Dinah saw his hands shaking as he closed the door behind them.

As they walked away up the hill, towards Michael's house, she glanced over her shoulder. There were no lights in the AIU now, but she was sure she glimpsed a dark shape at the window.

A dark shape with white hands that glimmered in the shadows.

Chapter 10

Hiding Dinah

Lloyd woke up very early the next morning. The moment he opened his eyes, he thought, *I hope Dinah phones soon*. He was desperate to know whether she and Michael had managed to sneak into the AIU.

At eight o'clock, the phone rang, and he came rattling down the stairs, but his mother beat him to it. By the time he got there, she was shaking the phone and looking annoyed.

'There really is something wrong with this,' she said. 'I spent hours last night trying to phone Claudia, to tell Dinah about *Your Wildest Dreams*, but all I got was crackling. And now there's someone trying to get through to us, and I can't make out a word. Listen.'

Lloyd listened, but all he could hear was a noise like gargling underwater. Before he could decide what to do, the person at the other end gave up and rang off.

Mrs Hunter frowned. 'We'll have to get someone to look at the phone.'

'I don't think it's just *our* phone,' said Lloyd. 'I think there's something wrong with the whole system. All over the country.'

'Don't be silly. It's been going on for days. We'd have seen something in the papers. There's nothing about telephones.'

Mrs Hunter tossed the morning paper across the room. Lloyd caught it and looked down at the headlines. There certainly wasn't anything about telephones:

Great-gran celebrates 100th birthday
Conservatives slam Labour promises
Weather still dry

He turned the pages. 'There's no real news at all. Don't you think *that's* peculiar, too?'

Mrs Hunter started to laugh. 'Oh, Lloyd! What are you trying to say? That there's some kind of conspiracy?'

She picked up the phone and dialled, but it was no better. After a moment or two, she put it down in disgust.

'It's ridiculous! Dinah can't miss out on her wildest dream, just because the phone's not working. I'll have to go and get her.'

'No, I'll go,' Lloyd said quickly. 'Harvey and the others can come too.'

'*Would* you?' Mrs Hunter looked relieved. 'It would be a big help. I've got the plumber coming this morning.'

'No problem.' Lloyd gave his mother an angelic smile.

He didn't think Dinah should go anywhere near the *Wildest Dreams* studio, but he was delighted to have an excuse to go and see her. He had to find out what had happened.

Three quarters of an hour later, Lloyd and Harvey were setting out for the university with Ian and Mandy. Ingrid had refused to come.

'I promised to go to the café. Kate and I are going to try and get some more news on Crazyspace.'

Mandy pulled a face at her. 'It'll take hours to get anything. The phones are dreadful.'

'We'll try and try and try once more,' Ingrid rapped back at her. 'We've got to beat the emerald paw!'

Her hand shot out towards Mandy's face, with all the fingers wriggling. Mandy jumped back with a shriek.

'Don't! That's creepy!'

'The Green Hand *is* creepy,' Ingrid said. 'That's why Kate and I are staying with the chat. We want to get in touch with Plum and Jelly again, to find out why they've got so many badges at that Outdoor Centre.'

'Good idea,' said Lloyd. 'You concentrate on that, and we'll go and find out what Dinah and Michael have discovered.'

'And see how Dinah feels about having her name picked by the Dream Machine,' said Ian.

'The Dream Machine picked out *what?*' Dinah said.

She and Michael were in Tim Dexter's study, doing something on the computer. Mrs Barnes had sent the others up to join them, and Lloyd hadn't wasted any time getting to the point.

Dinah spun round on the computer chair and stared at him in amazement.

'It picked out your name,' Lloyd said. 'Dinah Hunter. If you go to the studio before midday, they'll make your wildest dream come true.'

Dinah went white. 'It's the Headmaster, isn't it? He's trying to get me.'

'But you said he wouldn't know who you were.' Harvey looked accusingly at her. 'You said he wouldn't remember.'

'I thought he wouldn't,' Dinah said, in a shaky voice. 'But I was wrong. He's got that security video from the Research Centre. It shows me talking to him, so he's seen my face, and he knows we've met.'

'Are you sure?' Lloyd said.

Dinah nodded. 'Can we show them, Michael? Can you get into the Hyperbrain from here?'

Michael nodded. 'Easy. Just keep out of sight. If I request a link with the Hyperbrain, that'll activate the video eye up there.'

'What on earth's that?' Lloyd said.

Dinah explained, as she ducked out of sight. 'It's so the Hyperbrain can recognize him. He has to give his name, and then it finds a picture of his face and checks it's the same person.'

'So you couldn't log in if you forgot your name?' Harvey said.

Ian patted him on the head. 'Don't worry. We know you find it hard to remember things.'

Harvey growled at him—and then stopped to grin as Michael's school photograph appeared on the screen. 'Brilliant picture, Mike!'

Michael blinked, as if he didn't quite understand the joke. Then he typed a request into the computer. '*Picture of Dinah Hunter?*'

He was online to the Hyperbrain now, and it responded immediately.

YOU ARE NOT MY MASTER, BUT I WILL CO-OPERATE WITH THIS REQUEST.

'What does that mean?' Dinah looked at Michael.

'Don't know.' He pulled a face. 'It's not supposed to have a master. Dad said it was going to co-operate with anyone who asked.'

Dinah and Lloyd glanced at each other, but they didn't say anything. Michael didn't notice because, at that moment, the screen filled with a picture of Dinah, standing straight and defiant. And facing her, looking icily furious, was the Headmaster. The images were grey and fuzzy, but they were perfectly recognizable.

Lloyd shuddered. 'That's where the Headmaster got your face from, then. But if *Your Wildest Dreams* is something to do with him he must know your name as well.'

'I suppose Claudia told him,' Dinah said miserably. 'It's lucky I forgot to give her our new address, or she would have brought him—' She stopped, choking.

Mandy squeezed her hand. 'It's not Claudia's fault. You know it isn't. He made her tell him.'

'But how did he know she knew?' Lloyd bit his lip. 'Has he ever seen you together, Di?'

Dinah thought about it. 'I don't see when he could have done.'

'He's been spying!' Harvey said shrilly. 'He's going to kidnap Di, isn't he? She'll vanish for ever, like Michael's dad!'

There was a little, soft gasp from Michael. Lloyd glared at Harvey.

'Don't be such a pinhead! Michael's dad hasn't vanished for ever. And Dinah's not going to vanish either.'

'She is in danger though,' Mandy said.

Lloyd nodded. 'We ought to get her out of the way for a bit. But where can she go?'

He looked round at them all. Everyone stared back blankly.

Then Ian's face brightened. 'She can come with Dad and me!'

'What?' Dinah said.

'On the lorry! Dad's going to Manchester today. I've often been with him, and he's always on at me to bring a friend.'

Lloyd beamed. 'That's great. The Headmaster'll never track Di down if she's in a lorry. How long can you keep her away?'

'Till tomorrow, probably. When Dad goes to Manchester, he usually stays the night with Gran on the way back.'

'And Di could go too?'

'No problem. Gran's got fourteen grandchildren. She's always having unexpected visitors.'

'Brilliant!' Lloyd beamed. 'Can you catch your dad before he goes?'

Ian looked at his watch. 'I reckon. If we shift a bit.'

'Go on then.' Lloyd gave Dinah a push. 'We'll sort things out here.'

Dinah hesitated. 'It seems like running away.'

'Don't be stupid!' Mandy said. 'We'll investigate much better if we haven't got to worry about you.'

'Yes I know, but—' Dinah was still reluctant.

It was Ian who worked out a way to persuade her. 'Hey!' he said. 'Isn't that Outdoor Centre near Manchester? The one where Plum and Jelly are?'

'That's right!' Mandy said excitedly. 'You could get your dad to drop you off near it—say you're going for a walk or something. And you could go and investigate.'

'Great!' Lloyd grinned at her. 'See if you can find out why they've got so many badges, Di.'

'But . . .' Dinah was still hesitating. 'I haven't got the right shoes for walking. And suppose it rains—'

'You'll be fine in your trainers,' Lloyd said firmly. 'And you can take Mandy's cagoule.' He snatched it up, without bothering to ask Mandy, and pushed it into Dinah's hands. 'Go *on*!'

Grabbing Dinah's shoulders, he spun her round and Ian seized her arm, pulling her out of the room. The others stood and listened to the footsteps as the two of them went downstairs and out of the house.

When the front door closed, Michael shuddered. 'I wish we knew what was going on. I still don't understand why the Controller wants to get hold of Dinah.'

'It's not for any *good* reason,' Harvey said grimly.

Mandy nodded. 'He may be a clone, but he hasn't changed. He's grabbing all the knowledge and—'

Her voice stopped, suddenly. Something on the computer screen had caught her eye.

'What's the matter?' Lloyd spun round.

Mandy didn't need to explain. He understood the moment he saw the odd, wobbly picture on the screen. It was jerking around like a shot from a hand-held camera, but there was no mistaking the people it showed.

It was Dinah and Ian. They were standing by the bus stop, on the edge of the university campus. Suddenly, Ian pointed up the road and said something. Lloyd couldn't make out the words, but he heard the noise as a bus pulled in to the kerb.

'I don't understand,' Mandy said. 'That must be happening now! But how—?'

Dinah and Ian stepped into the bus and it pulled away. Almost immediately, another bus drew up in its place and the shot they were watching changed suddenly. All at once, they were on the second bus, with the driver looking up at them. For an instant, they saw two hands come forward, holding out money and reaching for a ticket.

Harvey blinked. 'What's going on? Is it a camera? How can he be holding it?'

The next moment, the shot changed again. Now they were looking at another part of the university altogether, about half a mile away. There didn't seem to be any connection with the first lot of shots, except that there was the same kind of bumpy movement.

'What's the computer doing?' Mandy said. 'Where are these pictures coming from?'

'Straight out of the Hyperbrain.' Michael was looking puzzled too. 'People must be walking round with digital cameras. Radioing the pictures straight back to the Hyperbrain. Did you see anyone like that when you came in?'

Mandy shook her head. 'We didn't really see anyone at all. Only a group of weird students—'

'That's it!' Lloyd said. It came to him suddenly, in a horrible flash. When the others turned to look at him, he couldn't see why they hadn't realized too. 'Those weird students all looked the same—*and they were all wearing Green Hand badges!*'

'So?' Harvey said.

'So that's what the badges are for! *They're miniature cameras, spying for the Hyperbrain!* That's how the Headmaster found out that Claudia knows Dinah. He must have seen Di, through Claudia's badge.'

Michael gasped. 'You mean that's why Claudia came hunting for Dinah? Because he told her to?'

Mandy turned pale. 'But that's terrible!'

'Why?' Lloyd said.

The others turned to look at her. Her eyes were round and frightened.

'We sent Di away to keep her safe,' she whispered, '. . . and we've just made things worse! She's going to the Outdoor Centre, isn't she? And there are hundreds of badges there!'

Chapter 11

Plum and Jelly

Dinah and Ian had no idea that they were travelling into danger. Ian's father was delighted to have company. He even found them a couple of maps to help with their walk.

But he was rather puzzled about why they wanted to do it.

'You sure you really mean it?' he said, as they drew near to the drop-off point. 'It looks like rain. Why not stay in the lorry and come to Manchester?'

'We'll be fine,' said Ian. 'We've got cagoules. And those sandwiches you bought us.'

Dinah nodded. 'And there's loads of time. We can have a couple of hours at the Outdoor Centre before we need to start back.'

Ian's father swung the wheel as they went round a corner. 'So who are these friends you're going to see?'

'They . . . er . . .' Dinah had been hoping he wouldn't ask that. What could she say? *We've never met them, but their Crazyspeak names are Plum and Jelly?* 'They're very keen on computers, and—'

Luckily, at that moment, someone cut in front of them, dangerously close. Ian's father braked and flashed his lights and by the time he'd finished saying what he thought about careless drivers he had forgotten his question.

Just before the next crossroads, there was a service area. He pulled in there and Dinah and Ian slid out of the cab.

'Thanks a lot, Dad!'

'We'll meet you back here this evening,' said Dinah.

Ian's father nodded. 'Don't be too late. We want to get to Gran's in time for one of her amazing meals.' He grinned and drew away, waving his hand.

Dinah looked at Ian. 'Off we go, then.' She hadn't got a clue what they were going to find at the Outdoor Centre.

Nor had Ian. 'Into the unknown! And keep your eyes peeled for Green Hand badges!'

There were plenty of badges around. They walked through three little villages on their way and, by one o'clock, they had seen at least six. One was on a postman who was emptying a pillarbox, three were on drivers going in the opposite direction, and two were on village shopkeepers, peering through their shop windows.

Both the shops had scrawled notices outside.

Sorry, no Advertiser this week

'That'll be the local paper,' Dinah muttered. 'Those are disappearing too, are they?'

'So's the library.' Ian nodded across the road at the sign sellotaped to its door:

Closed until further notice.

Dinah shuddered. 'It's the same everywhere, isn't it?' She stopped and pulled out the map. 'We go on another footpath now, round behind the church.'

The footpath went through some trees and up a hill. Towards the top of the hill, it turned right, to run along a fence. Dinah studied the fence.

'If we want to get in secretly, we've got to climb that.'

'We can do it along there. There's a stile.' Ian stepped off the path and through the rhododendron bushes.

They climbed the stile and went on to the top of the hill. Ian stopped in a clump of trees.

'That building down there must be the Outdoor Centre. If we eat our lunch here, we can watch it for a bit and decide what to do.'

'Good idea.' Dinah flopped down under the tree and pulled on Mandy's cagoule. 'I wish I'd had time to go home and get some proper shoes. My feet are really sore.'

'Having a few blisters is better than getting caught by the Headmaster,' Ian said grimly.

'I know.' Dinah leaned back against the tree and unwrapped her sandwiches. 'What do you think he wants?' She took a bite and stared thoughtfully down the hill.

'Maybe—' Ian began.

But he didn't get any further. Dinah leaned forward and grabbed his arm.

'Look at that!'

'Ouch!' Ian pulled his arm away and rubbed it. 'No need to be violent!'

'Sorry, but I thought I saw—yes, look. There it is again.'

Dinah pointed across the valley to the trees on the opposite hill. There was a sudden flash of light. And then another.

Ian shrugged. 'It's just the sun reflecting off something.'

'Of course it is!' Dinah said impatiently. 'Someone's got a mirror. But can't you see the pattern in the flashes? *Look.* Short, long, long. Short, long. Long. Long, short, long, short.'

Still watching, she pulled out her pocket notebook and began to write down what she could see.

.—–/.—/–/–.—./.…/—–/..–/–/

.—./–––/...–/.—.—./–––/––/../–./—–/

96

After the first few dots and dashes, Ian started looking interested. The moment the flashing stopped, he grabbed the pen and began to write letters underneath the marks Dinah had made.

·— —/·—/—/·—·—·/····/—— —/···—/—/

  w   a   t   c   h   o   u   t

·— —·/—— —/···/···/·/·—·—·/—— —/—/··/—·—·/

  p   o   s   s   e   c   o   m i n g

'Morse code,' he said.

Dinah still didn't understand. 'But what does it mean? *Watch out, posse coming.* What posse?'

'Perhaps we ought to ask *them*,' Ian said softly.

He pointed down the slope in front of them and Dinah peered through the trees. A little way down the hill there were two figures huddled together whispering. Putting his finger to his lips, Ian began to crawl towards them and Dinah followed, keeping under cover of the rhododendron bushes.

When they got closer, Dinah could see that the two figures were a boy and a girl. The boy had a book in his hand, and he was calling out letters.

'S. S again. E.'

The girl was writing the letters on a piece of paper. As she copied the last one down, she sighed. 'We're so *slow*. We'll never be fast enough to pass on long messages.'

'Don't be so soft. We've got to do something now the telephone's packed up. And we're getting faster all the time.' The boy bent down and pulled the paper out of her hand. '*Watch out posse coming*,' he read.

Dinah took a step closer, to hear what he said next—but she wasn't careful enough about where she put her feet. There was a rustle of leaves, and a twig snapped.

The girl jumped, nervously. 'There's someone watching us!'

'OK, Jen. Don't panic.' The boy raised his voice. 'We know you're there. Who are you?'

Dinah looked at Ian and shrugged. Feeling rather stupid, they crawled out from behind the bush.

'We weren't really spying,' Dinah said. 'We just wanted to know about the message.' She smiled.

The boy didn't smile back. 'Take off your cagoules,' he said sharply.

Dinah pulled off the cagoule she was wearing, feeling uneasy. The boy was looking at her in an odd way, scanning the front of her jacket. And so was the girl. What—?

Then their eyes switched to Ian's sweatshirt—and Dinah understood.

'You're looking for Green Hand badges!'

'I—' The girl looked anxious and took a step backwards.

'It's all right,' Dinah said quickly. 'We haven't got them!'

'We don't want them, either,' growled Ian. 'We hate what's going on.'

'Like?' the girl said cautiously.

'Like libraries closing!' said Dinah.

'Television news vanishing!' Ian said.

'No decent newspapers!'

'Teletext going crazy!'

'The Internet packing up!'

'Faxes going bananas.'

The boy and the girl looked wary. Dinah racked her brain for something that would make them trust her and Ian.

It was Ian who found it. Suddenly, he grinned and held out his hand. 'I know who you are! You're Plum and Jelly, aren't you?'

'We . . .' The boy hesitated.

'We've come looking for you,' Ian said eagerly. 'We're Boff and ManUfan.'

It was like magic. The boy beamed and grabbed Ian's hand. 'That's right! I'm Paul, and this is my sister, Jenny. But what are you doing here?'

'We're investigating,' Dinah said. 'We want to know why you've got so many Green Hand badges round here. Is it a centre, or something?'

'It certainly is!' Paul said. 'Our father—'

Jenny grabbed at his hand. 'Not here!' she hissed. 'Remember there's a posse—'

She was too late. There was a sound of tramping feet coming up the hill towards them. Paul and Jenny shrank back towards the bushes, but there was nowhere to hide. They could only stand watching as a group of people came marching through the trees. There were a dozen of them, all around sixteen, and they were all wearing Green Hand badges.

When they saw Ian and Dinah they stopped and looked at them.

'They're our friends,' Jenny said quickly.

One or two of the posse smiled, but Dinah barely noticed. She couldn't stop staring at the glinting Green Hand badges pinned to their chests. She could see her own face reflected back towards her a dozen times, surrounded by the long, grasping fingers on the badge.

'Come on,' Jenny whispered. 'Let's get out of here.'

She pushed past the posse and led the way down the hill towards the Outdoor Centre, slipping between the rhododendron bushes to stay out of sight.

Dinah and Ian followed, with Paul. They had only moved a few yards when a man came out of the barn at the bottom of the hill. Dinah was sure they were invisible from where he was standing, but he headed up the hill, making straight for them.

Paul groaned. 'Oh no! He always comes out when there are people here. How does he know?'

They dodged sideways, into a copse of trees, but it was no use. The man strode up the slope and into their hiding place. He didn't bother to ask any questions. He just began to shout at Dinah and Ian.

'You're trespassing!'

A Green Hand badge glinted on the front of his jacket. Dinah didn't look at it. She was starting to hate the sight of them.

'They're not trespassing,' Paul said quickly. 'They're our friends.'

The man raised his eyebrows. 'Really?' His face was disbelieving. 'Suppose you tell me their names, then.'

'Yes. Um. Of course.' Paul looked helplessly sideways.

Ian jumped in to rescue him. 'I'm Ian.'

But the man didn't seem to be interested in him. It was Dinah he was staring at. 'How about the girl?' he said. 'What's her name?'

In the nick of time, Dinah realized what to do. 'I'm Mandy,' she said.

The man gave her a strange look. 'Are you sure?'

'Do you think I don't know my own name?' Coolly, Dinah held out the cagoule she had just taken off, turning it inside out to show the name sewn into the back of the neck.

Mandy's name.

The man read it and grunted. Without a word of apology, he pushed past Dinah and walked on, up the hill. A second later, they heard him giving instructions to the posse.

'You've got two hours to get to the places marked on your maps.'

There was a burst of muttering, and a girl's voice wafted down the slope. 'Can you tell us—?'

'You have enough information!' the man barked.

'But I can't help being curious—'

The answer came thundering down the hill. 'Curiosity is the curse of the human brain.'

Dinah caught her breath. Beside her, Jenny gave a little moan.

'Don't get upset, Jen,' whispered Paul. 'It must be an illness or something. You *know* Dad's not really like that!'

The horrible man was their father? Dinah felt almost as upset as Jenny. 'Don't worry!' she hissed fiercely. 'Paul's right. It's not his fault. It's got something to do with those Green Hand badges!'

Slowly, Jenny lifted her head, and she and Paul looked at each other. Paul nodded.

'That makes sense. Dad was fine until he got that badge.'

'Where did it come from?' said Ian.

Jenny glanced up the slope. Her father was still busy giving orders, but she lowered her voice anyway. 'He got it from a conference. He went to read a paper on physical and spatial intelligence. That's what he studies here.'

'What he *used* to study,' Paul said bitterly. He scowled. 'All he does now is dish out Green Hand badges to people and send them snooping round the villages in posses. Then they go back to their own towns. He's filling the whole country with Green Hands.'

'And you try and keep track of them?' Dinah said.

Jenny nodded. 'Edward helps us. He's our friend—the one you saw signalling—and his mother's a journalist. She went to report on the conference Dad went to, and she came back with a badge as well. Now she won't write about anything except gardens and cookery.'

'And if Edward asks a question . . .' Jenny pulled a face and chanted. '*Curiosity is the curse of the human brain.*'

The posse above them was moving off now. Dinah looked up, watching everyone go. Seeing the Green Hand badges carried off in all directions.

'Does Edward's mother give out badges, like your dad?'

Paul shook his head. 'No, it's only Dad who does that. He came back from the conference with boxes of them.'

Dinah looked thoughtful. 'I'm sure they're the key to the whole thing. You couldn't get hold of one, could you?'

Paul and Jenny looked at each other. Then Paul stepped back and glanced up the hill. Their father was walking away from them, towards the stile.

Paul waited until he had climbed over. Then he said, 'OK.'

He went flying down the hill towards the Outdoor Centre, and Dinah took a step out of the rhododendrons, to see where he went.

As she did so, she saw another glint of light from the opposite hill. Jenny saw it too. Immediately, she pulled the notebook out of her pocket and started to note down the dots and dashes. Ian grinned at Dinah.

'It's a great system, isn't it? Who needs the Internet?'

He was only joking, but Dinah almost stopped breathing.

'You're right! We don't need the Internet. Or Crazy-space. We can keep in touch with people even if all those things collapse!'

Chapter 12

SPLATweb

Crazyspace was certainly collapsing. Lloyd had spent most of the day in the cybercafé, and he was getting crosser and crosser.

'We *need* to tell people that the badges are spying on them. Can't you get it over to them, Ing?'

'I'm doing my best,' Ingrid said sulkily.

She'd certainly been working hard. Over and over again, she had typed in the same message.

Hands have ears and fists have eyes!
Badges can be snoopy spies!
They may bring danger too, I fear.
Don't let them see! Don't let them hear!

It had looked fine on the screen, and it should have made sense to the people who had chatted to them before. But it wasn't getting across—as far as they could tell from the messages they were getting back.

M $, is yo¶r c❤n↕ecti❤n b❤d!
Scr❤mbl↕d le♣♣ers ❤re re❤l¶y s❤d!

Michael stared gloomily at the screen. 'We're wasting our time, aren't we?'

For the tenth or eleventh time, the words flickered and disappeared and another message took its place.

LINE ERROR
CONNECTION LOST

It was a message they were getting sick of. Kate glowered at the computer.

'*Horrible* thing!' Ingrid said sulkily. 'I think it's teasing us!'

Lloyd grinned. 'It's not the Hyperbrain, you know.'

'Even the Hyperbrain hasn't got a sense of humour,' Michael said. His voice was thin and tense and he looked as though he hadn't had any sleep for three days now.

Ingrid pulled a funny face, trying to cheer him up.

'Can the Hyperbrain laugh like a drain?' she chanted.

'Can it make us laugh till we crack in half?

'Does it pass the time with a nonsense rhyme?

'Or give a little wriggle as it starts to giggle?

'Or—'

'Stop! Stop!' Lloyd put his hands over his ears. 'That would drive anyone mad. Even the Hyperbrain.'

Ingrid punched the air. 'That's the idea! It's our secret weapon. Ingrid's SLS!'

'Ingrid's *what*?' said Mandy.

'Special Laughter Service! Want to hear a joke?'

'No!' Lloyd put his hands over his ears. 'I can't bear it.' He nodded to Kate. 'Turn that computer off. There's no point in doing anything else tonight. We'll come back tomorrow morning and try again. Maybe Dinah and Ian will have some good ideas.'

'Good ideas?' Dinah said the next morning. 'I've got the *best* idea you've heard for years!'

Ian's father had dropped her and Ian off right outside the café and they had come running in, looking pink and excited.

'It's brilliant!' Ian said. 'But we need to try and tell people about it before Crazyspace packs up altogether.'

'We won't need it for long,' Dinah said. 'Because we're going to start a network of our own—'

'A SPLATweb,' interrupted Ian. 'With mirrors—'

'And torches—'

'And flags—'

'*Flags?*' Lloyd stared at them. Had they gone mad?

'Flags for semaphore!' Dinah said impatiently. 'Don't you see? It'll be faster than passing on news by post.'

'Safer, too,' Ian said. 'If we start getting sacks full of letters, someone with a Green Hand badge is sure to notice. But they won't spot SPLATweb if it uses lots of different things.'

Lloyd hadn't quite got what they meant, but Michael understood. He jumped out of his seat.

'We could use homing pigeons, too! I know someone who has those.'

'Great!' Dinah grinned at him. 'And we can send messages with lorry drivers, like Ian's dad, and find people with CB radios—'

'Like my uncle and his friend!' Mandy was getting the idea as well.

'Everything. Anything. All we've got to do is set up the network. And we can use Crazyspace for that. No one's going to spot it, as long as we keep the messages sounding like nonsense.'

'Better hurry,' Lloyd said grimly. 'It's been going on and off all morning.'

Dinah sat down. 'Let's see if we can get a connection, then.'

'I'll do it.' Kate pulled her chair up to the terminal. 'And Ingrid can tell me what to say. She's good at nonsense.'

Ingrid stuck out her tongue, but she didn't waste time arguing. As soon as Kate got the connection, she was ready to rap.

'Keep in touch with all your might
'Using flags and sounds and light.
'Pigeons, milkmen—any way
'To get your message here today.
'Flash it, squeak it, send a bird—
'Any way to get it heard.
'If you want the Green Hands gone,
'Get the news and pass it on!'

Everyone was leaning forward to watch the screen and wait for the answers.

Except Michael.

He was standing behind the others. Glancing back, Lloyd saw him staring at Dinah and Ian. His fists were clenched and he was biting his lip. Lloyd knew exactly what he wanted. The question in his mind was so clear he might just as well have been yelling it.

Have you seen my dad?

Lloyd nudged Dinah, and she understood the moment she looked round. She pulled her chair away from the others, so that she could talk quietly to Michael.

'We haven't got fantastic news,' Lloyd heard her say. 'But we have found out something. They give out Green Hand badges at the Outdoor Centre. Loads and loads of them.'

'We've even got one!' Ian said over his shoulder. 'Show them, Di.'

'*What?*' Lloyd jumped up in horror. 'You haven't—?'

'Oh yes we have.' Dinah was smiling. 'Look.' She put her hand into her pocket.

'No!'

Lloyd threw himself forward. As Dinah's hand came out of her pocket, he snatched the badge from her fingers.

Then he grabbed Ian's cagoule, which was lying on the next table, and bundled it round and round, muffling the badge in as many layers as possible.

Dinah stared. 'What on earth are you doing?'

'You don't understand!' Harvey hissed. 'The badges are for spying on people. Mini cameras and microphones. They feed information back to the Hyperbrain.'

'*What?*' Dinah went white.

Michael nodded. 'We saw you on the screen, in Dad's study. When you and Ian got on that bus at the university, *we were watching you.*'

'What have you done since you got that badge?' Lloyd looked round wildly, half-expecting to see the Headmaster appear in the café. 'Has it picked up your face? And where you've been?'

Dinah shook her head slowly. 'No, it's been in my pocket all the time. But—' She sank into a chair and put her head in her hands.

'Don't worry,' Mandy patted her shoulder. 'It's not that bad.'

'Isn't it?' Dinah muttered. Lloyd couldn't see her face, but her voice was shaking.

'What's the matter?' he said.

Dinah lowered her hands. 'Don't you see?' she said. 'There are badges everywhere, pinned on to all sorts of people. And everything they see is being fed straight back to the Hyperbrain. The Headmaster's beaten us, hasn't he?'

'Why?' Mandy said.

Dinah gave her a weary smile. 'If he's in control of the Hyperbrain, he's got all the information in the world. Everything that's on computers and in books, *and* everything that people can hear and see. And we've got nothing. We can't even phone each other. How can we possibly fight back?'

Lloyd had never seen her so near to giving up. He grabbed her arm and shook it. 'Don't be so feeble! We've got our own eyes and ears, haven't we? And we've got each other. We have to go on!'

Michael echoed him. 'We *have* to!' His voice was desperate.

Dinah clenched her fists. 'It's so awful not being able to find out anything. It's like . . . like being blindfolded.'

'Then find things out!' Lloyd said fiercely. 'People didn't always have the Internet. They didn't always have books. They just had to go out and see things for themselves. If we can't do anything else, we'll have to do that!'

Dinah stared down at her fists for a moment. Then she looked up. Her face was still pale, but it was determined now. 'You're absolutely right. That's what we've got to do. And that means I've got to go back to the university.'

'What?' Harvey almost shrieked.

Mandy was looking horrified too. 'You can't! The Headmaster's hunting for you, and he knows what you look like. It's much too dangerous.'

'So?' Dinah said. She stood up. 'I've got to find out what he's up to—and I'm not going to do that by sitting around here. You can set up the SPLATweb perfectly well without me.'

Lloyd looked at her. He knew he ought to argue. He knew she was stupid to be walking into danger like that. But—he knew she was right. If they were ever going to discover what the Headmaster was planning, someone had to go to the university. And Dinah was the best person to go.

'Be careful,' he said.

Dinah nodded and picked up her bag. 'I will. And you get SPLATweb going, as fast as you can. I've got a feeling we're going to need it soon. Borrow those CB radios Mandy was talking about. Find people who travel around a lot. Get Michael to talk to his friends about the pigeons.'

'I'm not staying to talk about pigeons,' Michael said quietly. He was scribbling an address on a piece of paper. 'This is where they are, Ingrid. Can you and Kate sort it out? I'm going with Dinah.'

Ingrid took the paper and grinned. 'Pigeons? No problem!'

Dinah looked at Michael for a second and then she nodded. 'OK. Come on.'

The two of them set off across the café. As they reached the door, Ingrid called after them.

'Hey! Di!' They both looked round and she waved. 'SPLAT for ever!'

'SPLAT for ever!' Dinah said gravely.

Then she and Michael went off together.

Chapter 13

Not Just a Computer . . .

When Dinah and Michael reached the university, it was almost lunch time. It took them a long while to get near the AIU, because they had to keep dodging groups of weird students wearing Green Hand badges.

'We'll need a place to hide,' Dinah said. 'Is there somewhere we can watch the AIU without being seen?'

'There's a garden by the English Faculty building. I used to play at spying on Dad when I was little. And we had signals—' Michael's voice wobbled a bit, and he stopped.

Dinah could see how much he was missing his father. She wanted to tell him it was going to be all right, that Tim Dexter would come back and be the same as before, but there was no point in pretending. None of them knew what was going to happen.

'Let's go to the garden,' she said quickly. 'We'll watch who goes in and out of the Unit and see if we can work out anything from that. Where do we go?'

Michael led the way up the hill opposite. The garden was tucked round one side of the English building and there was a bench where they could sit, shielded by a big rose bush. There was a wonderful view of the campus from there.

Dinah settled herself on the bench and took out her notebook. 'Let's make a note of everyone who goes in and out.' She handed the book to Michael. 'You'll recognize people. You write the names.'

She was pretty sure she would remember anything important, without writing it down, but the writing would give Michael something to do. That was better than sitting and fretting.

He took the book and turned to a clean page. Very neatly, he wrote two headings:

GOING IN   *COMING OUT*

Then they settled down to watch.

By five o'clock, their list was quite long:

GOING IN	*COMING OUT*
2 weird students	*1 weird student*
Claudia (with Molecular Storage Unit)	*Claudia (without Molecular Storage Unit)*
3 weird students	*2 weird students*
5 weird students	*4 weird students*
Green Hand van (unloading)	
Green Hand van (unloading)	
2 weird students	

Dinah pulled a face at it. 'It's not much help. I can't even tell which of those students are which. They all look the same to me.'

'Why do they keep going in and out?'

'The Headmaster must be giving them orders.'

'But what orders?' Michael twisted his fingers together miserably. 'And why did Claudia take in that Molecular Storage Unit? What's going on?'

He twisted his fingers the other way, and the pencil snapped suddenly, with a dull crack. Dinah wished she knew how to cheer him up. Her mother would have hugged him

113

and Mandy would have had something comforting to say, but she just felt helpless.

The only way *she* could help Michael was by trying to find his father. She frowned down at the list again—and this time she noticed something odd about it.

'We haven't seen that woman yet. The one we met in the lab. She said she worked with the Hyperbrain, but she doesn't seem to be around.'

'Maybe she's not here today.' Michael's eyes flicked up from the paper, towards the front door of the AIU. 'Or maybe—'

He broke off. Clutching at Dinah's sleeve, he pointed to the door. A young man in jeans was walking out of the Unit, looking vague and distracted.

Dinah frowned. 'Who's that? Another weird student?'

Michael shook his head and stood up. 'It's Peter Giles! My dad's postgraduate student!' he said excitedly. 'He might know where Dad is!'

Nervously, Dinah scanned the windows of the AIU building. 'I think we ought to be careful—'

'You can be careful if you like! I want to talk to Peter!'

Dropping her arm Michael ran out of the garden and slithered down the slope towards the main path, calling as he went.

'Peter! Peter, wait for me!'

The young man didn't react at all. He just went on walking, in the same vague way, almost as if he were asleep. Michael slid down the last few feet to the path and landed right in front of him.

'Hi, Peter,' Dinah heard him say. 'Didn't you hear me? I—'

He stopped. The student was staring straight past him, with unfocused eyes.

'Peter? It's *me*. Michael Dexter. Don't you recognize me?'

There was no answer. Peter's face was completely blank. Michael stood staring at him in bewilderment.

Then the man in the brown anorak came hurrying out of the Unit. Ignoring Michael, he went up to Peter and put a hand on his shoulder. She couldn't hear what he said, but when he moved off Peter went with him, like a zombie.

Michael stood motionless, watching them climb into a car and drive off. Then he clambered up the slope, back to the garden. His face was white and frightened as he sat down on the bench again.

'That was horrible,' he whispered.

'He didn't know who you were?'

'He didn't know anything. It was like talking to some-one—' Michael shuddered. 'Like talking to someone who wasn't *there*. His eyes—'

Dinah forgot about not being like her mother or Mandy, and put an arm round his shoulders.

'Don't worry. The Headmaster's terrible, but he's never won yet. We'll beat him! When we find out what's going on.'

'But that's just what we can't do!' Michael said. It was almost a wail. 'Every day it gets harder to find things out. All the knowledge is disappearing. And now—'

He stopped. Dinah could feel his whole body shaking.

'It's always worse if you keep things to yourself,' she said. 'What's really scaring you? Tell me.'

Michael spoke slowly, as if he had to force the words out. 'First the Hyperbrain was taking the knowledge out of

libraries and newspapers and things. That was bad enough. Then we found it was using the Green Hand badges to snatch the knowledge from under people's noses—the things they actually see and hear. That felt much more dangerous. And now—'

'With Peter?' Dinah said.

Michael nodded. 'It's as if the Hyperbrain actually got inside his head and snatched the knowledge out. I think it's using—'

There was a long silence. Then he said three more words, speaking so softly that Dinah had to lean closer to hear.

'Direct Brain Access.'

Direct Brain Access, Dinah thought. *DiBrAc.* She was horribly afraid he was right. But she wasn't going to tell him that.

'You told me your dad wouldn't work on that! And you said no one knew how to do it!'

Michael twisted his fingers together. 'Maybe they do now. Maybe someone's worked it out.'

'Like who?'

'Like . . . the Hyperbrain.'

Dinah hadn't been expecting that. She stared. 'The Hyperbrain? By itself?'

'I keep telling you—it's not just a computer. It thinks, like us. It's curious and it wants to *know*.'

Dinah sat in silence for a moment, trying to work out what that meant. 'You're saying that it's the Hyperbrain itself that wants all this information?'

Michael nodded. 'I think so. I think it wants more and more and more. As if it can never be satisfied.'

'But why would the Headmaster let it grab everything? If he's in charge—'

'What makes you so sure he *is* in charge?' Michael said. He looked up, challenging her. 'How do you know the Hyperbrain hasn't outwitted him?'

Dinah felt as if a terrifying black space had opened up in front of her. She stared down at the AIU building and thought about the Headmaster and the Hyperbrain.

What was really going on in there?

Chapter 14

Mrs Hunter Steps In

Lloyd and Harvey were trying to find out what was going on too. But they were doing it with mirrors.

They were at home, helping to set up SPLATweb's Morse Code Link. There was a chain of mirrors and flags and Lloyd was reading the flashes from one mirror— Mirror Three—and calling them out to Harvey, so that Harvey could wave his flags and pass the message on to Mirror Four.

.../–/.–/–/..–/– – –/–.../.–/.../– –/–/.–/.– – –/– – ./.../...

s t a t i o n h a s t w o   g h b s

Harvey was getting flustered.

'I can't signal fast enough!' he grumbled, when there was a pause. 'Why can't we do something simpler? Like the CB radios or the pigeons? Or being in charge, at the cybercafé?'

Lloyd wasn't sympathetic. 'You'll get a turn. But we've got to start this going too. We need all the news we can get.' He frowned. 'I just wish we could hear something from Di.'

Harvey nodded. 'I thought you'd give her one of those CB radios.'

'What?' Lloyd stopped looking out of the window. He turned to stare at Harvey. 'Say that again.'

Harvey shrugged. 'Dinah could have had one of those CB radios, couldn't she? From Mandy's uncle. Why didn't you make her take one?'

'Because I didn't think of it, you dodo!' Frantically, Lloyd began to push his feet into his trainers.

'What are you doing?' Harvey said.

'I'm going to Mandy's, of course! To get a radio and take it to Di.'

'But it's almost tea time.'

'Danger doesn't stop for meals.' Scornfully, Lloyd banged out of the room. Harvey heard the front door slam behind him as he left the house.

Mrs Hunter called from upstairs. 'Was that Lloyd going out?'

'He . . . er . . .' Harvey dithered.

'Where has he gone? It's a bit late.'

'Not . . . um . . . not really,' Harvey was floundering. As his mother came downstairs, he switched on the television, to distract her. 'Look, it's only just time for *Your Wildest Dreams*.'

The picture swam into focus and they saw the screen twinkling with stars.

'Yes, folks!' said a fake-American voice. 'We're here to show you a dream come true! In just a few minutes, we'll be picking next week's lucky dreamer, but first let's meet the girl whose name was chosen last time.'

'What?' Mrs Hunter sat down abruptly on the couch. 'Is Dinah there after all?'

Harvey sat down too. *She can't be!* he was thinking. *She wouldn't go there—*

But it sounded as if she had.

'What a dreamer she is!' said the presenter's voice. 'You're going to love watching her favourite fantasy come true. Ladies and gentlemen, please give a big welcome to—'

No!

'—Miss Dinah Hunter!'

There was a terrifying pause. Trumpets blew a fanfare and Harvey gripped the arms of his chair, feeling sick.

119

Then a small, skinny figure marched on to the screen. She was wearing high heels and a very short mini-skirt and there was a large tattoo on her left arm. Her wild red hair was permed into a frizz.

'What on earth—?' Mrs Hunter said.

'It's the wrong Dinah Hunter!' Harvey was so relieved that he started laughing. And once he started, he couldn't stop. He rolled sideways on the couch, punching at the cushions.

Mrs Hunter was baffled. 'What's so funny? If there's another Dinah Hunter, it means that *our* Dinah's missed out. Don't you care?'

'Yes, of course,' Harvey gasped. 'I . . . I—'

But he couldn't hold his giggles back. He kept imagining the Headmaster marching into the studio, thinking he'd caught the right Dinah Hunter. And then seeing— The thought of that set Harvey laughing again.

It was a bad mistake. Mrs Hunter lost her temper.

'You're all being very peculiar. Something's going on, isn't it? First Dinah goes off to the university and now Lloyd's walked out. I don't like it, and I'm not getting any sense out of you. I'm going to Claudia's to fetch Dinah back. *She'll* tell me what's up.'

That stopped Harvey's laughter. He sat up sharply. 'But you can't—! I mean—'

'No?' His mother gave him a long, hard look. 'Why not?'

'Because . . . I mean . . .' The whole story flew through Harvey's mind, at top speed. He didn't see how he could ever explain. 'I mean . . . you can't go on your own,' he said at last. 'I'll come too.'

He didn't know what he was going to do, but at least he would be *there*.

*　　*　　*

120

Mrs Hunter drove on to the campus and parked in the multi-storey car park.

'All right,' she said. 'Now where's Claudia going to be? At home or in her office?'

'I'm . . . not sure,' Harvey stuttered. 'I know she works late sometimes but—'

Mrs Hunter was in no mood to hang around. 'We'll start in the Biological Sciences building, then.'

She strode out on to the campus and Harvey followed, frantically trying to slow her down. 'Look at those students, Mum! They're all exactly like each other! Look at their funny badges!'

It was useless. Mrs Hunter kept straight on, heading for the Biological Sciences building. Even when Harvey grabbed her arm, she didn't slow down. Sweeping into the building, she entered the lift, and pressed the button for the top floor. Harvey had to move quickly to get inside before the doors closed.

He stared out through the glass, wishing he could catch sight of Dinah. Or Lloyd. Or Michael. But the only person he saw was a thin man in a brown anorak, coming out of the Artificial Intelligence Unit.

When the lift reached the top, Mrs Hunter stepped out and knocked briskly on the door opposite, which had Claudia's name on it. Claudia opened the door.

Harvey was shocked by how stiff and unfriendly her face was. Mrs Hunter didn't seem to notice, though. She launched straight into a little speech she had obviously been planning.

'Hallo, Claudia. Thank you for having Dinah to stay for so long. I was just passing, so I thought I'd come and pick her up.'

'You . . . what?' The stiffness vanished, and Claudia looked bewildered.

Mrs Hunter gave her a sharp glance. 'You don't remember me, do you? I'm Dinah Hunter's mother.'

The words had an amazing effect. Suddenly, Claudia stopped looking cold and distant, and a warm smile spread across her face.

'Mrs Hunter! Of course! How's Dinah? It seems ages since I saw her.'

'I'm sorry?' Mrs Hunter looked puzzled. Slowly she turned to Harvey.

'Honestly, Mum, I can explain—'

He was desperately trying to invent a sensible explanation when his eye caught a glint of green on Claudia's shirt. He froze, staring in horror.

He'd forgotten Claudia's Green Hand badge! Everything they said was going straight to the Hyperbrain. And the Headmaster.

Harvey grabbed his mother's hand. 'We mustn't waste time. Dinah's not here. She—'

But Mrs Hunter wouldn't be distracted. She shook him off and took a step nearer to Claudia. 'I don't understand. Didn't you phone up and ask Dinah to stay? Lloyd said she was at the university, so I assumed she was with you. If you haven't seen her—where is she?'

Inside his head, Harvey groaned. The Headmaster must be gloating! He'd probably caught every word of that. *Lloyd said she was at the university* . . . Now the Headmaster would know that Dinah was on the campus.

Where *was* she? Harvey peered over his shoulder, hoping, wildly, that she would appear. But he couldn't see anything much except the entrance of the Artificial Intelligence Unit, and Dinah wasn't going to pop up there. She'd promised not to go in. He sighed and started to turn back to his mother and Claudia.

And then he saw something that turned him icy-cold.

There was a figure in the doorway of the Unit. A tall figure with pale hair and dark glasses.

Harvey thought he was going to faint. He couldn't hear what his mother and Claudia were saying. He forgot they were there. He just stood staring down in horror.

It was *him*! The Headmaster. There was no mistaking that cold, stern face, and the scornful way it looked round at the campus. He was there—and he was just the same as before!

He wasn't on his own, either. A whole group of weird students with Green Hand badges had followed him out of the building. He was busy giving orders, sending them out in all directions.

What was he doing?

Harvey was trying to see, when Mrs Hunter shook his arm.

'Harvey? What's the matter?'

'I . . . er . . . nothing.' He gulped and turned round.

'I expect he's worrying about Dinah,' Claudia said calmly. 'But there's no need. She's probably with Michael Dexter. Come into my office and I'll try and get through to them.'

With a last backward glance at the Headmaster, who was walking away from the AIU building, Harvey reluctantly followed his mother into the office. Claudia picked up her telephone, dialled, and frowned.

'Not *again*! The phone's completely dead. We'll have to go over to the Dexters' house—'

She was interrupted by a flicker on the computer screen and she smiled apologetically.

'I'll just take a look at my e-mail.' She laughed. 'You never know. It might be Dinah.'

Harvey read the message over her shoulder.

Please send Mrs Hunter and Harvey to the AIU laboratory.

'That looks like the answer to your problem,' Claudia said. 'Dinah must be there.'

'Typical!' Mrs Hunter grinned. 'Trust her to find a lab!' She turned and headed out of the office. 'Just wait till I get hold of her! Come on, Harvey.'

'But—'

Harvey couldn't make sense of it. Dinah had *promised* not to go to the AIU. That message couldn't be from her. But it couldn't be from the Headmaster, either. He'd just walked away from the Unit.

So who *had* sent it?

There was no time to think about it. Mrs Hunter was getting impatient. 'Come *on*, Harvey. Do you know where we have to go?'

'I'll show you,' Claudia said. She walked out on to the landing with them, and pointed down at the AIU building. 'That's it. There's a security thing at the entrance. Buzz and give your name, and someone will let you in.' She waved them into the lift.

As they slid down towards the ground, Harvey stood staring out at the campus. He could still see the tall figure of the Headmaster in the distance, striding away from them. By the time the lift stopped, he was completely out of sight.

Harvey followed his mother out of the Biological Sciences building and across to the AIU. She was peering ahead, at the entrance.

'Did Claudia say there was a buzzer?'

It was beside the front door. Harvey pressed it, and his mother leaned forward ready to speak her name into the grille.

But no one asked her to. Instead, the door clicked open and a voice came out of the speaker. A woman's voice.

'Good afternoon, Mrs Hunter. Good afternoon, Harvey. Please come in, and walk through to the back of the building.'

Harvey looked at his mother. 'Funny voice,' he said. 'It's too—' But he couldn't find the right word.

'Everyone sounds odd through those things,' said Mrs Hunter briskly. 'Come on.'

Pushing the door open, she walked into the building. There were office doors on each side of them and straight ahead, on the far side of the entrance hall, was a door marked *Laboratory*. They walked towards it, and the woman's voice spoke again, from behind the door.

'Please come in, Mrs Hunter. We must discuss something to do with Dinah. Harvey can wait outside.'

'Don't go!' Harvey whispered. 'It doesn't feel right.'

'Don't be silly,' Mrs Hunter said. 'I won't be long.'

She pushed the door open and went in. Harvey peered over her shoulder, trying to catch a glimpse of the woman who had spoken, but he couldn't see anything except an armchair and a large computer screen.

'Please close the door,' the woman's voice said.

Mrs Hunter turned, gave Harvey a rather worried smile and shut the door behind her.

Harvey crept up and put his ear to the door. He heard the murmur of two voices, but he couldn't make out any words.

After about ten minutes, the voices stopped. He pressed his ear closer to the wood, straining to catch a sound, but all he could hear was his own hair rustling. And an odd movement of the air that wasn't really sound at all. More like a kind of tingling.

Then the woman's voice spoke again, loud enough for him to hear clearly. 'Come in, Harvey.'

He reached for the door handle, and found that his hand was shaking. Taking a deep breath, he pushed the door open and walked through. His mother was sitting in the armchair, with her back to him. He couldn't see anyone else in the room.

'Mum?' he said uncertainly.

She didn't turn round.

'Mum!'

The mocking voice that answered him came out of the empty air.

'You won't get her to speak to you. You're not clever enough to work out how . . .'

Chapter 15

The Trap

At that very moment, Lloyd was racing across the campus to Michael's house. It had taken him ages to get the CB radio from Mandy, and then the bus had been late. He felt as if he'd never get to Dinah.

Even something as simple as crossing the campus was harder than usual. Everywhere he looked, there were weird students with Green Hand badges. They seemed to be stopping people and talking to them.

Lloyd dodged the first two, keeping out of sight of their badges, but the third one stepped in front of him, blocking his way.

'Excuse me,' he said. 'I'd just like to ask—'

Lloyd saw his own face, reflected very small in the student's badge. *Keep calm*, he told himself firmly. *The Headmaster won't recognize your face.* He forced himself to smile politely.

'Er . . . sorry. What did you say?'

'Excuse me.' The student repeated exactly the same words as before. 'I'd just like to ask whether you've seen this girl. She's somewhere on the campus.' He held out a sheet of computer printing.

Lloyd found himself staring at a grey, fuzzy picture of Dinah's face. He made himself study it for ten seconds or so before he looked up and shook his head. 'Haven't a clue.'

'Thank you,' the student said, mechanically.

He moved on down the path, towards the next person. As Lloyd began to run, he heard him start up again.

'Excuse me. I'd just like to ask whether you've seen . . .'

There was no time to waste! Lloyd tore through the campus, to Michael's house, and banged on the door.

Mrs Barnes opened it, looking startled. 'Yes, dear?'

'I . . . er . . . sorry. Is Michael—?'

'Up in the study. First door at the top of the stairs. Spends too much time with that computer, if you ask me.'

She waved Lloyd on, and he ran upstairs and knocked. There was a pause, and a shuffling noise. Then Michael opened the door. When he saw Lloyd, he grinned.

'It's all right, Dinah. You can come out. You're safe.'

Lloyd looked sharply at Dinah as she crawled out from behind the desk. 'You're *not* safe. The Headmaster's got his students out hunting for you. You mustn't go out.'

'But I've got to,' Dinah said impatiently. 'I won't find out anything in here.'

'It's not going to help if the Headmaster catches you. He—'

'Ssh!' Michael said suddenly.

The door bell was ringing again. They all heard Mrs Barnes shuffle to the door, and Lloyd pointed at the desk, meaning that Dinah ought to hide again.

But there was no chance of that. Before she could move, feet came running up the stairs and someone flung the door open. A frantic voice shouted at them all.

'You've got to help! It's Mum!'

Dinah had never seen Harvey so distraught. His face was red from running and he was gasping and wheezing.

'Calm down,' she said, even though her own heart was thudding. 'Get your breath back, so you can tell us properly.'

Harvey flopped down on to the bed, panting desperately. The moment he could speak, he launched into a great flood of words.

'It's Mum! She went to tell Claudia you had to come home . . . and there was an e-mail saying we had to go to the AIU . . . but there was nobody there only a voice . . . and it's got Mum and she's just sitting in a chair as if her mind's gone or something . . . and I saw the Headmaster go back in . . . and Mum's there—' He stopped for another gasp of air.

Dinah and Michael looked at each other.

DiBrAc, Dinah thought, with a terrible shuddering of her heart. She dropped on to her knees beside Harvey.

'You think Mum's had something done to her?'

Harvey's face twisted. 'It's horrible. I couldn't make her speak to me, and the voice kept saying: *You're not clever enough to solve this, Harvey Hunter. You're not clever enough to rescue your mother. That's why I came to get you.* I thought—'

So that's it, Dinah thought. *That's what I have to do.* She closed her eyes for a second and then stood up. Perfectly calm.

'I'll have to go to the AIU,' she said.

'But you can't!' Lloyd stared at her. 'Didn't you hear what Harvey said? The Headmaster's in there. It must be a trap!'

'I know!' Dinah said fiercely. 'But what else can I do?'

'You won't help by walking straight into the Headmaster's clutches. You know he's trying to catch you! He sent Claudia after you when he saw your face in her badge. He tried to catch you by fixing *Your Wildest Dreams*. And this is his next plan.'

'But—'

Dinah made herself stop. Quarrelling with Lloyd wasn't going to do any good. She had to *think*.

'We must get the Headmaster out of the AIU,' she said slowly.

Lloyd nodded. 'That's sensible. But how?'

'I know!' Michael jumped up excitedly. 'Dinah could walk past one of those peculiar students, with the badges. Then the Headmaster would see her and come out to chase her—'

'And he'd probably catch her,' Lloyd said. 'That wouldn't help.'

'Not if . . . she wasn't really there,' Harvey said. He'd got his breath back now, and he was working something out. 'Suppose *we* trick *him*. There's that badge that Dinah and Ian got at the Outdoor Centre. If one of us put that on—'

'Brilliant!' Dinah beamed at him.

Lloyd nodded. 'Well done, Harvey.' He unzipped his jacket and took out the CB radio. 'I'll get Ian to bring it. Hallo? Hallo?'

Ian's voice came crackling out of the radio. 'SPLATweb here!'

'It's Lloyd. Is everything OK?'

'Incredible! We've got messages pouring in.' Ian sounded amazed. 'We've just had a letter delivered by motorbike. And someone in that big block of flats is passing on semaphore messages. And there's a pigeon as well. How about you?'

'We've got . . . a problem,' Lloyd said cautiously. He didn't think the Headmaster could possibly be eavesdropping

131

on their call, but he wasn't taking any risks. 'We need the . . . er . . . the emerald fist thing that Plum and Jelly gave you.'

'The emerald—?' For a second, Ian didn't get it. Then he laughed. 'OK. Where are you?'

Lloyd hesitated. Dinah saw that he couldn't think of a nonsense way to explain.

'In the lost scientist's den,' she hissed.

Lloyd grinned and passed it on. 'We're lurking in the lost scientist's den.'

'I'll be right over!' Ian said.

It took him half an hour. By that time, they had the whole plan worked out and Lloyd explained it, pointing out the places on a plan of the university.

Ian looked at Dinah. 'Are you sure you want to do this? It's pretty dangerous.'

'It's just as dangerous for all of you,' Dinah said.

Harvey nodded. 'We're all in it together. SPLAT for ever!'

'OK, then.' Ian picked up the plan, looked at it one last time and folded it up. 'Let's get going.'

They crept down to the front door and peered out. The campus was crowded, but there was no sign of any of the weird students. Ian held out his cagoule, with the Green Hand badge rolled inside, and Lloyd took it. He put his finger to his lips.

'Total silence now. Don't let the Headmaster hear anything except what we want him to hear.'

Carefully, he unrolled the cagoule and took out the badge. Keeping it covered with his hand, he pinned it on to

Ian's sweatshirt. He looked round, to make sure the others were all out of view, and then dodged out of the way himself.

Right? he mouthed at Dinah.

She nodded. Deliberately, she stepped in front of Ian and began to walk away from him, towards the main road. When she was about fifty metres away, Harvey shouted. 'Hey! Dinah Hunter! Stop!'

Dinah turned to look back, staring straight at the badge on Ian's sweatshirt. Giving it a good view of her face.

'Stop!' Harvey yelled again. 'Come back!'

He dodged in front of Ian and Dinah raced away, round the side of a building. Harvey started after her, with Ian following. The two boys ran between the buildings, twisting and turning, as if Dinah were just ahead of them.

But she wasn't. She ran right round the first building and came back to Lloyd's side.

'Great!' he said. He nodded at Michael. 'Off you go. You've got to meet the others up by the bus stop.'

Michael ran off, and Lloyd grinned at Dinah. 'That was perfect. Let's get up to the AIU and see if it tricked the Headmaster. Is there somewhere we can hide?'

'There's a little garden.' Dinah led the way. 'We can watch from there.'

They didn't have long to wait. They had barely reached the garden when three of the weird students came hurrying out of the AIU. They ran off towards the main road.

Lloyd looked down at his watch and grinned at Dinah. 'Brilliant. The Headmaster's sent them to catch you up by the bus stop. Harvey should be ready to distract them. And Michael and Ian ought to be on the bus by now.'

'If it wasn't late,' Dinah said. She was frowning.

'Don't *worry*.'

'But suppose they catch Harvey—?'

Lloyd grinned. 'They won't even see him. He's brilliant at dodging. They'll just hear him calling your name, leading them on a wild goose chase.'

Dinah bit her lip and looked down at the AIU. She wished she could be as confident as Lloyd.

He was checking his watch again. 'Michael and Ian will be jumping *off* the bus now. It only takes a couple of minutes to get to the other end of the university. Michael will be pinning the badge on, and Ian will be shouting your name. The Headmaster should send someone else out in around thirty seconds. Twenty. Ten—'

It went like clockwork. As Lloyd's countdown finished, Claudia came running out of the building. Without hesitating, she headed for the far end of the university.

Miserably, Dinah stared after her. 'She's going to try and catch me.'

'It's not her fault,' Lloyd said. 'It's the Headmaster. And we're going to stop him. Right?'

'Right,' Dinah said.

But inside her head she added, *I hope*. They were all concentrating on getting her into the AIU, as if she would magically solve everything once she was inside. But what was she going to do?

Lloyd was still checking the time.

'OK. Ian's doing the dodging and shouting now. He'll keep Claudia busy. And Michael's racing off to the Sports Centre. If we're lucky, we might see him. Watch that gap between the buildings.'

He pointed and Dinah held her breath. She couldn't believe the plan would work so exactly.

But it did. For a split second, they saw Michael in the distance, racing across the opposite slope that led up to the Sports Centre. He disappeared round the side of the Centre, and Lloyd started working things out again.

'He'll have to find somewhere to prop the badge. Then he'll get in front of it and start calling you. And then—'

It could only have taken two or three minutes, but it seemed like hours. Dinah's fists were screwed up tight, and her brain was whirring, thinking of all the things that could go wrong.

Then Lloyd caught his breath.

'There he is,' he said softly.

The Headmaster was standing in the doorway of the AIU.

Until that moment, Dinah hadn't quite believed that it was him. She'd worked it out, logically, but that was quite different from seeing him actually standing there, real and solid.

Exactly the same.

The moment she saw that cold, stern face, she stopped worrying about the things that might go wrong. Nothing could be allowed to go wrong. They had to stop the Headmaster from taking over. Because if he got a grip on things he would fill the whole world with his own cruel efficiency.

There would be no room for feelings, or differences, or imagination.

Dinah clenched her fists and began to concentrate on what she might do.

The Headmaster didn't stand in the doorway for long. He glanced up and down the campus once, and then set off towards the Sports Centre.

Lloyd stood up. 'Ready?'

Dinah gave him the best grin she could manage. 'Let's go.'

They ran down the slope towards the AIU. Michael had told them the security code, but they didn't need it. The moment Dinah touched the entry button, the door swung open by itself. She looked at Lloyd and he shrugged.

'The Headmaster must have forgotten to shut it.'

Dinah didn't think he had, but she wasn't going to argue. 'You'll stay here and keep watch?'

Lloyd nodded. 'Good luck.'

Dinah turned and walked into the building. It was very quiet inside. All the doors were open and she could see that the offices were empty. She made straight for the lab. For a second she paused, to catch her breath. Then she opened the door and went in.

Her mother was sitting in an armchair, with her back to the door.

'Mum?' Dinah said.

There was no answer. Slowly, Dinah walked round the chair. Her mother was wearing a strange headband, with lots of equipment fixed to it. And she was staring straight ahead, with unfocused eyes.

'Mum?' Dinah said again.

There was no reaction.

Stepping forward, Dinah caught hold of her arm. It was warm, and her mother was breathing in an easy, relaxed way, but she didn't make any response. She just went on sitting and staring with the same utterly blank expression.

Slowly, Dinah turned and looked round the room. There was no one else there, but she was aware of something. A sort of presence.

'Where are you?' she shouted. '*Who* are you? What do you want?'

The answer came from behind her, in a woman's voice. Smooth and sweet.

'Hallo, Dinah Hunter. I've been waiting for you.'

Chapter 16

'Which Side Are You On, Dinah Hunter?'

Lloyd couldn't understand why Dinah was being so long. Everyone had left the AIU, hadn't they? Why didn't she just bring Mum out, so that they could escape?

He stuck his head inside the building, but he couldn't hear what was happening, even though the door of the lab was ajar. He was on the verge of going after Dinah when there was a crackle from the CB radio in his hand.

'SPLATbase here!' said Ingrid's voice. 'I've just been pecked by a pigeon.'

'Ssh!' Lloyd hissed. 'I can't talk now!'

'But you've got to!' Ingrid said urgently. 'I've got to tell you the message. From the pigeon.'

'But I can't—'

'Listen!' Ingrid began to read, without giving him any more time to protest:

'News from a hacker—Stop the Hand!
'It's got control of all the land!
'Tonight, at midnight, on the hour
'It'll get the army in its power.
'If it controls our fighting men
'No one will defeat it then!'

Lloyd felt his heart thump. 'Do you think it's true? I mean—is the Hyperbrain really taking over the army?'

'Sounds like it,' Ingrid said. Her voice was scared. 'We've got to do something, Lloyd. We've got to stop him—'

'Don't worry,' Lloyd said. 'We will. We—'

He stopped suddenly. He'd been so busy talking to Ingrid that he had forgotten to keep watch. Now it was too late. The Headmaster was striding down the slope from the Sports Centre. And he was dragging Michael with him.

'Emergency!' Lloyd hissed into the radio. 'Keep silence until I call!'

Sliding the aerial down, he slipped the radio into his pocket. It was too late to warn Dinah. It was too late to hide. All he could do was stand there and watch the Headmaster heading towards him.

Michael was looking at him with helpless, terrified eyes—but the Headmaster barely gave him a glance. As he reached the door, he waved impatiently.

'Out of my way, boy!' he snapped.

It was the eeriest moment of Lloyd's life. He was staring straight into the Headmaster's face, straight at the dark glasses that hid those cold, sea-green eyes. He knew that face almost as well as he knew his own. He had even seen it in his dreams. But the Headmaster didn't recognize him.

Putting out an arm, he brushed Lloyd out of the way. 'Take that toy radio somewhere else,' he said.

He pulled Michael into the AIU and pushed at the door to close it behind them. Just in time, Lloyd stuck out his hand. Instead of shutting, the door swung on to his fingers. He hardly noticed the pain. Holding his breath, he crept through the door and slipped into one of the empty offices.

Inside the lab, Dinah was bending over her mother's chair. Suddenly she felt someone watching her and she straightened and spun round.

A figure had appeared on the far side of the lab, in front of the shelves. It was the woman Dinah and Michael had seen before, and she was standing in exactly the same place.

'Who *are* you?' Dinah said. 'What have you done to my mother?'

The woman gave her a long, slow stare. 'Your mother has . . . provided me with information,' she said at last.

'It's DiBrAc, isn't it? You've destroyed her mind.'

'Nothing is destroyed. Your mother's knowledge is here. Safely stored.'

The woman gestured towards the shelves behind her, at the Molecular Storage Units. They were heaped up, just as they had been last time Dinah saw them. But, this time, three of them were translucent and glittering.

'Three?' Dinah said softly.

'They hold the knowledge from three human brains. This one—' The woman pointed. '—is Tim Dexter's.'

Dinah caught her breath. 'Where is he? What have you—'

'He is perfectly safe,' the woman said smoothly. 'And his knowledge has been extremely useful. Especially his design for an interface for the Hyperbrain.'

She smiled, a small, strange smile, and Dinah felt her skin prickle.

'What about the others?' she said.

'The next one comes from a meddling student who came asking questions about Tim Dexter.'

'Peter Giles,' Dinah said.

'That is correct. And this—' The woman made a small gesture towards the third cylinder. Dinah had to fight the scream that exploded inside her.

'That's Mum, isn't it? But why did you do it to *her*? She's not a scientist.'

The woman didn't answer directly. 'I know all about you now, Dinah Hunter. I know how you were adopted. I know that you like sausages and hate ravioli. I know the pattern on your pyjamas and the marks on your last school report. I know—'

'You've destroyed my mother's brain for *that*?'

'Your mother's brain is not destroyed. She can have it back whenever you choose. If—'

If.

Of course there was an if. Dinah had known that, all along. This was a trap, and her mother was the bait. It seemed that the Headmaster and this strange woman both wanted something that only she could give them.

She wished she knew what it was.

'If what?' she said.

The woman glided closer. Her feet were eerily silent on the floor. 'I want to know about the man who says he is the master of the Hyperbrain,' she said.

'You want to know about the Headmaster? Is that *all*?' Dinah felt like crying with relief. 'What do you want to know?'

But the woman shook her head. 'Telling is not enough. You might lie. Or forget. The knowledge must go straight from your mind into the mind of the Hyperbrain. Then I can be sure that I have it all.'

Dinah's eyes travelled to the next empty, opaque Molecular Storage Unit, and the woman nodded.

'I can see that you are intelligent and well informed. I shall enjoy exploring your mind.' For a second, her eyes flickered hungrily.

Dinah shuddered. 'Why should I let you destroy my brain as well?'

'Your brain will not be destroyed. And I will make a bargain with you. Give me what I want, and I will restore the rest of your knowledge. And your mother's.'

'What about Tim Dexter?' Dinah said quickly. 'And Peter Giles?'

The woman looked surprised. 'Why should you care about them?'

'Because they're people!'

For a moment, the woman hesitated, considering. Then she nodded. 'Give me Direct Access to your brain and I will give you all the used Storage Units, and tell you what to do with them. And where to find the people who provided the information.'

Dinah looked at her mother's blank, unmoving face and knew that she would have to accept the bargain. But . . . she was being offered everything that she asked. What did she know that was worth so much?

The woman was obviously growing impatient, because she began to murmur in her soft, sweet voice. 'Maybe I have miscalculated. I thought you would want to save your mother. But she's not your *real* mother, is she? Why should you risk your life to save her?'

'Of course she's my real mother!' Dinah said fiercely. 'Nobody could be a realer mother than she is to me! Of course I'll take the risk.' She struggled to stay calm and think clearly, but it was hard when the woman knew everything about her. And how to manipulate her.

'What do you want me to do?' she said.

The woman took another silent step towards her. 'You see the headband your mother is wearing? Take it off, and put it on your own head.'

Dinah undid the headband. Her mother didn't seem aware of what was happening, but Dinah did it very gently, trying to send messages through her fingers. *I'm looking after you, Mum. It's going to be all right.*

Trembling slightly, she lifted the headband, put it on her own head and adjusted it to fit. It was studded with tiny magnetic sensors and transdermal conductors and she had a pretty good idea of the way it would access her brain. But how would it channel the information back to the Hyperbrain?

There had to be a connection somewhere, but she couldn't see it.

The woman didn't explain. She simply waited until the headband was fastened. Then she said, 'Let us waste no more time.' She began to move towards Dinah.

But before she was half-way there, the door was flung open and a tall figure came striding into the room, dragging Michael behind him by one hand.

'Stop!' he shouted. 'Don't let her take what you know, Dinah Hunter—or she will rule the world!'

It was the Headmaster.

Defiantly, Dinah spun round to face him. 'Why should I take your side, against her? You want to rule the world as well, don't you?'

The Headmaster didn't answer in words. Instead, he took hold of Michael's shoulders and pushed him forward, straight at the woman.

Michael staggered, reaching out to save himself from falling. Dinah saw his hands touch the woman's arm. But they didn't stop there. They went on moving, as though there was nothing solid in their way. Michael fell forward and for one brief second—impossibly—he and the woman both occupied the same space.

Then he tumbled to his knees, falling right through the woman's body, and sprawled full length on the floor.

'She is not human,' the Headmaster said. 'She is a hologram. Do you want *that* to rule the world?'

The woman stood perfectly still, expressionless. Michael looked up at her, from the floor.

'You're the interface, aren't you?' he said, in an awed, wondering voice. 'The new interface my father designed.'

Gravely, she nodded. 'Tim Dexter's mind was full of useful knowledge,' she said smoothly.

The Headmaster looked triumphantly at Dinah. 'You see? She is an illusion. When you talk to her, you are really talking to the Hyperbrain. A computer with no human feelings. Do you want to give the world to *that*?'

The woman smiled her small, strange smile and glided soundlessly nearer to Dinah. 'Maybe that would be better than giving the world to *him*,' she murmured.

'I—' Dinah didn't know what to say.

The Headmaster didn't give her a chance to think. He stepped closer too. 'You cannot hand over the whole human race to a machine.'

'And you cannot hand it over to a monster,' said the woman. 'What are you going to do, Dinah Hunter?'

'*Me?*' Dinah said. 'What's it got to do with me?'

All at once, the room was very quiet. Even the air seemed to have grown still. Michael lay motionless on the floor. Mrs Hunter sat unmoving in the chair. The Headmaster and the woman both had their eyes fixed on Dinah.

She looked back steadily. 'What do I know that's so important? Why does the Hyperbrain want *my* knowledge?'

'She doesn't want it for herself,' the Headmaster said impatiently. 'She wants to keep me from getting it. You know the one thing I need to stop her,' the Headmaster said.

'Why do you need anything? I thought you were the Controller of the Hyperbrain.'

'I am. The Hyperbrain is programmed to obey me, and no one else. I am its master.' A faint frown crossed the

145

Headmaster's face. 'But Tim Dexter made a blunder in his programming. To take over, I need two words. Unless I have them, no one will be able to master the Hyperbrain. It will be out of control, and that woman will run the world to satisfy her thirst for knowledge.'

'And what would you do?' Dinah said.

'I would run it sensibly. Efficiently. Without allowing people to ruin it with their stupid wishes.' The Headmaster dropped his voice suddenly. Instead of shouting at Dinah, he started to croon. 'You know me, Dinah Hunter, don't you? You know what I'm like. Tell these other people. Tell them who I am.'

What was he up to? Dinah took a step back, looking warily at him.

'Tell them who I am,' he crooned. 'Tell them my name. What is it, Dinah?'

'Your name?' Dinah blinked. 'What does that prove?'

'Tell them my name . . .'

Michael sat up suddenly. 'No!' he shouted. 'That's it, Dinah! That's what he needs to take over.'

'What?' Dinah blinked.

'It's the security procedure! He made Dad programme the Hyperbrain to obey a single master. But he didn't tell him to suspend the security procedure. The Hyperbrain won't recognize him until he gives his name.'

Suddenly Dinah understood everything. 'He's got the old Headmaster's face—but he hasn't got his memory. So he doesn't know his name!'

'Don't tell him,' said the woman, from half-way across the room. 'If you do, he will take over the Hyperbrain, and rule the world.'

'And if you don't,' shouted the Headmaster, 'the Hyper-brain will rule the world by itself. Which side are you on, Dinah Hunter?'

Helplessly, Dinah looked from the smooth hologram of the woman's head to the Headmaster's pale, stern face.

What on earth am I going to do? she thought.

Chapter 17

All the Knowledge in the World

Lloyd had crept right up to the door. He watched in horror as Dinah turned towards the Headmaster.

No! he thought. *You can't take his side!*

Then she turned the other way, towards the beautiful, inhuman interface.

No! Not her either!

All the while, the Headmaster's voice was murmuring on and on. 'My name, Dinah Hunter! Tell me my name. My name . . .'

Dinah looked from one to the other, faster and faster. At last, she laughed harshly. 'Your name's . . . Rumpelstiltskin!'

Lloyd knew it was just a desperate, unfunny joke—but the Headmaster obviously didn't. For an instant, a smile of triumph spread across his face.

'Rumpel Stiltskin! My name—'

Then the woman began to rattle out words. Not in her usual sweet, syrupy way, but in a ragged, erratic voice, as though something had disturbed her. 'Rumpelstilt . . . skin is a . . . dwarf in . . . German fairytale . . . not real name . . . nonsense . . .'

Lloyd saw Dinah's face light up, the way it did when she made a wonderful new discovery. Flinging back her head, she began to chant in a loud, cheerful voice.

''Twas brillig and the slithy toves
Did gyre and gimble in the wabe,
All mimsy were the borogoves
And the mome raths outgrabe!'

The Headmaster glared at her. 'What are you saying? Why are you wasting time like this—?'

Oh good! thought Lloyd gleefully. *That's upset him. He doesn't like nonsense. He—*

And then he saw the interface, and for a second he forgot all about the Headmaster. Because she was even more disturbed. Behind her, the big computer screen was buzzing and flashing, and her body was beginning to shake and judder. The hologram image had started to turn fuzzy.

'Beware the Jabberwock, my son!' Dinah was chanting,

'The jaws that bite, the claws that catch!

Beware the Jub-jub bird—'

All of a sudden, Michael realized what she was trying to do. Jumping to his feet, he began to chant as well.

'As I was going up the stair

I met a man who wasn't there—'

The Headmaster shook his head from side to side, as if he were trying to get rid of the rubbish Michael and Dinah were speaking. And the woman was growing more and more shapeless. Jagged black stripes were shooting across her image, and flashes of green light were exploding from her shoulders.

It was the nonsense! The Hyperbrain couldn't cope with jokes and nonsense! Lloyd felt like shouting and cheering, but there wasn't time for that yet. Stepping away from the lab doorway, he flicked on the CB radio.

'Calling SPLATweb! Calling SPLATweb! Everyone who's near a Green Hand badge must talk rubbish to it! TALK NONSENSE NOW!'

Mandy stood in the cybercafé and stared at her CB radio. What was going on? Had Lloyd gone mad?

Ingrid reacted faster. 'Let me have the keyboard, Kate! And you and Mandy send out this message every way you can! Get the pigeons going! Catch the milkman! *Anything!*'

She began to type at top speed, trying to contact anyone who could still get Crazyspace.

They like logic, they like fact,
Fantasy will have them whacked!
Talk rubbish no one understands
To all those grabby greenish hands!
Give them nonsense overload!
Netspeak junk till they explode!

Mandy understood now. She began to scribble messages on little pieces of paper, fixing them into rings for the pigeons' legs . . . *Talk rubbish no one understands* . . .

Kate was up at the window with a mirror, signalling for all she was worth. Sending out the message to Mirror One, so that it could flash on to Mirror Two and Mirror Three . . . *Give them nonsense overload* . . .

Back in the lab, Dinah still thought she was on her own, except for Michael. She was racking her brains to keep up a constant stream of gibberish.

'One fine day in the middle of the night,
Two dead men got up to fight . . .'

She couldn't concentrate properly, because she knew the Headmaster wouldn't let himself be defeated that easily. He was bound to try something—

'Back to back they faced each other . . .'

She was right. Just as she was searching for the next line, his hand went up to his dark glasses. *No!* she thought. Backing away, she screwed up her eyes to stop herself from seeing those strange green eyes. She heard him chanting as he pulled off the glasses.

'Why are you talking when you are so sleepy, Dinah Hunter? So very, very sleepy . . .'

I'm not sleepy! I'm not! She raised her voice and went on shouting, with her eyes tightly closed.

'And with their swords they shot one another!'

But she couldn't keep her eyes shut. There was a sudden shriek from Michael.

'Dinah! Watch out behind you!'

Whisking round, she saw the hologram woman gliding towards her. She hardly looked human now. Her shape was blurred and jagged and whole sections of her body were breaking down into patterns of swirling dots. But her hands were still the shape they should have been, and they were stretching out towards Dinah. Reaching for her head. Big square hands, with long green fingers reaching out to grab. Once she had the knowledge from Dinah's brain, she would never let it go.

Dinah didn't wait to work out what a hologram could do to her. Instinctively she dodged sideways, spinning away.

And she found herself looking at the Headmaster again.

'You are very sleepy . . .' he was crooning.

She had never felt so lonely and desperate in her life.

But she wasn't alone. All over the country, children were getting the message. Gazing at flashing mirrors. Pulling pieces of paper from their pigeons' legs.

They like logic, they like fact,
Fantasy will have them whacked!

151

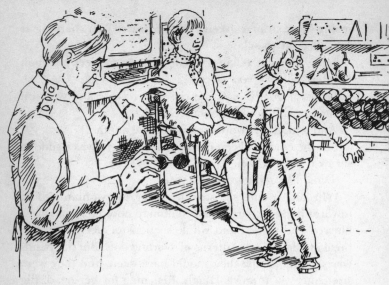

Ham radio fans were sending it on in Morse code, and boys and girls in the streets were banging on doors and shouting to their friends.

Talk rubbish no one understands
To all those grabby greenish hands!

SPLATweb was working at full stretch. Everywhere people were running towards the nearest Green Hand badge as they deciphered Ingrid's rap.

Give them nonsense overload!
Netspeak junk till they explode!

'Squeeble greezzerpop!' Dinah shouted, with her hands over her face. 'Criadion boogledrip!'

She had got beyond remembering nonsense rhymes. And she didn't dare look up because, if she did, the Headmaster

would hypnotize her and find out his name. She mustn't let him get it.

'Poodle-noodle farby jerrup! Fiddle-diddle hayrake!'

Somewhere very close, Michael was shouting too, and she could tell that he was near the end of his tether as well.

'Grass is kinder than a horse is blue. How Thursday are you, my dear soup? No pale is motorbike mania.'

The nonsense was disrupting the Hyperbrain. Dinah could hear the computer struggling and buzzing—but it was still going. She and Michael couldn't produce enough nonsense on their own.

'Di!' It was Lloyd's voice, from the doorway. 'Watch out! That woman—'

Frantically, Dinah opened her eyes and spun round. But she was too late. The woman was there, close enough to touch her. Her whole shape was juddering and disintegrating, but her arms were reaching up, up towards Dinah's head. And those horrible green hands were closing round the headband. Grabbing for knowledge.

Dinah had one last moment of clear thinking. *So that's how it's done! There's a force field round the hologram that makes the connection—*

Then the green hands reached the headband she was wearing, and something caught hold of her brain, squeezing it into unconsciousness . . .

'No!' shouted Lloyd. 'Let her go! You can't—'

He ran into the room, but before he was half-way to Dinah he saw the Headmaster's scornful face.

'You fool!' the Headmaster said coldly. 'If you interrupt the DiBrAc process, she will die.'

'But we can't—'

'We can do nothing. The Hyperbrain will not stop now until her mind has gone. Until she is like Tim Dexter and that woman in the chair.'

'But the woman promised she would be all right!' Lloyd said frantically.

The Headmaster looked even more scornful. 'Why should anyone keep a promise?'

Desperately, Lloyd looked at Dinah's blank, white face, trapped between those clutching green hands. It looked small and empty. What could he do? There must be something!

Like magic, a voice spoke out of the air.

Twinkle twinkle little bat!

'What?' The Headmaster frowned and looked round.

How I wonder what you're at, the voice went on cheerfully.
Up above the world so high—
Before it could finish the line, it was joined by another voice.
Far and few, far and few
Are the lands where the Jumblies live—
'What?' said the Headmaster again. 'Who?'
And another.
Little Nanny Etticoat
In a white petticoat—
The woman's glittering hands began to shake and tremble. Suddenly—gloriously—Lloyd knew what they were hearing. It was SPLATweb!

Children all over the country were talking nonsense into Green Hand badges, and their voices were being relayed through the Hyperbrain. The woman was getting the full blast of it. She lost colour completely, so that she became a trembling black shape.

And Dinah's closed eyes opened wide.

'Hold on, Di!' Lloyd yelled. 'It's going to be all right!'

But Dinah wasn't smiling. Her eyes opened wider still. And suddenly she was shouting.

'It's gone into reverse! All the knowledge is coming *into* my brain! It's . . . it's—'

Good? Bad? Looking at her twisted face, Lloyd couldn't tell.

But the Headmaster jumped forward, with a shout of fury. 'You? *You* are getting all the world's knowledge? Give me that headband!'

'You don't . . . understand . . .' Dinah gasped. 'It's not—'

He didn't listen. Plunging his arms full into the black turmoil of the hologram woman's hands, he pulled at the headband, wrenching it off Dinah's head. She staggered forward, stumbling against Lloyd and Michael.

The Headmaster jammed the headband on to his own head and, for a moment, his eyes glowed with triumph.

'Knowledge is power! All the knowledge in the world will be mine!'

Then a fresh surge of nonsense billowed out of the loudspeakers, as dozens more voices joined in.

Doctor Foster went to Gloucester . . .

Purple rabbit, purple rabbit, catch me if you can . . .

High over Colchester the moon eats chips . . .

Lloyd didn't recognize any of the voices, but Dinah did. She spun round, joyfully. 'Plum!' she shouted. 'Jelly!'

It sounded like more nonsense. For the Hyperbrain, it was obviously the last straw. With a terrible shriek, the woman exploded into a million emerald stars. The computer screen went blank, and the Headmaster crumpled and fell to the ground.

The lab was eerily, abruptly silent.

The silence was broken by the sound of feet running into the building. Ian and Harvey pushed open the lab door.

'What's going on?' Ian said.

'What's happening to Mum?' said Harvey.

Dinah bent down and unstrapped the headband from the Headmaster's head. Then she walked over to the shelves on the far side of the lab and took down three glittering cylinders. When she turned round, Lloyd could see that she was exhausted, but she didn't falter.

'It's going to be all right,' she said wearily. 'I know exactly what to do. And I know where your father is, Michael. And Peter Giles. Someone go and phone for an ambulance for the Headmaster, and then I'll start.'

'What I want to know,' said Ingrid, 'is what it was *like*. Having all the knowledge in the world flooding into your head.' She took a large bite of her cream bun.

Dinah looked round the university library, where they were standing. It was crowded with people who'd come to celebrate the re-opening, but she wasn't looking at them. She waved her hand at the shelves full of books.

'Imagine someone trying to squash all that into your head, in twenty seconds.'

Mandy shuddered. 'If the Headmaster hadn't snatched that headband, you'd probably be in a coma in hospital, like him. Knowledge is wonderful, but you can't keep it *all* in your head.'

'Well, you got the right bits,' Lloyd said. 'If the Hyperbrain hadn't gone into reverse, you'd never have found out how to get Mum back to normal.' He glanced across the library, to where Mrs Hunter was chatting to Tim Dexter. 'Do you think they realize what happened?'

Michael shook his head. 'Dad thinks he was ill for a bit. And your mum told me she dropped off to sleep. Dad's already trying to redesign the Hyperbrain so it doesn't overload again. He had a long talk to Mr Smith about it yesterday.'

Lloyd frowned. 'Mr Smith.' He looked across at the man in the brown anorak who had just joined Tim Dexter and Mrs Hunter. 'Of course! He's in Intelligence, isn't he?'

'Artificial Intelligence?' said Mandy.

Lloyd shook his head. 'Spies and stuff, I think.'

Ian whistled. 'And even *he* got hypnotized by the Headmaster? It's frightening, isn't it?'

'No, it's not,' Ingrid said cheerfully. 'Because *we beat the Headmaster*! Mr Smith ought to be grateful to us. I'm going to go and ask him about spying.'

She bounded forward and the others raced after her, to make sure she didn't say anything dreadful.

Dinah was left on her own. She stood for a moment, staring round at the library. It was safe now. Like the newspapers and the Internet and everything else. For a moment she wondered what life would have been like if they hadn't defeated the Headmaster. And the Hyperbrain.

Then Claudia came over from the other side of the library, and greeted her with a warm, happy smile.

'Dinah! Just the person I wanted to see. I've had a brilliant new thought about that creeper . . .'

She started explaining it, and Dinah forgot all about the Headmaster.

Everyone forgot him, except the nurse who was sitting beside his bed, in Intensive Care.

Waiting to see if his eyes would open . . .

Other titles by
DARREN SHAN

THE SAGA OF DARREN SHAN

THE DEMONATA

*Also available on audio

DARREN SHAN

SONS OF DESTINY

THE SAGA OF DARREN SHAN
BOOK 12

HarperCollins *Children's Books*

Discover your Destiny with Darren Shan on the web at
www.darrenshan.com

First published in Great Britain by HarperCollins *Children's Books* 2004
This edition published 2009
HarperCollins *Children's Books* is a division of HarperCollins*Publishers* Ltd,
77-85 Fulham Palace Road, Hammersmith,
London, W6 8JB

The HarperCollins website address is:
www.harpercollins.co.uk

1

Text copyright © Darren Shan 2004

ISBN-13   978 0 00 794560 3

For:

Bas, Biddy and Liam — my three pillars

OBE's
(Order of the Bloody Entrails) to:

"Lucky" Aleta Moriarty

A and Bo — Bangkok's best banshees
Emily "Lilliputian" Chuang
Jennifer "Stacey" Abbots

Saga Editors:
Domenica De Rosa, Gillie Russell, Zoë Clarke and
Julia Bruce — you done good, girls!!!

Bloody Brilliant Buccaneers:
The Christopher Little Cutthroats

And an extra special thank you to all of my Shansters,
especially those who have kept me company on Shanville.
Even in death may you all be triumphant!

PROLOGUE

If my life was a fairy tale and I was writing a book about it, I'd start with, "Once upon a time there were two boys called Darren and Steve..." But my life's a horror story, so if I were to write about it, I'd have to begin with something like this instead:

Evil has a name — Steve Leopard.

He was born Steve Leonard, but to his friends (yes — he had friends once!) he was always Steve Leopard. He was never happy at home, didn't have a dad, didn't like his mum. He dreamt of power and glory. He yearned for strength and respect, and time in which to enjoy it. He wanted to be a vampire.

His chance came when he spotted a creature of the night, Larten Crepsley, performing in the wondrous magical show, the Cirque Du Freak. He asked Mr Crepsley to blood him. The vampire refused — he said Steve had bad blood. Steve

hated him for that and vowed to track him down and kill him when he grew up.

Some years later, as Steve was preparing for his life as a vampire hunter, he learnt about the purple-skinned, red-eyed vampaneze. In legends, vampires are wicked killers who suck humans dry. That's hysterical rubbish — they only take small amounts of blood when they feed, causing no harm. But the vampaneze are different. They broke away from the vampire clan six hundred years ago. They live by laws of their own. They believe it's shameful to drink from a human without killing. They always murder when they feed. Steve's sort of people!

Steve went in search of the vampaneze, certain they'd accept him. He probably thought they were as twisted as he was. But he got it wrong. Although the vampaneze were killers, they weren't inherently evil. They didn't torture humans and they tried not to interfere with vampires. They went about their business quietly and calmly, keeping a lower-than-low profile.

I don't know this for sure, but I'm guessing the vampaneze rejected Steve, just like Mr Crepsley did. The vampaneze live by even stricter, more traditional rules than vampires. I can't see them accepting a human into their ranks if they knew he was going to turn out bad.

But Steve found a way in, thanks to that eternal agent of chaos — Desmond Tiny. Most just call him Mr Tiny, but if you shorten his first name and put it with his surname, you get Mr *Destiny*. He's the most powerful person in the world,

immortal as far as anyone knows, a meddler of the highest order. He gave the vampaneze a present many centuries earlier, a coffin which filled with fire whenever a person lay within it, burning them to ash within seconds. But he said that one night someone would lie in the coffin and emerge unharmed. That person would be the Lord of the Vampaneze and had to be obeyed by every member of the clan. If they accepted this Lord, they'd gain more power than they'd ever imagined. Otherwise they'd be destroyed.

The promise of such power proved too much for Steve to ignore. He decided to take the test. He probably figured he had nothing to lose. He entered the coffin, the flames engulfed him, and a minute later he stepped out unburnt. Suddenly, everything changed. He had an army of vampaneze at his command, willing to give their lives for him and do anything he asked. He no longer had to settle for killing Mr Crepsley — he could wipe out the entire vampire clan!

But Mr Tiny didn't want the vampaneze to crush the vampires too easily. He thrives on suffering and conflict. A quick, assured victory wouldn't provide him with enough entertainment. So he gave the vampires a get-out clause. Three of them had the ability to kill the Vampaneze Lord before he came fully into his powers. They'd have four chances. If they were successful and killed him, the vampires would win the War of the Scars (that's what the battle between the vampires and vampaneze was known as). If they failed, two would die during the hunt, while the third would survive to witness the downfall of the clan.

Mr Crepsley was one of the hunters. A Vampire Prince, Vancha March, was another. The last was also a Prince, the youngest ever, a half-vampire called Darren Shan — and that's where *I* come in.

I was Steve's best friend when we were kids. We went to the Cirque Du Freak together, and through Steve I learnt of the existence of vampires and was sucked into their world. I was blooded by Mr Crepsley and served as his assistant. Under his guidance I studied the ways of vampires and travelled to Vampire Mountain. There I undertook my Trials of Initiation — and failed. Fearing death, I fled, but during my escape I uncovered a plot to destroy the clan. Later I exposed it, and as a reward I was not only accepted into the fold, but made a Vampire Prince.

After six years in Vampire Mountain, Mr Tiny set me on the trail of the Lord of the Vampaneze, along with Mr Crepsley and Vancha. One of Mr Tiny's Little People travelled with us. His name was Harkat Mulds. Little People are grey-skinned, stitched-together, short, with large green eyes, no nose, and ears sewn beneath the flesh of their heads. They're created from the remains of dead people. Harkat didn't know who he used to be, but we later found out he was Kurda Smahlt in his previous life — the vampire who'd betrayed the clan in the hope of preventing the War of the Scars.

Not knowing who the Vampaneze Lord was, we missed our first chance to kill him when Vancha let him escape, because he was under the protection of Vancha's vampaneze

brother, Gannen Harst. Later, in the city of Mr Crepsley's youth, I ran into Steve again. He told me he was a vampaneze hunter and, fool that I was, I believed him. The others did too, although Mr Crepsley was suspicious. He sensed something wrong, but I convinced him to grant Steve the benefit of the doubt. I've made some terrible mistakes in my life, but that was certainly the worst.

When Steve revealed his true colours, we fought, and twice we had the power to kill him. The first time we let him live because we wanted to trade his life for Debbie Hemlock's — my human girlfriend. The second time, Mr Crepsley fought Steve, Gannen Harst and an impostor, who was pretending to be the Lord of the Vampaneze. Mr Crepsley killed the impostor, but then was knocked into a pit of stakes by Steve. He could have taken Steve down with him, but let him live so that Gannen and the other vampaneze would spare the lives of his friends. It was only afterwards that Steve revealed the truth about himself, and made the bitter loss of Mr Crepsley all the more unbearable.

There was a long gap between that and our next encounter. I went with Harkat to find out the truth about his past, to a waste world full of monsters and mutants, which we later discovered was Earth in the future. Upon my return I spent a couple of years travelling with the Cirque Du Freak, waiting for destiny (or Des Tiny) to pit Steve and me together again for one final clash.

Our paths finally crossed in our old home town. I'd returned with the Cirque Du Freak. It was strange revisiting

the past, walking the streets of the town where I'd grown up. I saw my sister Annie, now a grown woman with a child of her own, and I ran into an old friend, Tommy Jones, who'd become a professional footballer. I went to watch Tommy play in an important cup game. His team won, but their celebrations were cut short when two of Steve's henchmen invaded the pitch and killed a lot of people, including Tommy.

I chased after the murderous pair, straight into a trap. I faced Steve again. He had a child called Darius with him — his son. Darius shot me. Steve could have finished me off, but didn't. It wasn't the destined time. My end (or his) would only come when I faced him with Vancha by my side.

Crawling through the streets, I was rescued by a pair of tramps. They'd been recruited by Debbie and an ex-police inspector, Alice Burgess, who were building a human army to help the vampires. Vancha March linked up with me while I was recovering. With the ladies and Harkat, we returned to the Cirque Du Freak. We discussed the future with Mr Tall, the owner of the circus. He told us that no matter who won the war, an evil dictator known as the Lord of the Shadows would rise to rule and destroy the world.

As we were trying to come to terms with the shocking news, two of Steve's crazed followers struck — R.V. and Morgan James, the pair who'd killed Tommy. With the help of Darius, they slaughtered Mr Tall and took a hostage — a young boy called Shancus. Half human, half snake, he was the son of one of my best friends, Evra Von.

As Mr Tall lay dying, Mr Tiny and a witch called Evanna mysteriously appeared out of nowhere. It turned out that Mr Tiny was Mr Tall's father, and Evanna his sister. Mr Tiny stayed to mourn the death of his son, while Evanna followed us as we chased after her brother's killers. We managed to kill Morgan James and capture Darius. As the others hurried after R.V. and Shancus, I stole a few words with Evanna. The witch had the ability to see into the future and she revealed that if I killed Steve, I would take his place as the dreaded Lord of the Shadows. I'd become a monster, murder Vancha and anybody else who got in my way, and destroy not just the vampaneze, but humanity as well.

As shocked as I was, there was no time to brood. With my allies, we tracked R.V. to the old cinema where Steve and I had first met Mr Crepsley. Steve was waiting for us, safe on the stage, separated from us by a pit which he'd had dug and filled with stakes. He mocked us for a while, then agreed to trade Shancus's life for Darius's. But he lied. Instead of releasing the snake-boy, he killed him brutally. I still had hold of Darius. In a blind, cold rage, I prepared to murder him for revenge. But just before I stabbed the boy, Steve stopped me with his cruellest revelation yet — Darius's mother was my sister, Annie. If I murdered Steve's son, I'd be killing my own nephew.

And with that he departed, cackling like the demon he was, leaving me to the madness of the blood-drenched night.

PART ONE

CHAPTER ONE

Sitting on the stage. Gazing around the theatre. Remembering the thrilling show I saw the first time I came. Comparing it to tonight's warped 'entertainment'. Feeling very small and lonely.

Vancha didn't lose his head, even when Steve played his trump card. He kept going, picked his way through the pit of stakes to the stage, then raced down the tunnel which Steve, Gannen and R.V. had fled by. It led to the streets at the rear of the theatre. No way of telling which way they'd gone. He returned, cursing with fury. When he saw Shancus, lying dead on the stage like a bird with a broken neck, he stopped and sank to his knees.

Evra was next across, following Vancha's route through the stakes, crying out Shancus's name, screaming for him not to die, even though he must have known it was too late, that his son was already dead. We should have held him back — he fell

and pierced himself several times, and could easily have perished – but we were frozen with shock and horror.

Fortunately Evra made it to the stage without injuring himself too severely. Once there, he slumped beside Shancus, desperately checked for signs of life, then howled with loss. Sobbing and moaning with grief, he cradled the dead boy's head in his lap, tears dripping on to his son's motionless face. The rest of us watched from a distance. We were all crying bitterly, even the normally steel-faced Alice Burgess.

In time, Harkat also climbed through the stakes. There was a long plank on the stage. He and Vancha extended it over the pit, so that the rest of us could join them. I don't think anybody really wanted to go up there. For a long moment none of us moved. Then Debbie, sobbing with deep, wracking gulps, stumbled to the plank and hauled herself up.

Alice crossed the pit next. I brought up the rear. I was shaking uncontrollably. I wanted to turn and run. Earlier, I thought I knew how I'd feel if our gamble backfired and Steve killed Shancus. But I'd known nothing. I never truly expected Steve to murder the snake-boy. I'd let R.V. march the boy into Steve's den, certain no harm would come to my honorary godson.

Now that Steve had made a fool of me (yet again) and slaughtered Shancus, all I wanted was to be dead. I couldn't feel pain if I was dead. No shame. No guilt. I wouldn't have to look Evra in the eye, knowing I was responsible for his son's needless, shocking death.

We'd forgotten about Darius. I hadn't killed him — how

could I kill my own nephew? Following Steve's triumphant revelation, the hatred and anger which had filled me like a fire, drained away from me in an instant. I released Darius, having lost my murderous interest in him, and just left him on the far side of the pit.

Evanna was standing near the boy, idly picking at one of the ropes which encircled her body — she preferred ropes to ordinary clothes. It was clear from the witch's stance that she wouldn't interfere if Darius made a break for freedom. It would have been the simplest thing in the world for him to escape. But he didn't. He stood, sentry-like, trembling, waiting for us to summon him.

Finally Alice stumbled over to me, wiping tears from her face. "We should take them back to the Cirque Du Freak," she said, nodding at Evra and Shancus.

"In a while," I agreed, dreading the moment I'd have to face Evra. And what about Merla, Shancus's mother? Would *I* have to break the terrible news to her?

"No — now," Alice said firmly. "Harkat and Debbie can take them. We need to straighten some things out before we leave." She nodded at Darius, tiny and vulnerable under the glare of the lights.

"I don't want to talk about this," I groaned.

"I know," she said. "But we must. The boy might know where Steve is staying. If he does, this is the time to strike. They won't expect—"

"How can you even think about such things?" I hissed angrily. "Shancus is dead! Don't you care?"

She slapped my face. I blinked, stunned. "You're not a child, Darren, so don't act like one," she said coldly. "Of course I care. But we can't bring him back, and we'll achieve nothing by standing around, moping. We need to act. Only in swift revenge can we maybe find a small sliver of comfort."

She was right. Self-pity was a waste. Revenge was essential. As hard as it was, I dug myself out of my misery and set about sending Shancus's body home. Harkat didn't want to leave with Evra and Debbie. He wanted to stay and chase Steve with us. But somebody had to help carry Shancus. He accepted his task reluctantly, but made me promise we wouldn't face Steve without him. "I've come too far with you to … miss out now. I want to be there when you … cut the demon down."

Debbie threw her arms around me before leaving. "How could he do it?" she cried. "Even a monster couldn't … wouldn't…"

"Steve's more than a monster," I replied numbly. I wanted to return her embrace, but my arms wouldn't work. Alice pried her away from me. She gave Debbie a handkerchief and whispered something to her. Debbie sniffed miserably, nodded, gave Alice a hug, then went to stand beside Evra.

I wanted to talk with Evra before he left, but I could think of nothing to say. If he'd confronted me, maybe I'd have responded, but he had eyes only for his lifeless son. Dead people often look like they're sleeping. Shancus didn't. He'd

been a vibrant, buzzing, active child. All that vitality was lost now. Nobody could have looked upon him and thought he was anything but dead.

I remained standing until Evra, Debbie and Harkat had departed, Harkat carrying Shancus's body tenderly in his thick, grey arms. Then I slid to the floor and sat there for ages, staring around in a daze, thinking about the past and my first visit here, using the theatre and my memories as a barrier between me and my grief.

Eventually Vancha and Alice approached. I don't know how long the pair had been talking together, but when they came to stand before me they'd wiped their faces clean of tears and looked ready for business.

"Will I talk to the boy or do you want to?" Vancha asked gruffly.

"I don't care," I sighed. Then, glancing at Darius, who still stood alone with Evanna in the vastness of the auditorium, I said, "I'll do it."

"Darius," Alice called. His head rose immediately. "Come here."

Darius went straight to the plank, climbed up and walked across. He had an excellent sense of balance. I found myself thinking that was probably a by-product of his vampaneze blood — Steve had pumped some of his own blood into his son, turning him into a half-vampaneze. Thinking that, I began to hate the boy again. My fingers twitched in anticipation of grabbing him by the throat and...

But then I recalled his face when he'd learnt he was my nephew — shock, terror, confusion, pain, remorse — and my hatred for the boy died away.

Darius walked directly up to us. If he was afraid — and he must have been — he masked it bravely. Stopping, he stared at Vancha, then at Alice, finally at me. Now that I studied him closely, I saw a certain family resemblance. Thinking about that, I frowned.

"You're not the boy I saw before," I said. Darius looked at me uncertainly. "I went to my old home when we first came to town," I explained. "I watched from behind the fence. I saw Annie. She was bringing in laundry. Then you arrived and came out to help her. Except it wasn't *you*. It was a chubby boy with fair hair."

"Oggy Bas," Darius said after a second's thought. "My friend. I remember that day. He came home with me. I sent him out to help Mum while I was taking my shoes off. Oggy always does what I tell him." Then, licking his lips nervously, he looked around at all of us again and said, "I didn't know." It wasn't an apology, just a statement of fact. "Dad told me vampires were evil. He said you were the worst of the lot. 'Darren the cruel, Darren the mad, Darren the baby-killer.' But he never mentioned your surname."

Evanna had crossed the plank after Darius and was circling us, studying us as if we were chess pieces. I ignored her — there'd be time for the witch later.

"What did Steve tell you about the vampaneze?" I asked Darius.

"That they wanted to stop vampires killing humans. They broke away from the clan several hundred years ago and had battled to stop the slaughter of humans ever since. They drank only small amounts of blood when they fed, just enough to survive."

"You believed him?" Vancha snorted.

"He was my dad," Darius answered. "He was always kind to me. I never saw him like I saw him tonight. I'd no reason to doubt him."

"But you doubt him now," Alice noted wryly.

"Yes. He's evil." As soon as he said it, Darius burst into tears, his brave front collapsing. It can't have been easy for a child to admit his father was evil. Even in the midst of my grief and fury, I felt pity for the boy.

"What about Annie?" I asked when Darius had recovered enough to speak again. "Did Steve feed her the same sort of lies?"

"She doesn't know," Darius said. "They haven't spoken since before I was born. I never told her I was meeting him."

I breathed a small sigh of relief. I'd had a sudden, terrifying flash of Annie as Steve's consort, having grown up as bitter and twisted as him. It was good to know she wasn't part of this dark insanity.

"Do you want to tell him the truth about vampires and vampaneze, or will I?" Vancha asked.

"First things first," Alice interrupted. "Does he know where his father is?"

"No," Darius said sadly. "I always met him here. This is

where he was based. If he has another hideout, I don't know about it."

"Damn!" Alice snarled.

"No ideas at all?" I asked. Darius thought for a moment, then shook his head. I glanced at Vancha. "Will you set him straight?"

"Sure." Vancha quickly filled Darius in on the truth. He told him that the vampaneze were the ones who killed when they drank, though he was careful to describe their ways in detail — they kept part of a person's spirit alive within themselves when they drained a human dry, so they didn't look upon it as murder. They were noble. They never lied. They weren't deliberately evil.

"Then your father came along," Vancha said, and explained about the Lord of the Vampaneze, the War of the Scars, Mr Tiny's prediction and our part in it.

"I don't understand," Darius said at the end, forehead creased. "If the vampaneze don't lie, how come Dad lied all the time? And he taught me how to use an arrow-gun, but you said they can't use such weapons."

"They're not supposed to," Vancha said. "I haven't seen or heard of any others breaking those rules. But their Lord's above such laws. They worship him so much — or fear what will happen if they disobey him — that they don't care what he does, as long as he leads them to victory over the vampires."

Darius thought about that in silence for a long time. He was only ten years old, but he had the expression and manner of someone much older.

"I wouldn't have helped if I'd known," he said in the end. "I grew up thinking vampires were evil, like in the movies. When Dad came to me a few years ago and said he was on a mission to stop them, I thought it was a great adventure. I thought he was a hero. I was proud to be his son. I'd have done anything for him. I *did*..."

He looked like he was about to cry again. But then his jaw firmed and he stared at me. "But how did *you* get involved in this?" he asked. "Mum told me you died. She said you broke your neck."

"I faked my death," I said, and gave him a very brief rundown of my early life as a vampire's assistant, sacrificing everything I held dear to save Steve's life.

"But why does he hate you if you saved him?" Darius shouted. "That's crazy!"

"Steve sees things differently," I shrugged. "He believes it was his destiny to become a vampire. He thinks I stole his rightful place. He's determined to make me pay."

Darius shook his head, confused. "I can't understand that," he said.

"You're young." I smiled sadly. "You've a lot to learn about people and how they operate." I fell silent, thinking that those were some of the many things poor Shancus would never learn.

"So," Darius said a while later, breaking the silence. "What happens now?"

"Go home," I sighed. "Forget about this. Put it behind you."

"But what about the vampaneze?" Darius cried. "Dad's still out there. I want to help you find him."

"Really?" I looked at him icily. "You want to help us kill him? You'd lead us to your own father and watch while we cut his rotten heart out?"

Darius shifted uneasily. "He's evil," he whispered.

"Yes," I agreed. "But he's still your father. You're better off out of this."

"And Mum?" Darius asked. "What do I tell her?"

"Nothing," I said. "She thinks I'm dead. Let her go on thinking that. Say nothing of this. The world I live in isn't a fit world for children — and as a child who's lived in it, I should know! Take back your ordinary life. Try not to dwell on what's happened. In time you might be able to dismiss all this as a horrible dream." I placed my hands on his shoulders and smiled warmly. "Go home, Darius. Be good to Annie. Make her happy."

Darius wasn't pleased, but I could see him making up his mind to accept my advice. Then Vancha spoke. "It's not that easy."

"What?" I frowned.

"He's in. He can't opt out."

"Of course he can!" I snapped.

Vancha shook his head stubbornly. "He was blooded. The vampaneze blood is thin in him, but it will thicken. He won't age like normal children, and in a few decades the purge will strike and he'll become a full-vampaneze." Vancha sighed. "But his real problems will start long before then."

"What do you mean?" I croaked, though I sensed what he was getting at.

"*Feeding*," Vancha said. He turned his gaze on Darius. "You'll need to drink blood to survive."

Darius stiffened, then grinned shakily. "So I'll drink like you guys," he said. "A drop here, a drop there. I don't mind. It'll be kind of cool, in a way. Maybe I'll drink from my teachers and—"

"No," Vancha growled. "You can't drink like us. In the beginning, vampaneze were the same as vampires, except in their customs. But they've changed. The centuries have altered them physically. Now a vampaneze *must* kill when he feeds. They're driven to it. They have no choice or control. I was once a half-vampaneze, so I know what I'm speaking about."

Vancha drew himself up straight and spoke sadly but firmly. "In a few months the hunger will grow within you. You won't be able to resist. You'll drink blood because you have to, and when you drink, because you're a half-vampaneze — you'll *kill!*"

CHAPTER TWO

We marched in silence, in single file, Darius leading the way like Oliver Twist at the head of a funeral procession. Following the massacre at the stadium after the football match, a series of road blocks had been set in place around the town. But there weren't many in this area, so we made good time, having to take only a couple of short detours. I was at the back of the line, a few metres behind the others, worrying about the meeting to come. I'd agreed to it easily enough in the theatre, but now that we were getting closer, I was having second thoughts.

While I was running through my words, thinking of all the things I could and should say, Evanna slipped back to walk along beside me. "If it helps, the snake-boy's soul has flown straight to Paradise," she said.

"I never thought otherwise," I replied stiffly, glaring at her hatefully.

"Why such a dark look?" she asked, genuine surprise in her mismatched green and brown eyes.

"You knew it was coming," I growled. "You could have warned us and saved Shancus."

"No," she snapped, irritated. "Why do you people level the same accusations at me over and over? You know I have the power to see into the future, but not the power to directly influence it. I cannot act to change that which is to be. Nor could my brother."

"Why not?" I snarled. "You always say that terrible things will happen if you do, but what are they? What could be worse than letting an innocent child die at the hands of a monster?"

Evanna was quiet a moment, then spoke softly, so that only I could hear. "There are worse monsters than Steve Leonard, and worse even than the Lord of the Shadows — be he Steve or you. These other monsters wait in the timeless wings around the stage of the world, never seen by man, but always seeing, always hungering, always eager to break through.

"I am bound by laws older than mankind. So was my brother and so, to a large extent, is my father. If I took advantage of the present, and tried to change the course of a future I knew about, I'd break the laws of the universe. The monsters I speak of would then be free to cross into this world, and it would become a cauldron of endless, bloody savagery."

"It seems that way already," I said sourly.

"For you, perhaps," she agreed. "But for billions of others it is not. Would you have everyone suffer as you have — and worse?"

"Of course not," I muttered. "But you told me they were going to suffer anyway, that the Lord of the Shadows will destroy mankind."

"He will bring it to its knees," she said. "But he will not crush it entirely. Hope will remain. One day, far in the future, humans might rise again. If I interfered and unleashed the real monsters, hope would become a word without meaning."

I didn't know what to think about these other monsters of Evanna's — it was the first time she'd ever spoken of such creatures — so I brought the conversation back to centre on the monster I knew all too much about. "You're wrong when you say I can become the Lord of the Shadows," I said, trying to change my destiny by denying it. "I'm not a monster."

"You would have killed Darius if Steve hadn't said he was your nephew," Evanna reminded me.

I recalled the hateful fury which had flared to life inside me when I saw Shancus die. In that moment I became like Steve. I didn't care about right or wrong. I only wanted to hurt my enemy by killing his son. I'd seen a glimpse of my future then, the beast I could become, but I didn't want to believe it was real.

"That would have been in revenge for Shancus," I said bitterly, trying to hide from the truth. "It wouldn't have been the act of an out-of-control beast. I wouldn't become a monster just because of a single executioning."

"No?" Evanna challenged me. "There was a time when you thought differently. Do you remember when you killed your first vampaneze, in the caves of Vampire Mountain? You wept afterwards. You thought killing was wrong. You believed there were ways to resolve differences other than through violence."

"I still do," I said, but my words sounded hollow, even to me.

"You would not have tried to take the life of a child if you did," Evanna said, stroking the hairs of her beard. "You have changed, Darren. You're not evil like Steve, but you carry the seeds of evil within you. Your intentions are good, but time and circumstance will see you become that which you despise. This world will warp you and, despite your noble wishes, the monster within you will grow. Friends will become enemies. Truths will become lies. Beliefs will become sick jokes.

"The path of revenge is always lined with danger. By following the ways of those you hate, you risk turning into them. This is your destiny, Darren Shan. You cannot avoid it. Unless Steve kills you and he becomes the Lord of the Shadows instead."

"What about Vancha?" I hissed. "What if he kills Steve? Can't *he* become your bloody Lord of the Shadows?"

"No," she said calmly. "Vancha has the power to kill Steve and decide the fate of the War of the Scars. But moving beyond that, it's either you or Steve. There is no other. Death or monstrosity. Those are your options."

She moved ahead of me then, leaving me with my troubled, frantic thoughts. Was there truly no hope for me or the world? And if not, if I was trapped between death at the hands of Steve or replacing him as the Lord of the Shadows, which was preferable? Was it better to live and terrorize the world — or die now, while I was still halfway human?

I couldn't decide on an answer. There didn't seem to be one. And so I trudged along miserably and let my thoughts return to the more pressing issue — what to say to my grown-up sister who'd buried me as a child.

Twenty minutes later, Darius opened the back door and held it ajar. I paused, staring at the house, filled with a sense of foreboding. Vancha and Alice were behind me, and Evanna further behind them. I looked back at my friends pleadingly. "Do I really have to do this?" I croaked.

"Yes," Vancha said. "It would be wrong to risk his life without informing his mother first. She must decide."

"OK," I sighed. "You'll wait out here till I call?"

"Aye."

I gulped, then stepped over the threshold into the house where I'd lived as a boy. After eighteen long years of wandering, I'd finally come home.

Darius guided me to the living room, though I could have found my way blindfolded. Much had changed within the house — new wallpaper and carpets, furniture and light fittings — but it felt the same, warm and comfy, layered

with memories of the distant past. It was like walking through a ghost house — except the house was real and I was the ghost.

Darius pushed the living-room door open. And there was Annie, her brown hair tied up in a bun, sitting in a chair in front of the TV, sipping hot chocolate, watching the news. "Decided to come home at last, did you?" she said to Darius, catching sight of him out of the corner of her eye. She laid the cup of hot chocolate down. "I was worried. Have you seen the news? There's—"

She saw me entering the room after Darius. "Is this one of your friends?" she asked. I could see her thinking I looked too old to be his friend. She was instantly suspicious of me.

"Hello, Annie," I said, smiling nervously, advancing into the light.

"Have we met before?" she asked, frowning, not recognizing me.

"In a way," I chuckled drily.

"Mum, it's—" Darius started to say.

"No," I interrupted. "Let her see for herself. Don't tell her."

"Tell me what?" Annie snapped. She was squinting at me now, uneasy.

"Look closer, Annie," I said softly, walking across the room, stopping less than a metre away from her. "Look at my eyes. They say the eyes never really change, even if everything else does."

"Your voice," she muttered. "There's something about…" She stood — she was the same height as me — and gazed steadily into my eyes. I smiled.

"You look like somebody I knew a long time ago," Annie said. "But I don't remember who…"

"You did know me a long time ago," I whispered. "Eighteen years ago."

"Nonsense!" Annie snorted. "You'd have only been a baby."

"No," I said. "I've aged slowly. I was slightly older than Darius when you last saw me."

"Is this a joke?" she half laughed.

"Look at him, Mum," Darius said intently. "Really *look* at him."

And she did. And this time I saw something in her expression and realized she'd known who I was the second she saw me — she just hadn't admitted it to herself yet.

"Listen to your instincts, Annie," I said. "You always had good instincts. If I'd had your nose for trouble, maybe I wouldn't have gotten into this mess. Maybe I'd have had more sense than to steal a poisonous spider…"

Annie's eyes widened. "No!" she gasped.

"Yes," I said.

"You can't be!"

"I am."

"But … *No!*" she growled, firmly this time. "I don't know who put you up to this, or what you think you'll achieve by it, but if you don't get out quick, I'll—"

"I bet you never told anyone about Madam Octa," I cut her off. She trembled at mention of the spider's name. "I bet you kept that secret all these years. You must have guessed she had something to do with my 'death'. Maybe you asked Steve about it, since he was the one she bit, but I bet you never told Mum or—"

"*Darren?*" she wheezed, confused tears springing to her eyes.

"Hi, sis," I grinned. "Long time no see."

She stared at me, appalled, and then did something I thought only happened in corny old movies — her eyes rolled up, her legs gave way, and she fainted!

Annie sat in her chair, a fresh mug of hot chocolate cupped between her hands. I sat opposite her in a chair I'd dragged over from the other side of the room. Darius stood by the TV, which he'd turned off shortly after Annie fainted. Annie hadn't said much since recovering. Once she'd come to, she'd pressed back into her chair, gazed at me, torn between horror and hope, and simply gasped, "*How?*"

I'd spent the time since then filling her in. I spoke quietly and rapidly, starting with Mr Crepsley and Madam Octa, explaining the deal I'd struck to save Steve's life, giving her a quick rundown of the years since then; my existence as a vampire, the vampaneze, the War of the Scars, tracking the Vampaneze Lord. I didn't tell her Steve was the Lord or involved with the vampaneze — I wanted to see how she reacted to the rest of the story before

hitting her with that one.

Her eyes didn't betray her feelings. It was impossible to guess what she was thinking. When I got to the part of the story involving Darius, her gaze slid from me to her son, and she leant forward slightly as I described how he'd been tricked into aiding the vampaneze, again being careful not to refer to Steve by name. I finished with my return to the old cinema theatre, Shancus's death, and the Vampaneze Lord's revelation that Darius was my nephew.

"Once Darius knew the truth, he was horrified," I said. "But I told him he mustn't blame himself. Lots of older and wiser people than him have been fooled by the Lord of the Vampaneze."

I stopped and awaited her reaction. It wasn't long coming.

"You're insane," she said coldly. "If you *are* my brother – and I'm not a hundred per cent convinced – then whatever disease stunted your growth also affected your brain. Vampires? Vampaneze? My son in league with a killer?" She sneered. "You're a madman."

"But it's true!" Darius exclaimed. "He can prove it! He's stronger and faster than any human. He can—"

"Be quiet!" Annie roared with such venom that Darius shut up instantly. She glared at me furiously. "Get out of my house," she snarled. "Stay away from my son. Don't ever come back."

"But—" I began.

"No!" she screamed. "You're not my brother! Even if you are, you're not! We buried Darren eighteen years ago. He's

dead and that's the way I want him to stay. I don't care if you're him or not. I want you out of my life — *our* lives — immediately." She stood and pointed at the door. "*Go!*"

I didn't move. I wanted to. If it hadn't been for Darius, I would have slunk out like a kicked dog. But she had to know what her son had become. I couldn't leave without convincing her of the danger he was in.

While Annie stood, pointing at the door, hand trembling wildly, face twisted with rage, Darius stepped away from the TV. "Mum," he said quietly. "Don't you want to know how I fell in with the vampaneze and why I helped them?"

"There are no vampaneze!" she yelled. "This maniac has filled your imagination with lies and—"

"Steve Leonard's the Lord of the Vampaneze," Darius said, and Annie stopped dead. "He came to me a few years ago," Darius went on, edging slowly towards her. "At first we just went for walks together, he took me to the cinema and for meals, stuff like that. He told me not to say anything to you. He said you wouldn't like it, that you'd make him go away."

He stopped in front of her, reached up, took hold of her pointing hand and gently bent her arm down. She was staring at him wordlessly. "He's my dad," Darius said sadly. "I trusted him because I thought he loved me. That's why I believed him when he told me about vampires. He said he was telling me for my protection, that he was worried about me — and *you*. He wanted to protect us. That's where it began. Then I got more involved. He taught me how to use a knife, how to

shoot, how to kill."

Annie sank back into her chair, unable to respond.

"It was Steve," Darius said. "Steve who got me into trouble, who killed the snake-boy, who made Darren come back to see you. Darren didn't want to — he knew he'd hurt you — but Steve left him with no choice. It's true, Mum, everything he said. You've got to believe us, because it was Steve, and I think he might come back — come after *you* — and if we aren't ready ... if you don't believe..."

He ground to a halt, running out of words. But he'd said enough. When Annie looked at me again, there was fear and doubt in her eyes, but no scorn. "*Steve?*" she moaned. I nodded unhappily and her face hardened. "What did I tell you about him?" she screamed at Darius, grabbing the boy and shaking him angrily. "I told you never to go near him! That if you ever saw him, you had to run and tell me! I said he was dangerous!"

"I didn't believe you!" Darius cried. "I thought you hated him just because he ran away, that you were lying! He was my dad!" He tore himself away from her and collapsed on the floor, weeping. "He was my dad," he sobbed again. "I loved him."

Annie stared at Darius crying. Then she stared at me. And then she also started to cry, and her sobs were even deeper and more painful than her son's.

I didn't cry. I was saving my tears. I knew the worst was yet to come.

CHAPTER THREE

Later. After the tears. Sitting around the living room. Annie had recovered from the worst of the shock. All three of us were drinking hot chocolate. I hadn't called the others in yet — I wanted some personal time with Annie before I dumped the full fallout from the War of the Scars upon her.

Annie made me tell her more about my life. She wanted to hear about the countries I'd visited, the people I'd met, the adventures I'd had. I told her some of the highlights, leaving out the darker aspects. She listened, dazed, touching me every few minutes to make sure I was real. When she heard I was a Prince, she laughed with delight. "Does that make me a princess?" she smiled.

"Afraid not," I chuckled.

In return, Annie told me what her life had been like. The hard months after I'd 'died'. Slowly returning to normal. She was young, so she recovered, but Mum and Dad never really

got over it. She raised the question of whether or not they should be told I was alive. Then, before I could speak, she said, "No. They're happy now. It's too late to change the past. Best not to drag it up again."

I paid close attention when she spoke about Steve. "I was a teenager," she said angrily, "mixed-up and unsure of myself. I had some friends but not many. And no serious boyfriend. Then Steve came back. He was only a few years older than me, but he looked and acted grown-up. And he was interested in me. He wanted to talk to me. He treated me like an equal."

They spent a lot of time together. Steve put on a good act — kind, generous, loving. Annie thought he cared for her, that they had a future together. She fell in love with him, and gave her love to him. Then she found out she was expecting a baby.

"His face lit up when he heard," she said, shivering from the memory. Darius was by her side, solemn, silent, listening intently. "He made me believe he was delighted, that we'd get married and have lots of children together. He told me not to tell anyone — he wanted to keep it secret until we were husband and wife. He went away again. He said it was to earn money, to pay for our wedding and the baby's upkeep. He stayed away a long time. He returned late one night, while I was sleeping. Woke me up. Before I could say anything, he clamped a hand over my mouth and laughed. 'Too late to stop it now!' he mocked me. He said other things, horrible things. Then he left. I haven't heard from him since."

She had to tell Mum and Dad about the baby then. They were furious — not with her, but with Steve. Dad would have

killed Steve if he'd found him. But nobody knew where Steve was. He'd vanished.

"Raising Darius was hard," she smiled, ruffling his hair, "but I wouldn't give up a day of it. Steve was wicked, but he gave me the most marvellous gift anyone could have ever given me."

"Soppy old cow," Darius grunted, fighting hard not to smile.

I was quiet a long time after that. I wondered if Steve had meant to use Darius against me even then. This was back before he met the vampaneze and learnt of his abominable destiny. But I bet he was already planning my downfall, one way or the other. Did he deliberately get Annie pregnant, so he could use his nephew or niece to hurt me? Knowing Steve as I did, I guessed those were his exact intentions.

Annie started telling me about her life with Darius, from how Mum and Dad helped rear him until they moved away, how the pair were managing now on their own. She worried about him not having a father, but her experience with Steve had made her wary of men, and she found it hard to trust anyone. I could have listened to Annie talk all night, telling tales about Mum, Dad and Darius. I was catching up on all those missed years. I felt like part of the family again. I didn't want it to stop.

But we were in the middle of a crisis. I'd delayed the moment of truth, but now I had to tell her about it. The night was drawing on, and I was keen to conclude the business I'd come about. I let her finish the story she was

telling – about Darius's first week in school – then asked if I could introduce her to some of my friends.

Annie wasn't sure what to make of Vancha, Alice and Evanna. Alice dressed normally, but Vancha in his animal hides, with his straps of throwing stars and green hair, and the hirsute, deliriously ugly Evanna draped in ropes ... They would have stuck out like a couple of gargoyles anywhere!

But they were my friends (well, Vancha and Alice were, whatever about the witch), so Annie welcomed them — though I could tell she didn't entirely trust the trio. And I knew she sensed they weren't here just to make up the numbers. She guessed that something bad was coming.

We made small talk for a while. Alice told Annie about her years on the police force, Vancha described some of his Princely duties and Evanna gave her tips on how to breed frogs (not that Annie had any interest in that!). Then Darius yawned. Vancha looked at me meaningfully — it was time.

"Annie," I started hesitantly, "I told you Darius pledged himself to the vampaneze. But I didn't tell you what precisely that means."

"Go on," Annie said when I stalled.

"Steve blooded him," I said. "He transferred some of his vampaneze blood to Darius. The blood isn't very strong within him, but it will strengthen. The cells will multiply and take over."

"You're saying he'll become like you?" Annie's face was ashen. "He won't age normally? He'll need to drink blood to survive?"

"Yes." Her face crumpled — she thought that was the worst, the part I'd been holding back. I wished I could spare her the truth, but I couldn't. "There's more," I said, and she stiffened. "Vampires can control their feeding habits. It isn't easy — it requires training — but we can. Vampaneze can't. Their blood forces them to kill every time they feed."

"No!" Annie moaned. "Darius isn't a killer! He wouldn't!"

"He would," Vancha grunted. "He'd have no choice. Once a vampaneze gets the taste of blood, his urges consume him. He goes into a kind of trance and feeds until he's drained the source dry. He can't stop."

"But there must be some way to help him!" Annie insisted. "Doctors … surgery … medicine…"

"No," Vancha said. "This isn't a human disease. Your doctors could study him, and restrain him while he was feeding — but do you want your son to spend his life imprisoned?"

"Also," I said, "they couldn't stop him when he was older. As he comes into his full powers, he'll grow incredibly strong. They'd have to keep him comatose to control him."

"No!" Annie shouted, her face dark with stubborn rage. "I won't allow this! There must be a way to save him!"

"There is," I said, and she relaxed slightly. "But it's dangerous. And it won't restore his humanity — it will merely drive him towards a different corner of the night."

"Don't talk in riddles!" Annie snapped. "What does he have to do?"

"Become a vampire," I said.

Annie stared at me in disbelief.

"It's not as bad as it sounds," I went on quickly. "Yes, he'd age slowly, but that's something you and he could learn to cope with. And yes, he'd have to drink blood, but he wouldn't harm when he drank. We'd teach him to master his urges."

"No," Annie said. "There must be another way."

"There isn't," Vancha huffed. "And even this way isn't certain. Nor is it safe."

"I'll have to trade blood with him," I explained. "Pump my vampire cells into his body, and accept his vampaneze cells into mine. The vampire and vampaneze cells will attack each other. If all goes well, Darius will become a half-vampire and I'll carry on as before."

"But if it fails, you'll become a half-vampaneze and Darius won't change?" Annie guessed, trembling at the thought of such a horrible fate.

"No," I said. "It's worse than that. If it fails, I'll die — and so will Darius."

And then I sat back numbly and awaited her decision.

CHAPTER FOUR

Annie didn't like it — nobody did! — but we eventually convinced her that there was no other solution. She wanted to wait, think it over and discuss it with her doctor, but I told her it was now or never. "Vancha and I have a mission to complete," I reminded her. "We might not be able to come back later."

When we'd first discussed the transfusion, Vancha had volunteered. He didn't think it was safe for me to try. I was in the middle of the purge — my vampire cells were taking over, turning me into a full-vampire, and my body was in a state of flux. But when I pressed him, he admitted there was no real reason for thinking that the purge would have any affect on the procedure. It might even work in our favour — since my vampire cells were hyperactive, they might stand a better chance of destroying the vampaneze cells.

We'd tried to quiz Evanna about the dangers. She could look into the future and tell us whether it would succeed or

not. But she refused to be drawn. "This has nothing to do with me," she'd said. "I will not comment on it."

"But it must be safe," I'd pressed, hoping for reassurance. "We're destined to meet Steve again. We can't do that if I die."

"Your final encounter with Steve Leonard is by no means set in stone," she'd replied. "If you die beforehand, he will become the Lord of the Shadows by default and the war will swing the way of the vampaneze. Do not think you are immune to danger because of your destiny, Darren — you *can* and perhaps *will* die if you attempt this."

But Darius was my nephew. Vancha didn't approve — he would have preferred to overlook Darius for the time being, and focus on Steve — but I couldn't leave the boy this way, with such a threat hanging over him. If I could save him, I must.

We could have handled the blood transfer with syringes, but Darius insisted on the traditional fingertips method. He was excited, despite the danger, and wanted to do it the old way. "If I'm going to be a vampire, I want to be a real one," he growled. "I don't want to hide my marks. It's all or nothing."

"But it'll be painful," I warned him.

"I don't care," he sniffed.

Annie's doubts remained, but in the end she agreed to the plan. She might not have if Darius had wavered, but he stuck to his guns with grim determination. I hated to admit it — and I didn't say it out loud — but he had his father's sense of commitment. Steve was insanely evil, but he always did what

he set out to do, and nothing could change his mind once he'd made it up. Darius was the same.

"I can't believe this is happening," Annie sighed as I sat opposite Darius and prepared to drive my nails into the tips of his fingers. "Earlier tonight I was only thinking about doing the shopping tomorrow, and being here to let Darius in when he got home from school. Then my brother walks back into my life and tells me he's a vampire! And now, as I'm just getting used to that, I might lose him as swiftly as I found him — and my son too!"

She almost called it off then, but Alice stepped up behind her and said softly, "Would you rather lose him when he's human, or when he's a killer like his father?" It was a cruel thing to say, but it steadied Annie's nerves and reminded her of what was at stake. Trembling fiercely, weeping quietly, she stepped away and let me proceed.

Without any warning, I dug my nails into the soft flesh at the tips of Darius's fingers. He yelped painfully and jerked back in his chair. "Don't," I said as he raised his fingers to his mouth to suck them. "Let them bleed."

Darius lowered his hands. Gritting my teeth, I dug my right-hand nails into my left-hand fingertips, then did it the other way round. Blood welled up from ten fleshy springs. I pressed my fingers against Darius's and held them there while my blood flowed into his body, and his into mine.

We remained locked for twenty seconds ... thirty ... more. I could feel the vampaneze cells as soon as his blood entered my veins, itching, burning, sizzling. I ignored the

pain. I could see that Darius was also aware of the change, and that it was hurting him more than me. I pressed closer against him, so it was impossible for him to break away.

Vancha stood guard, observing us, calculating. When he thought the time was right, he grabbed my arms and pulled my hands away. I gasped out loud, stood, half smiled, then fell to the floor, writhing in agony. I hadn't expected the cells to kick in so soon, and was unprepared for the brutal speed of the reaction.

During my convulsions, I saw Darius twisting sharply in his chair, eyes bulging, making choking noises, arms and legs thrashing wildly. Annie hurried towards him but Vancha knocked her aside. "Don't interfere!" he barked. "Nature must take its course. We can't get in its way."

For several minutes I jackknifed wildly on the floor. It felt like I was on fire inside my skin. I'd experienced blinding headaches and loads of discomfort during the purge, but this took me to new heights of pain. Pressure built at the back of my eyes, as though my brain was going to bulge out through my eye sockets. I dug the heels of my hands hard into my eyes, then into the sides of my head. I don't know if I was roaring or wheezing — I could hear nothing.

I vomited, then dry-heaved. I crashed into something hard — the TV. I rolled away from it and smashed into a wall. I dug my nails into the plaster and brick, trying to make the pain go away.

Finally the pressure subsided. My limbs relaxed. I stopped dry-heaving. Sight and sound returned, though my fierce

headache remained. I looked around, dazed. Vancha was crouching over me, wiping my face clean, smiling. "You've come through it," he said. You'll be OK — with the luck of the vampires."

"Darius?" I gasped.

Vancha raised my head and pointed. Darius was lying on the couch, eyes closed, perfectly still, Annie and Alice kneeling beside him. Evanna sat in a corner, head bowed. For a horrifying moment I thought Darius was dead. Then I saw his chest lift softly and fall, and I knew he was just asleep.

"He'll be fine," Vancha said. "We'll have to keep a close eye on the two of you for a few nights. You'll probably have further fits, less severe than this one. But most who attempt this die of the first seizure. Having survived that, the odds are good for both of you."

I sat up wearily. Vancha took my fingers and spat on them, rubbing his spit in to help close the wounds.

"I feel awful," I moaned.

"You won't improve any time soon," Vancha said. "When I turned from vampanizm to vampirism it took my system a month to settle down, and almost a year to get back to normal. And you've got the purge to contend with too." He chuckled wryly. "You're in for some rough nights, Sire!"

Vancha helped me back to my chair. Alice asked if I'd like water or milk to drink. Vancha said blood would be better for me. Without blinking, Alice used a knife to cut herself and let me feed directly from the wound. Vancha closed the cut with

his spit when I was finished. He beamed up at Alice. "You're some woman, Miss Burgess."

"The best," Alice replied dryly.

I leant back, eyes half closed. "I could sleep for a week," I sighed.

"Why don't you?" Vancha said. "You've only recently recovered from a life-threatening wound. You're in the middle of the purge. You've pulled off the most dangerous blood transfusion known to vampires. By the black blood of Harnon Oan, you've earned a rest!"

"But Steve..." I muttered.

"Leonard can wait," Vancha grunted. "We'll send Annie and Darius out of town – Alice will escort them – then get you settled in at the Cirque. A week in your hammock will do you the world of good."

"I guess," I said unhappily. I was thinking about Evra and Merla, and what I could find to say to them. There was Mr Tall to consider too — everyone at the Cirque Du Freak had loved him. Like Shancus, he was dead because of his association with me. Would the people there hate me because of that?

"Who do you think will take over from Mr Tall?" I asked.

"I've no idea," Vancha said. "I don't think anybody ever expected him to die, certainly not in such sudden circumstances."

"Maybe they'll break up," I mused. "Go their own ways, back to whatever they did before they joined. Some might have left the stadium already. I hope–"

"What was that about a stadium?" Annie interrupted. She was still tending to Darius — he was snoring lightly — but she'd overheard us talking.

"The Cirque Du Freak's camped in the old football stadium," I explained. "We're going back there when you leave, but I was saying to Vancha that—"

"The news," Annie interrupted again. "You didn't see tonight's news?"

"No."

"I was watching it when you came in," she said, eyes filling with fresh worry. "I didn't know that's where you were based, so I didn't connect it with you."

"Connect what?" I asked edgily.

"Police have surrounded the stadium," Annie said. "They say the people who killed Tom Jones and the others at the football match are there. I should have put it together earlier, when you were telling me about Tommy, but…" She shook her head angrily, then continued. "They're not letting anyone in or out. When I was watching the news, they hadn't moved in yet. But they said that when they did, they'd go in with full, lethal force. One of the reporters—" She stopped.

"Go on," I said hoarsely.

"He said he'd never seen so many armed police before. He…" She gulped and finished in a whisper. "He said they meant to go in as hard as they could. He said it looked like they planned to kill everyone inside."

CHAPTER FIVE

First things first — make sure Annie and Darius got away safely. I couldn't concentrate on helping my friends trapped inside the stadium if I was worrying about my sister and nephew. Once they were free of Steve's influence, safe somewhere he couldn't find them, I could focus on business entirely. Until that time I would only be a distracted liability.

Annie didn't want to go. This was her home and she wanted to fight to protect it. When, after telling her about some of the atrocities Steve had committed over the years, I convinced her they had to leave, she insisted I go with them. For years she'd believed I was dead. Now she knew otherwise, she didn't want to lose me again so quickly.

"I can't come," I sighed. "Not while my friends are in danger. Later, when it's over, I'll find you."

"Not if Steve kills you!" Annie cried. I had no answer for

that one. "What about Darius?" she pressed. "You said he needs training. What will he do without you?"

"Give us your mobile number," I said. "Alice will contact her people before we go to the stadium. In the worst case scenario, somebody will get in touch. A vampire will link up with you and instruct Darius, or guide him to Vampire Mountain, where Seba or Vanez can look after him."

"Who?" she asked.

"Old friends," I smiled. "They can teach him everything he'll ever need to know about being a vampire."

Annie kept trying to change my mind, telling me my place was with her and Darius, that I was her brother before I became a vampire and I should think of her first. But she was wrong. I left the human world behind when I became a Vampire Prince. I still cared for Annie and loved her, but my first loyalty was to the clan.

When she realized she couldn't win me round, Annie bundled Darius into the back of their car – he was still sound asleep – and tearfully went to gather some personal belongings. I told her to take as much as she could, and not to come back. If we defeated Steve, she and Darius could return. If not, somebody would fetch the rest of her stuff. The house would have to be sold, and they'd remain in hiding under the protection of the vampire clan, for as long as the clan was capable of looking after them. (I didn't say "Until the clan falls," but that's what I was thinking.) It wouldn't be an ideal life — but it would be better than winding up in the hands of Steve Leopard.

Annie hugged me with all her strength before getting into the car. "It's not fair," she wept. "There's so much you haven't told me, so much I want to know, so much I want to say."

"Me too," I said, blinking away tears. It was a weird feeling. Everything was happening at ten times the speed it should. It had only been a few hours since we returned to the Cirque Du Freak to chat with Mr Tall, but it felt like weeks had passed. His death, the chase, Morgan James's beheading, the theatre, Shancus being slaughtered by Steve, finding out about Darius, coming to see my sister ... I wanted to put my foot down on the brake, take time out, make sense of all that was going on. But life makes its own rules and sets its own pace. Sometimes you can rein it in and slow it down — other times you can't.

"You really can't come with us?" Annie tried one last time.

"No," I said. "I want to ... but no."

"Then I wish you all the luck in the world, Darren," she moaned. She kissed me, began to say something else, then broke down in tears. Hurling herself into the car, she checked on Darius, then started the engine and roared away, disappearing into the night, leaving me standing outside my old home — heartbroken.

"Are you all right?" Alice asked, creeping up behind me.

"I will be," I replied, wiping tears from my eyes. "I wish I'd been able to say goodbye to Darius."

"It's not goodbye," Alice said. "Just *au revoir*."

"Hopefully," I sighed, though I didn't really believe it. Win or lose, I had a sick feeling in my stomach that tonight was the last time I'd ever see Annie and Darius. I paused a

moment to wish them a silent farewell, then turned around, put them from my thoughts, and let all my emotions and energies centre on the problems to hand and the dangers faced by my friends at the Cirque Du Freak.

Inside the house, we discussed our next move. Alice was for getting out of town as quickly as possible, abandoning our friends and allies. "Three of us can't make a difference if there are hordes of police stationed around the stadium," she argued. "Steve Leonard remains the priority. The others will have to fend for themselves."

"But they're our friends," I muttered. "We can't just abandon them."

"We must," she insisted. "It doesn't matter how much it hurts. We can't do anything for them now, not without placing our own lives in jeopardy."

"But Evra ... Harkat ... *Debbie*."

"I know," she said, her eyes sad but hard. "But like I said, it doesn't matter how much it hurts. We have to leave them."

"I don't agree," I said. "I think..." I stopped, reluctant to voice my belief.

"Go on," Vancha encouraged me.

"I can't explain it," I said slowly, eyes flicking to Evanna, "but I think Steve's there. At the stadium. Waiting for us. He set the police on us before — when Alice was one of them — and I can't see him pulling the same trick twice. It would be boring the second time round. He craves originality and new thrills. I think the police outside are just for cover."

"He could have set a trap in the cinema theatre," Vancha mused, taking up my train of thought. "But that wouldn't have been as elaborate a setting as where we fought him before — in the Cavern of Retribution."

"Exactly," I said. "This is our big showdown. He'll want to go out on a high, with something outlandish. He's as much of a performer as anyone at the Cirque Du Freak. He loves theatrics. He'd relish the idea of a stadium setting. It would be like the ancient gladiator duels in the Colosseum."

"We're in trouble if you're wrong," Alice said uneasily.

"Nothing new about that," Vancha huffed. He cocked an eyebrow at Evanna. "Care to drop us a hint?"

To our astonishment, the witch nodded soberly. "Darren is right. You either go to the stadium now and face your destiny, or flee and hand victory to the vampaneze."

"I thought you couldn't tell us stuff like that," Vancha said, startled.

"The endgame has commenced," Evanna answered cryptically. "I can speak more openly about certain matters now, without altering the future."

"It'd alter it if we turned tail and ran like hell for the hills," Vancha grunted.

"No," Evanna smiled. "It wouldn't. As I said, that would simply mean the vampaneze win. Besides," she added, her smile widening, "you aren't going to run, are you?"

"Not in a million years!" Vancha said, spitting against the wall for added emphasis. "But we won't be fools about this either. I say we check out the stadium. If it looks like

Leonard's in residence, we'll force a way in and chop the fiend's head off. If not, we'll search elsewhere and the circus folk will have to make their own luck. No point risking our lives for them at this stage, aye, Darren?"

I thought of my freakish friends — Evra, Merla, Hans Hands and the rest. I thought of Harkat and Debbie, and what might happen to them. And then I thought of my people – the vampires – and what *would* happen to the clan if we threw our lives away trying to save our non-vampire allies.

"Aye," I said miserably, and though I knew I was doing the right thing, I felt like a traitor.

Alice and Vancha checked their weapons while I armed myself with some sharp kitchen knives. Alice made a few phone calls, arranging protection for Annie and Darius. Then, with Evanna in tow, we pulled out and I left my childhood home for the second time in my life, certain in my heart that I'd never again return.

CHAPTER SIX

The journey across town passed without incident. All the police seemed to have been sent or drawn to the stadium. We didn't run into any road blocks or foot patrols. In fact we met hardly anyone. It was eerily quiet. People were in their homes or in pubs, watching the siege on TV, waiting for the action to kick off. It was a silence I knew from the past, the silence that usually comes before battle and death.

Dozens of police cars and vans were parked in a ring around the stadium when we arrived, and armed guards stood watch at every possible entry or exit point. Barriers had been erected to keep back the public and media. Ultra-bright spotlights were trained on the walls of the stadium. My eyes watered from the glare of the lights, even from a long way off, and I had to stop to tie a strip of thick cloth around them.

"Are you sure you're up to this?" Alice asked, studying me doubtfully.

"I'll do what I have to," I growled, although I wasn't as convinced of my vow as I pretended to be. I was in rough shape, the roughest I'd been since my trip down the stream and through the stomach of Vampire Mountain when I'd failed my Trials of Initiation. The purge, my shoulder wound, overall exhaustion and the blood transfer had sapped me of most of my energy. I wanted only to sleep, not face a fight to the death. But in life we don't usually get to choose the time of our defining moments. We just have to stand and face them when they come, no matter what sort of a state we're in.

A large crowd had gathered around the barriers. We mingled among them, unnoticed by the police in the darkness and crush of people — even the weirdly dressed Vancha and Evanna failed to draw attention. As we gradually pushed our way to the front, we saw thick clouds of smoke rising from within the stadium, and heard the occasional gun report.

"What's happening?" Alice asked the people nearest the barrier. "Have the police moved in?"

"Not yet," a burly man in a hunter's cap informed her. "But a small advance team went in an hour ago. Must be some new crack unit. Most of them had shaved heads and were dressed in brown shirts and black trousers."

"Their eyes were painted red!" a young boy gasped. "I think it was blood!"

"Don't be ridiculous," his mother laughed. "That was just paint, so the glare of the lights wouldn't blind them."

We withdrew, troubled by this new information. As we were leaving, I heard the boy say, "Mummy, one of those women was dressed in ropes!"

His mother responded with a sharp, "Stop making up stories!"

"Sounds like you were right," Alice said when we were at a safe distance. "The vampets are here, and they generally don't go anywhere without their masters."

"But why did the police let them in?" I asked. "They can't be working for the vampaneze — can they?"

We looked at each other uncertainly. Vampires and vampaneze had always kept their battles private, out of the gaze of humanity. Although both sides were in the process of putting together an army of select human helpers, they'd kept the war secret from humans in general. If the vampaneze had broken that age-old custom and were working with regular human forces, it signalled a worrying new twist in the War of the Scars.

"I can still pass for a police officer," Alice said. "Wait here. I'll try to find out more about this."

She slipped forward, through the crowd and past the barrier. She was immediately challenged by a policeman, but following a quick, hushed conversation, she was led away to talk to whoever was in command.

Vancha and I waited anxiously, Evanna standing calmly nearby. I took the time to analyse my situation. I was weak, dangerously so, and my senses were going haywire. My head was pounding and my limbs were trembling. I'd told Alice I

was up for a fight, but in all honesty I couldn't say whether or not I'd be able to fend for myself. It would have been wiser to retreat and recover. But Steve had forced this battle. He was calling the shots. I'd have to struggle along as best I could and pray to the gods of the vampires for strength.

I started thinking about Evanna's prophecy again as I waited. If Vancha and I faced Steve this night, one of the three of us would die. If it was Vancha or me, Steve would become the Lord of the Shadows and the vampaneze would rule the night, as well as the world of mankind. But if Steve died, I'd become the Lord instead of him, turn on Vancha and destroy the world.

There must be some way to change that. But how? Try to make peace with Steve? Impossible! I wouldn't even if I could, not after what he'd done to Mr Crepsley, Tommy, Shancus and so many others. Peace wasn't an option.

But what other way was there? I couldn't accept the fact that the world was damned. I didn't care what Evanna said. There must be a way to stop the Lord of the Shadows from rising. There *must*...

Alice returned ten minutes later, her features dark. "They're dancing to a vampaneze tune," she said shortly. "I pretended I was an out-of-town chief inspector. I offered my assistance. The ranking officer said they had everything under control. I asked about the brown-shirted soldiers and he told me they were a special government force. He didn't say as much, but I got the feeling he's taking orders from them. I

don't know if they've bribed or threatened him, but they're pulling his strings, no doubt about it."

"So you couldn't persuade him to let us in?" Vancha asked.

"I didn't have to," Alice said. "A way's already open. One rear entrance has been left unblocked. The approaching path is being kept clear. The police around that point aren't to interfere with anyone going in."

"He told you that?" I asked, surprised.

"He was under orders to tell anyone who asked," Alice said. She spat on the ground with disgust. "Traitor!"

Vancha looked at me with a thin smile. "Leonard's in there, isn't he?"

"No doubt about it," I nodded. "He wouldn't miss something like this."

Vancha cocked a thumb at the walls of the stadium. "He's laid this on for our benefit. We're the guests of honour. Be a shame to disappoint him."

"We probably won't come out of there alive if we go in," I noted.

"That's negative thinking," Vancha tutted.

"Then we're going to proceed?" Alice asked. "We're going to push on, even though we're outnumbered and outgunned?"

"Aye," Vancha said after a moment's thought. "I'm too long in the tooth to start bothering with wisdom now!"

I grinned at my fellow Prince. Alice shrugged. Evanna remained as blank-faced as ever. Then, without discussing it any further, we slipped around back to the unguarded entrance.

* * *

The lights weren't as bright at the rear of the stadium, and there weren't many people. Lots of police were about, but they deliberately ignored us, as they'd been told to. As we were about to advance through the gap in the ranks of police, Alice stopped us. "I've had an idea," she said hesitantly. "If we all go in, they can close the net around us and we won't be able to punch our way out. But if we attack from two fronts at once…"

She quickly outlined her plan. It made sense to Vancha and me, so we held back while she made several phone calls. Then we waited an impatient hour, taking it easy, preparing ourselves mentally and physically. As we watched, the smoke thickened from the fires inside the stadium, and the crowd around the barriers grew. Many of the newcomers were tramps and homeless people. They mixed with the others and slowly pushed forwards, where they waited close to the barriers, quiet, unnoticed.

When all was as it should be, Alice handed me a pistol and we bade her farewell. The three of us joined hands and wished each other luck. Then Vancha and I set our sights on the unguarded door. With Evanna following us like a ghost, we boldly walked past the ranks of armed police. They averted their eyes or turned their backs on us as we passed. Moments later we left the brightness outside for the darkness of the stadium tunnels and our date with destiny.

We had entered the leopard's den.

CHAPTER SEVEN

The tunnel twisted a lot, but ran directly under the stands to the open interior of the stadium. Vancha and I walked side by side in absolute silence. If Steve was waiting, and the night went against us, one of us would die within the next few hours. There wasn't much to say in a situation like that. Vancha was probably making his peace with the vampire gods. I was worrying about what would happen after the fight, fixed on the idea that there must be some way to stop the coming of the Lord of the Shadows.

There were no traps along the way and we saw nobody. When we left the confines of the tunnel, we stood by the exit for a minute, numbly absorbing the chaos which Steve's troops had created. Evanna moved away slightly to our left, and she studied the carnage too.

The big top of the Cirque Du Freak, along with most of the vans and tents, had been set ablaze — the source of the

banks of smoke which clogged the air overhead. The performers and circus crew had been herded together about twenty metres ahead of the tunnel, clear of the stands. Harkat stood among them, near Evra and Merla. I'd never seen his grey face filled with such rage. They were surrounded by eight armed vampets, and spotlights which had been taken from inside the big top were trained upon them. Several dead bodies lay nearby. Most were backstage crew, but one was a long-serving star of the show — the skinny, supple, musical Alexander Ribs would never take to the stage again.

Ripping the piece of cloth away from my eyes, I let my sight adjust, then looked for Debbie among the survivors — there was no sign of her. In a panic, I examined the faces and forms of the corpses again, for fear she was lying among them — but I couldn't see her.

Several vampaneze and vampets patrolled the stadium, circling the burning tents and vans, controlling the flames. As I watched, Mr Tiny strolled out of the burning pyre of the big top, through a wall of fire, rubbing his hands together. He was wearing a red top hat and gloves — Mr Tall's. I understood instinctively that he'd left Mr Tall's body inside the tent, using it as a makeshift funeral pyre. Mr Tiny didn't look upset, but I could tell by his donning of the hat and gloves that, on some level, he'd been in some way affected by his son's death.

Between the burning tent and the surviving members of the Cirque Du Freak stood a new addition — a hastily constructed gallows. Several nooses hung from the crossbeam,

but only one was filled — with the poor, thin neck of the snake-boy, Shancus Von.

I cried aloud when I spotted Shancus and made to rush towards him. Vancha gripped my left wrist and jerked me back. "We can't help him now," he growled.

"But—" I started to argue.

"Lower your gaze," he said quietly.

When I did, I saw that a band of vampaneze was grouped beneath the crossbeam and knotted ropes. All were armed with swords or battle-axes. Behind them, standing on something that raised him above them, and smirking evilly, stood their master, the Lord of the Vampaneze — Steve Leopard. He hadn't seen us yet.

"Easy," Vancha said as I stiffened. "No need to rush." His eyes were sliding slowly left and right. "How many vampaneze and vampets are here? Are there more hiding in the stands or behind the burning vans and tents? Let's work out exactly what we have to deal with before we go barging ahead."

Breathing deeply, I forced myself to think calmly, then studied the lie of the land. I counted fourteen vampaneze – nine grouped around Steve — and more than thirty vampets. I didn't see Gannen Harst, but guessed he would be close by Steve, hidden by the group of circus folk between us and the gallows.

"I make it a dozen-plus vampaneze and three times that amount of vampets, aye?" Vancha said.

"More or less," I agreed.

Vancha looked sideways at me and winked. "The odds are in our favour, Sire."

"You think so?"

"Most definitely," he said with fake enthusiasm — we both knew it didn't look good. We were vastly outnumbered by enemies with superior weapons. Our only ace card was that the vampaneze and vampets couldn't kill us. Mr Tiny had predicted doom for them if anybody other than their Lord murdered the hunters.

Without saying anything, we started forward at the exact same moment. I was carrying two knives, one in either hand. Vancha had drawn a couple of throwing stars but was otherwise unarmed — he believed in fighting with his bare hands at close quarters. Evanna moved when we did, shadowing our every footstep.

The vampets surrounding the imprisoned Cirque Du Freak troupe saw us coming but didn't react, except to close a little more tightly around the people they were guarding. They didn't even warn the others that we were here. Then I saw that they didn't need to — Steve and his cronies had already spotted us. Steve was standing on a box, or something, staring happily at us, while the vampaneze in front of him bunched defensively, weapons at the ready.

We had to pass the circus prisoners to get to Steve. I stopped as we drew level with Evra, Merla and Harkat. Evra and Merla's eyes were wet with tears. Harkat's green globes were shining with fury, and he'd pulled down his mask to bare his sharp grey teeth (he could survive up to half a day without the mask).

I gazed sorrowfully at Evra and Merla, then at the body of their son, dangling from the gallows further ahead. The vampets guarding my friends watched me cautiously but made no move against me.

"Come on," Vancha said, tugging at my elbow.

"I'm sorry," I croaked to Evra and Merla, unable to continue without saying something. "I wouldn't ... I didn't ... if I could..." I stopped, unable to think of anything else to say.

Evra and Merla said nothing for a moment. Then, with a screech, Merla smashed through the guards around her and threw herself at me. "I hate you!" she screamed, scratching my face, spitting with rage. "My son's dead because of you!"

I couldn't react. I felt sick with shame. Merla dragged me to the ground, yelling and crying, beating me with her fists. The vampets moved forward to pull her off, but Steve shouted, "No! Leave them alone! This is fun!"

We rolled away from the vampets, Merla driving me back. I didn't even raise my hands to defend myself as she called me every name under the moon. I just wanted the earth to open and swallow me whole.

And then, as Merla lowered her face as though to bite me, she whispered in my ear, "Steve has Debbie." I gawped at her. She roared more insults, then whispered again, "We didn't fight. They think we're gutless, but we were waiting for *you*. Harkat said you'd come and lead us."

Merla cuffed me about the head, then locked gazes with me. "It wasn't your fault," she said, smiling ever so slightly

through her tears. "We don't hate you. Steve's the evil one — not you."

"But ... if I hadn't ... if I'd told Vancha to kill R.V..."

"Don't think that way," she snarled. "You're not to blame. Now help us kill the savages who *are!* Give us a signal when you're ready and we'll answer the call. We'll fight to the death, every last one of us."

She screamed at me again, grabbed me by the neck to strangle me, then fell off and punched the ground, sobbing pitifully. Evra pushed forward, collected his wife and led her back to the pack. He glanced at me once, fleetingly, and I saw the same thing in his expression that I'd seen in Merla's — sorrow for the loss of their son, hatred for Steve and his gang, but only pity for me.

I still felt at fault for what had happened to Shancus and the others. But Evra and Merla's sympathy gave me the strength to carry on. If they'd hated me, I doubt I could have continued. But now that they'd given me their backing, I not only felt able to push on — I felt that I had to. For their sakes, if not my own.

I got to my feet, acting shaken. As Vancha came to help me, I spoke quickly and quietly. "They're with us. They'll fight when we do."

He paused, then carried forward as though I hadn't spoken, checking my face where Merla had scratched me, loudly asking if she'd harmed me, if I was OK, if I wanted to rest a while.

"I'm fine," I grunted, pushing past him, showing my circus friends a stiff back, as if they'd insulted me. "Merla said Steve

has Debbie," I hissed to Vancha out of the side of my mouth, barely moving my lips.

"We might not be able to save her," he whispered back.

"I know," I said stonily. "But we'll try?"

A short pause. Then, "Aye," he replied.

With that, we quickened our pace and made a beeline for the gallows and the grinning, demonic, half-vampaneze beast waiting underneath, face half hidden by the shadow of the dangling Shancus Von.

CHAPTER EIGHT

"Halt!" one of the nine vampaneze in front of Steve shouted when we were about five metres away. We stopped. This close, I saw that Steve was actually standing on the body of one of the circus crew — Pasta O'Malley, a man who used to sleepwalk and even sleep-read. I could also see Gannen Harst now, just to Steve's right, sword undrawn, watching us intently.

"Drop your throwing stars," the vampaneze said to Vancha. When he didn't respond, two of the vampaneze raised spears and pointed them at him. With a shrug, Vancha slid the shurikens back into their holders and lowered his hands.

I glanced up at Shancus, swinging in the light breeze. The crossbeam creaked. The sound was louder than normal for me because of the purge — like the squeal of a wild boar.

"Get him down," I snarled at Steve.

"I don't think so," Steve replied lightly. "I like the sight of him up there. Maybe I'll hang his parents beside him. His brother and sister too. Keep the whole family together. What do you think?"

"Why do you go along with this madman?" Vancha asked Gannen Harst. "I don't care what Des Tiny says about him — this lunatic can bring nothing but shame upon the vampaneze. You should have killed him years ago."

"He is of our blood," Gannen Harst replied quietly. "I don't agree with his ways – he knows that – but we don't kill our kin."

"You do if they break your laws," Vancha grunted. "Leonard lies and uses guns. Any normal vampaneze would be executed if they did that."

"But he isn't normal," Gannen said. "He is our Lord. Desmond Tiny said we would perish if we did not follow him and obey. Whether I like it or not, Steve has the power to bend our laws, or even ignore them completely. I'd rather he didn't, but it's not my place to chastise him when he does."

"You can't approve of his actions," Vancha pushed.

"No," Gannen admitted. "But he has been accepted by the clan, and I am only a servant of my people. History can judge Steve. I'm content to serve and protect, in line with the wishes of those who appointed me."

Vancha glared at his brother, trying to stare him down, but Gannen only gazed back blankly. Then Steve laughed. "Aren't family get-togethers a joy?" he said. "I was hoping you'd bring Annie and Darius along. Imagine the fun all six of us could have had!"

"They're far away from here by now," I said. I wanted to dive for him and rip his throat open with my bare hands and teeth, but his guards would have cut me down before I struck. I had to be patient and pray for a chance to present itself.

"How's my son?" Steve asked. "Did you kill him?"

"Of course not," I snorted. "I didn't have to. When he saw you murder Shancus he realized you were a monster. I filled him in on your past *glories*. Annie told him some old stories too. He'll never listen to you again. You've lost him. He's your son no more."

I hoped to wound Steve with my words but he just laughed them off. "Oh well, I was never that fond of him anyway. A scrawny, moody kid. No taste for blood. Although," he chuckled, "I guess he'll develop one soon!"

"I wouldn't be too sure of that," I retorted.

"I blooded him," Steve boasted. "He's half-vampaneze."

"No," I smiled. "He's a half-vampire. Like me."

Steve stared at me uncertainly. "You re-blooded him?"

"Yes. He's one of us now. He won't need to kill when he feeds. Like I said, he's no longer your son — in any way whatsoever."

Steve's features darkened. "You shouldn't have done that," he growled. "The boy was mine."

"He was never yours, not in spirit," I said. "You merely tricked him into believing he was."

Steve started to reply, then scowled and shook his head gruffly. "Never mind," he muttered. "The child's not important. I'll deal with him – and his mother – later. Let's

get down to the good stuff. We all know the prophecy." He nodded at Mr Tiny, who was wandering around the burning tents and vans, paying no apparent interest to us. "Darren or Vancha will kill me, or I'll kill one of you, and that will decide the fate of the War of the Scars."

"If Tiny's right, or telling the truth, aye," Vancha sniffed.

"You don't believe him?" Steve frowned.

"Not entirely," Vancha said. "Tiny and his daughter–" He glared at Evanna –"have agendas of their own. I accept most of what they predict but I don't treat their predictions as absolute facts."

"Then why are you here?" Steve challenged him.

"In case they *are* correct."

Steve looked confused. "How can you not believe them? Desmond Tiny is the voice of destiny. He sees the future. He knows all that has been and will be."

"We make our own futures," Vancha said. "Regardless of what happens tonight, I believe my people will defeat yours. But I'll kill you anyway," he added with a wicked grin. "Just to be on the safe side."

"You're an ignorant fool," Steve said, shaking with outrage. Then his gaze settled on me. "I bet *you* believe the prophecy."

"Maybe," I replied.

"Of course you do," Steve smiled. "And you know it's you or me, don't you? Vancha's a red herring. You and I are the sons of destiny, the ruler and slave, the victor and vanquished. Leave Vancha behind, step up here alone, and I swear it will be a fair fight. You and me, man to man, one

winner, one loser. A Vampaneze Lord to rule the night — or a Vampire Prince."

"How can I trust you?" I asked. "You're a liar. You'll spring a trap."

"No," Steve barked. "You have my word."

"Like that means anything," I jeered, but I could see an eagerness in Steve's expression. His offer was genuine. I glanced sideways at Vancha. "What do you think?"

"No," Vancha said. "We're in this together. We'll take him on as a team."

"But if he's prepared to fight me fairly…"

"That demon knows nothing about fairness," Vancha said. "He'd cheat — that's his nature. We'll do nothing the way he wants."

"Very well." I faced Steve again. "Stuff your offer. What next?"

I thought Steve was going to leap over the ranks of vampaneze and attack me. He gnashed his teeth, hands twisted together, shivering furiously. Gannen Harst saw it too, but to my surprise, rather than step in to calm Steve down, he took a half-step back. It was as if he wanted Steve to leap, like he'd had enough of his insane, evil Lord, and wanted this matter settled, one way or the other.

But just when it seemed as if the moment of final confrontation had come, Steve relaxed and his smile returned. "I do my best," he sighed. "I try to make it easy for everybody, but some people are determined not to play ball. Very well. Here's 'what next'."

Steve put his fingers to his lips and whistled sharply. From behind the gallows, R.V. stepped out. The bearded, ex-eco-warrior was holding a rope between three lonely-looking hooks (Mr Tall had snapped the other hooks off before he died). When he tugged on the rope, a bound woman shuffled out after him — Debbie.

I'd been expecting this, so I didn't panic. R.V. walked Debbie forwards a few paces, but stopped a long way short of Steve. The one-time campaigner for peace and the protection of mother nature didn't look very happy. He was twitchy, head jerking, eyes unfocused, nervously chewing at his lower lip, which was bleeding from where he'd bitten through the flesh. R.V. had been a proud, earnest, dedicated man when I first met him, fighting to save the world from pollution. Then he'd become a mad beast, intent only on gaining revenge for the loss of his hands. Now he was neither — just a ragged, sorry mess.

Steve didn't notice R.V.'s confusion. He had eyes only for Debbie. "Isn't she beautiful?" he mocked me. "Like an angel. More warrior-like than the last time we met, but all the lovelier because of it." He looked at me slyly. "Be a shame if I had to tell R.V. to gut her like a rabid dog."

"You can't use her against me," I said softly, gazing at Steve without blinking. "She knows who you are and what's at stake. I love her, but my first duty is to my clan. She understands that."

"You mean you'll stand there and let her die?" Steve shrieked.

"Yes!" Debbie shouted before I could reply.

"You people," Steve groaned. "You're determined to annoy me. I try to be fair, but you toss it back in my face and..." He hopped off of Pasta O'Malley's back and ranted and raved, striding up and down behind his guards. I kept a close watch on him. If he stepped out too far, I'd strike. But even in his rage he was careful not to expose himself.

All of a sudden Steve stopped. "So be it!" he snarled. "R.V. — kill her!"

R.V. didn't respond. He was gazing miserably down at the ground.

"R.V.!" Steve shouted. "Didn't you hear me? Kill her!"

"Don't want to," R.V. mumbled. His eyes came up and I saw pain and doubt in them. "You shouldn't have killed the kid, Steve. He did nothing to hurt us. It was wrong. Kids are the future, man."

"I did what I had to," Steve replied tightly. "Now you'll do the same."

"But she's not a vampire..."

"She works for them!" Steve shouted.

"I know," R.V. moaned. "But why do we have to kill her? Why did you kill the kid? It was Darren we were meant to kill. *He's* the enemy, man. He's the one who cost me my hands."

"Don't betray me now," Steve growled, stepping towards the bearded vampaneze. "You've killed people too, the innocent as well as the guilty. Don't get moralistic on me. It doesn't become you."

"But ... but ... but..."

"Stop stuttering and kill her!" Steve screamed. He took another step forward and moved clear of his guards without being aware of it. I steeled myself to make a dash at him, but Vancha was one move ahead of me.

"*Now!*" Vancha roared, leaping forward, drawing a shuriken and launching it at Steve. He would have killed him, except the guard at the end of the line saw the danger just in time and threw himself into the path of the deadly throwing star, sacrificing himself to save his Lord.

As the other guards surged sideways to block Vancha's path to their Lord, I sheathed my knives, drew the pistol I'd borrowed from Alice before entering the stadium, aimed it at the sky and pulled the trigger three times — the signal for all-out riot!

CHAPTER NINE

Even before the echoes of the report of my third shot faded, the air outside the stadium filled with answering gunfire, as Alice and her band of vampirites opened fire on the police standing guard. She'd summoned the homeless people before Vancha and I entered the tunnel, and positioned them around the barrier outside the stadium. After years of surviving on the scraps other people threw away, this was their time to rise. They had only a small amount of training and basic weapons, but they had passion and anger on their side, and the desire to prove themselves. So now, at my signal, they leapt the barriers around the stadium and attacked as a unified force, throwing themselves upon the startled police, sacrificing themselves where necessary, fighting and dying not just for their own lives, but for the lives of those who considered them trash.

We weren't sure of the intentions of the police. Steve might have told them to remain outside regardless of what

happened within, in which case the attack by the vampirites would serve no purpose at all. But if they were there to support the vampaneze and vampets, to come to their aid if summoned, the vampirites could divert them and buy those of us inside the stadium a bit more space and time.

Most of the vampaneze guarding Steve moved to stop Vancha when he charged, but two lunged at me as I fired the pistol. They tackled me to the ground, knocking the gun from my hand. I struck out at them but they simply lay on top of me, pinning me down. They would have held me there, helpless, while their colleagues dealt with Vancha. Except…

The stars and crew of the Cirque Du Freak had also rallied to my signal. At the same time that the vampirites attacked the police, the prisoners inside the stadium turned on the vampets holding them captive. They attacked with their bare hands, driving the vampets back by sheer force of numbers. The vampets fired into the crowd and hacked wildly with their swords and axes. Several people fell, dead or wounded. But the group pushed on regardless, screaming, punching, kicking, biting — no force on Earth could hold them back.

While the bulk of the Cirque Du Freak troupe grappled with the vampets, Harkat led a small band towards the gallows. He'd grabbed an axe from a dead vampet and with one smooth swing he cut down a vampaneze who tried to intercept them, rushing past without breaking his stride.

Vancha was still locked in a struggle with Steve's guards, doing his best to break through to their Lord. He'd downed

two of them but the others were standing firm. He was cut in many places, knife and spear wounds, but none fatal. Looking around, I saw Gannen Harst push Steve away from the threat. Steve was arguing with him — he wanted to take Vancha on.

Behind Steve and Gannen Harst, R.V. had let go of Debbie's rope and was backing away from her, shaking his head, hooks crossed behind his back, wanting no part of this. Debbie was tugging at her bonds, trying to wriggle free.

The two vampaneze holding me down saw Harkat and the others racing towards them. Cursing, they abandoned me and lashed out at their attackers. They were too swift for the ordinary circus folk — three died quickly — but Truska was part of the group, and she wasn't so easily despatched. She'd let her beard grow while she'd been waiting to fight — the unnatural blonde hair now trailed down past her feet. Standing back, she made the beard rise — she could control the hairs as though they were snakes — then directed the twisting strands towards one of the vampaneze. The beard parted into two prongs, then curled around the startled vampaneze's throat and tightened. He sliced at the hair and at Truska, but she had him too firmly in her grip. He fell to his knees, purple features darkening even further as he choked.

Harkat took on the other vampaneze, chopping at him with his axe. The Little Person lacked the speed of a vampaneze, but he was very powerful and his round green

eyes were alert to his opponent's swift moves. He could fight as an equal, as he had many times in the past.

I circled around the vampaneze struggling with Vancha. I meant to go after Steve, but he and Gannen had linked up with three of the vampaneze who'd been roaming the grounds of the stadium. I didn't fancy the five-to-one odds, so I went to cut Debbie free instead.

"They surrounded the stadium shortly after Harkat and I arrived," she cried as I sliced through the ropes binding her arms. "I tried phoning, but it wouldn't work. It was Mr Tiny. He blocked my signal. I saw his watch glowing, and he was laughing."

"It's OK," I said. "We'd have come anyway. We had to."

"Is that Alice outside?" Debbie asked — the gunfire was deafening now.

"Yes," I said. "The vampirites seem to be enjoying their first taste of action."

Vancha lurched over to us, streaming blood. The vampaneze had given up on him and retreated, teaming up with the vampets and picking fights with the circus folk. "Where's Leonard?" Vancha bellowed.

I peered around the stadium but it was almost impossible to pick out any individuals in the press of bodies. "I had him in my sights a minute ago," I said. "He must be here somewhere."

"Not if Gannen flitted with him!" Vancha roared. He wiped blood clear of his eyes and looked for Steve and Gannen again.

"Are you badly wounded?" Debbie asked him.

"Scratches!" Vancha grunted. Then he shouted, "There! Behind the fat man!"

He rushed forward, bellowing madly. Squinting, I caught a glimpse of Steve. He was close to the enormous Rhamus Twobellies, warily backing away from him. Rhamus was literally falling on his opponents, squashing them lifeless.

Debbie darted away from me, picked the bodies of the dead vampaneze clean of their weapons, and returned with an array of knives and two swords. She gave one of the swords to me and hefted the other herself. It was too large for her, but she held it steady, face set. "You go get Steve," she said. "I'll help the others."

"Be—" I began, but she'd already raced out of earshot, "—careful," I finished softly. I shook my head, smiled briefly, then set off after Steve.

Around me the battle was raging. The circus folk were locked in bloody combat with the vampets and vampaneze, fighting clumsily but effectively, blind fury compensating for lack of military training. The gifted freaks were a huge help. Truska was causing havoc with her beard. Rhamus was an immovable foe. Gertha Teeth was biting off fingers, noses, sword tips. Hans Hands had tucked his legs behind his neck and was dodging between the enemy forces on his hands, too low for them to easily strike, tripping them up and dividing them.

Vancha had come to a halt, held up by the fighting. He started firing shurikens at those enemies ahead of him, to

clear a path. Jekkus Flang stepped up beside him and added his throwing knives to Vancha's stars. A deadly, efficient combination. I couldn't help thinking what a great show they could have put on if we'd been playing to an audience tonight instead of fighting for our lives.

Mr Tiny was picking his way through the mass of warring bodies, beaming merrily, admiring the corpses of the dead, studying the dying with polite interest, applauding those locked in especially vicious duels. Evanna was edging towards her father, disinterested in the carnage, bare feet and lower ropes stained with blood.

Gannen and Steve were still backing away from the massive Rhamus Twobellies, using him as a shield — it was hard for anybody else to get at them with Rhamus in the way. I tracked them like a hound, closing in. I was almost at the mouth of the tunnel through which we'd entered the stadium when fresh bodies burst through it. My insides tightened — I thought the police had come to the aid of their companions, meaning almost certain defeat for us. But then, to my astonished delight, I realized it was Alice Burgess and a dozen or so vampirites. Declan and Little Kenny — the pair who'd rescued me from the street when Darius shot me — were among them.

"Still alive?" Alice shouted as her troops laid into the vampaneze and vampets, faces twisted with excitement and battle lust.

"How'd you get in?" I yelled in reply. The plan had been for her to cause a diversion outside the stadium, to hold up the police — not invade with a force of her own.

"We attacked at the front, as planned," she said. "The police rushed to that point, to battle *en masse* — they lack discipline. Most of my troops fled with the crowd after a few minutes — you should have seen the chaos! — but I slipped around the back with a few volunteers. The entrance to the tunnel is completely unguarded now. We—"

A vampet attacked her and she had to wheel aside to deal with him. I did a very quick head count. With the addition of the vampirites, we seriously outnumbered the vampaneze and vampets. Although the fighting was brutal and disorganized, we had the upper hand. Unless the police outside recovered swiftly and rushed in, we'd win this battle! But that would mean nothing if Steve escaped, so I put all thoughts of victory on hold and went in pursuit of him again.

I didn't get very far. R.V. had backed away from the fighting. He was heading for the tunnel, but I was standing almost directly in his path. When he saw me, he stopped. I wasn't sure what to do — fight or let him escape so that I could go after Steve? While I was making up my mind, Cormac Limbs stepped in between us.

"Come on, hairy!" he roared at R.V., slapping his face with his left hand, jabbing at him with a knife held in his right. "Let's be having you!"

"No!" R.V. moaned. "I don't want to fight."

"The devil you don't, you big, bearded, bug-eyed baboon!" Cormac shouted, slapping R.V. again. This time R.V. lashed out at Cormac's hand with his hooks. He cut two of the

fingers off, but they immediately grew back. "You'll have to do better than that, stink-breath!" Cormac taunted him.

"Then I will!" R.V. shouted, losing his cool. Jumping forwards, he knocked Cormac over, knelt on his chest, and before I could do anything, he struck at Cormac's neck with his hooks. He didn't cut it clean off, but sliced about halfway through. Then, with a grunt, he hacked through the rest of it, and tossed Cormac's head aside like a ball.

"You shouldn't have messed with me, man!" R.V. groaned, rising shakily. I was about to attack him, to avenge Cormac's death, but then I saw that he was sobbing. "I didn't want to kill you!" R.V. howled. "I didn't want to kill anybody! I wanted to help people. I wanted to save the world. I..."

He ground to a halt, eyes widening with disbelief. Glancing down, I also came to a stunned stop. Where Cormac's head had been, two new heads were growing, shooting out on a pair of thin necks. They were slightly smaller than his old head, but otherwise identical. When they stopped growing, there was a short pause. Then Cormac's eyes fluttered open and he spat blood out of both mouths. His eyes came into focus. He looked at R.V. with one set and at me with the other. Then his heads turned and he stared at himself.

"So that's what happens when I cut my head off!" he exclaimed through both mouths at the same time. "I always wondered about that!"

"Madness!" R.V. screamed. "The world's gone mad! *Mad!*"

Spinning crazily, he rushed past Cormac, then past me, gibbering insanely, drooling and falling over. I could have

killed him easily — but I chose not to. Standing aside, I let the wretch pass, and watched sadly as he staggered down the tunnel, out of sight. R.V. had never been right in the head since losing his hands, and now he'd lost his senses completely. I couldn't bring myself to punish this pathetic shadow of a man.

And now, at last — Steve. He and Gannen were part of a small band of vampaneze and vampets. They'd been forced towards the centre of the stadium by the freaks, circus helpers and vampirites. Lots of smaller fights were still being waged around the stadium, but this was their last big stand. If this unit fell, they were all doomed.

Vancha was closing in on the group. I joined him. There was no sign of Jekkus Flang — I didn't know whether he'd fallen to the enemy or run out of knives, and this wasn't the time to make enquiries. Vancha paused when he saw me. "Ready?" he asked.

"Ready," I said.

"I don't care which of us kills him," Vancha said, "but let me go first. If—" He stopped, face twisting with fear. "No!" he roared.

Following the direction of his eyes, I saw that Steve had tripped. Evra stood over him, a long knife held in both hands, determined to take the life of the man who'd killed his son. If he struck, the Lord of the Vampaneze would die by the hand of one who wasn't destined to kill him. If Mr Tiny's prophecy was true, that would have dire results for the vampire clan.

As we watched, unable to prevent it, Evra stopped abruptly. He shook his head, blinked dumbly — then

stepped over Steve and left him lying on the ground, unharmed. Steve sat up, bleary-eyed, not sure what had happened. Gannen Harst stooped and helped him to his feet. The two men stood, alone in the crush, totally ignored by everyone around them.

"Over there," I whispered, touching Vancha's shoulder. Far off to our right, Mr Tiny stood, eyes on Steve and Gannen. He was holding his heart-shaped watch in his right hand. It was glowing redly. Evanna was standing beside him, her face illuminated by the glow of her father's watch.

I don't know if Steve and Gannen saw Mr Tiny and realized that he was protecting them. But they were alert enough to seize their chance and run for the freedom of the tunnel.

Mr Tiny watched the pair race free of danger. Then he looked at Vancha and me, and smiled. The glow of his watch faded and his lips moved softly. Even though we were a long way off, we heard him clearly, as if he was standing next to us. "It's time, boys!"

"Harkat!" I shouted, wanting him to come with us, to be there at the end, as he'd been by my side for so much of the hunt. But he didn't hear me. Nobody did. I glanced around the stadium at Harkat, Alice, Evra, Debbie. All of my friends were locked in battle with the vampaneze and vampets. None of them knew what was happening with Steve and Gannen Harst. They weren't part of this. It was just me and Vancha now.

"To the death, Sire?" Vancha murmured.

"To the death," I agreed miserably. I ran my eyes over the faces of my friends for what might be the final time, bidding silent farewells to the scaly Evra Von, the grey-skinned Harkat Mulds, the steely Alice Burgess and my beloved Debbie Hemlock, more beautiful than ever as she tore into her foes like an Amazonian warrior of old. Perhaps it was for the best that I couldn't bid them a proper farewell. There was so much to say, I don't know where I would have begun.

Then Vancha and I jogged after Steve and Gannen Harst, not rushing, sure that they wouldn't flit, not this time, not until we'd satisfied the terms of Mr Tiny's prophecy and Steve or one of us lay dead. Behind us, Mr Tiny and Evanna followed like ghosts. They alone would bear witness to the final battle, the death of one of the hunters or Steve — and the birth of the Lord of the Shadows, destroyer of the present and all-ruling monster of the future.

CHAPTER TEN

We followed Steve and Gannen down the hill at the rear of the stadium. They were fleeing towards the river, but they weren't racing at top speed. Either one of them was injured or, like ourselves, they'd simply accepted the fact that we had to fight, an evenly matched contest, to the bitter, bloody end.

As we jogged down the hill, leaving the stadium, lights and noises behind, my headache lessened. I would have been glad of that, except now that I was able to focus, I realized how physically drained I was. I'd been operating on reserve energy for a long time and had just about run dry. Even the simplest movement was a huge chore. All I could do was carry on as long as possible and hope I got an adrenaline burst when we caught up with our prey.

As we reached level ground at the bottom of the hill, I stumbled and almost fell. Luckily Vancha had been keeping an eye on me. He caught and steadied me. "Feel bad?" he asked.

"Awful," I groaned.

"Maybe you're not meant to go any further," he said. "Perhaps you should rest here and—"

"Save your breath," I stopped him. "I'm going on, even if I have to crawl."

Vancha laughed, then tilted my head back and examined my face, his small eyes unusually dark. "You'll make a fine vampire," he said. "I hope I'm around to celebrate your coming of age."

"You're not getting defeatist on me, are you?" I grunted.

"No." He smiled weakly. "We'll win. Of course we will. I just..."

He stopped, slapped my back and urged me on. Wearily, every step an effort, I threw myself after Steve and Gannen Harst again. I did my best to match Vancha's pace, swinging my legs as evenly as I could, keeping the rest of my body limp, relaxed, saving energy.

Steve and Gannen reached the river and turned right, jogging along the bank. As they came to the arch of a bridge spanning the river, they stopped. It looked like they were having an argument. Gannen was trying to pick Steve up — I assumed he meant to flit, with Steve on his back, as they'd escaped from us once before. Steve was having none of it. He slapped his protector's hands away, gesturing furiously. Then, as we closed upon them, Gannen's shoulders sagged and he nodded wearily. The pair turned away from the pass beneath the bridge, drew their weapons and stood waiting for us.

We slowed and walked the rest of the way. I could hear Mr Tiny and Evanna close behind — they'd caught up to us within the last few seconds — but I didn't turn to look back.

"You could use your shurikens," I whispered to Vancha as we came within range of Steve and Gannen Harst.

"That would be dishonourable," Vancha replied. "They've faced us openly, in expectation of a fair fight. We must confront them."

He was right. Killing mercilessly wasn't the vampire way. But I half wished he'd put his principles aside, for once, and fire his throwing stars at them until they dropped. It would be much simpler and surer that way.

We drew to a halt a couple of metres short of Steve and Gannen. Steve's eyes were alight with excitement and a slight shade of fear — he knew there were no guarantees now, no more opportunities for dirty tricks or games. It was a plain, fair fight to the death, and that was something he couldn't control.

"Greetings, brother," Gannen Harst said, bowing his head.

"Greetings," Vancha replied stiffly. "I'm glad you face us like true creatures of the night at last. Perhaps in death you can find again the honour which you abandoned during life."

"Honour will be shared by all here tonight," Gannen said, "both the living and the dead."

"They don't half go on a lot," Steve sighed. He squared up to me. "Ready to die, Shan?"

I stepped forward. "If that's what fate has in store for me — yes," I answered. "But I'm also ready to kill." With that I

raised my sword and struck the first blow of the fight which would decide the outcome of the War of the Scars.

Steve stood his ground, brought his own sword up — it was shorter and easier to handle than mine — and turned my blow aside. Gannen Harst stabbed at me with his long, straight sword. Vancha slapped the blade wide of its target and pulled me out of immediate range of his brother.

Vancha only gave me a relatively gentle tug, but in my weakened state I staggered backwards and wound up in an untidy mess on the ground, close to Mr Tiny and Evanna. By the time I struggled to my feet, Vancha was locked in combat with Steve and Gannen Harst, hands a blur as he defended himself against their swords with his bare palms.

"He's a fierce creature, isn't he?" Mr Tiny remarked to his daughter. "Quite the beast of nature. I like him."

Evanna didn't reply. All her senses were focused on the battle, and there was worry and uncertainty in her eyes. I knew in that moment that she'd told the truth and really didn't know which way this would go.

I turned away from the onlookers and caught quick flashes of the fight which was unfolding at superhuman speed. Steve nicked Vancha's left arm near the top — Vancha kicked him in the chest in return. Gannen's sword scraped down Vancha's left side, slicing a thin gouge from breast to waist — Vancha replied by grabbing his brother's sword hand and wrenching it back, snapping the bones of his wrist. Gannen gasped with pain as he dropped the sword, then ducked for it and grabbed it with his left hand. As he

came to his feet again, Vancha struck his head with his right knee. Gannen fell away with a heavy grunt.

Vancha spun round to deal with Steve, but Steve was already upon him, making short sweeps with his sword, keeping Vancha at bay. Vancha tried to grab the sword, but only succeeded in having the flesh of his palms cut open. I staggered up beside him. I wasn't of much use right then — I could barely raise my sword, and my legs dragged like dead weights — but at least it provided Steve with a double threat. If I could distract him, Vancha might be able to penetrate his defences and strike.

As I drew level with Vancha, panting and sweating, Gannen swung back into battle, dazed but determined, chopping angrily at Vancha, forcing him to retreat. I stabbed at Gannen, but Steve diverted my sword with his, then let go of the handle with one hand and punched me between the eyes. I dropped back, startled, and Steve drove the tip of his sword at my face.

If he'd had both hands on the sword, he'd have thrust it through me. But one-handed, he wasn't able to direct it as powerfully as he wished. I managed to knock it aside with my left arm. A deep cut opened up just below my elbow and I felt all the strength leave the fingers of that hand.

Steve stabbed at me again. I raised my sword to protect myself. Too late I realized he'd only feinted. Wheeling around, he threw himself into me, right shoulder first. He struck me heavily in the chest and I fell back, winded losing hold of my sword. There was a yell behind me and I

crashed into Vancha. Both of us went down, Vancha taken by surprise, arms and legs entangled with mine.

It took Vancha no more than a second to free himself — but that second was all Gannen Harst required. Darting forward, almost too fast for me to see, he stuck the tip of his sword into the small of Vancha's back — then shoved it all the way through and out the front of Vancha's stomach!

Vancha's eyes and mouth shot wide open. Gannen stood behind him a moment. Then he stepped away and pulled his sword free. Blood gushed out of Vancha, both in front and behind, and he collapsed in agony, face twisted, limbs thrashing.

"May your gods forgive me, brother," Gannen whispered, his face haggard, eyes haunted. "Though I fear I'll never forgive myself."

I scrabbled away from the downed Prince, chasing my sword. Steve stood close by, laughing. With an effort, Gannen regained control and set about securing victory. Hurrying over to me, he stood on my sword so that I couldn't lift it, sheathed his own blade and grabbed my head with his good left hand. "Hurry!" he barked at Steve. "Kill him quick!"

"What's the rush?" Steve muttered.

"If Vancha dies of the wound I gave him, we'll have broken the rules of Mr Tiny's prophecy!" Gannen shouted.

Steve pulled a face. "Bloody prophecies," he grumbled. "Maybe I'll let him die and see what happens. Maybe I don't care about Tiny or..." He stopped and rolled his eyes. "Oh, how *silly* we are! The answer's obvious — *I'll* kill Vancha

before he dies of your wound. That way we'll fulfil the requirements of the stupid prophecy *and* I'll get to hang on to Darren, so I can torture him later."

"Clever boy," I heard Mr Tiny murmur.

"Have it any way you wish!" Gannen roared. "But if you're going to kill him, kill him now, so that—"

"*No!*" someone screamed. Before anyone could react, a large shape shot out of the underpass beneath the bridge and hurled itself at Gannen, knocking him off me, almost toppling him into the river. Sitting up, I got a shocked fix on my most unlikely of rescuers — *R. V.!*

"Not gonna let you do it, man!" R.V. screamed, pounding Gannen Harst with his hooks. "You're evil!"

Gannen had been taken completely unawares, but he swiftly recovered, fumbled his sword free of its scabbard, and dug at R.V. with it. R.V. caught the sword with his gold right-handed hooks and smashed it against the ground, snapping it in two. With a roar of triumph, he slammed his silver left-handed hook into the side of Gannen's head. There was a crack and Gannen's eyes went blank. He slumped beneath R.V., unconscious. R.V. howled with joy, then drew both arms back to bring them down sharply and finish Gannen off.

Before R.V. could strike, Steve stepped up behind him and forced a knife up beneath his bushy beard, deep into his throat. R.V. shuddered and bowled Steve over. R.V. stood, spinning crazily, grabbing for the handle of the knife with his hooks. After missing it several times, he fell down, landing on his knees, head thrown back.

R.V. knelt there a moment, swaying sickeningly. Then his arms slowly rose. He gazed at the gold and silver hooks, his face glowing with wonder. "My hands," he said softly, and although his voice was gurgly with blood, his words were clear. "I can see them. My hands. They're back. Everything's OK now. I'm normal again, man." Then his arms dropped, his smile and pale red eyes froze in place, and his soul passed quietly on to the next world.

CHAPTER ELEVEN

I gazed at R.V.'s peaceful expression as he knelt in his death pose. He'd left his pain behind at last, for ever. I was glad for him. If he'd lived, he'd have had to carry around the memory of the evil he'd committed while in league with the vampaneze. Maybe he was better off this way.

"And now there's two — just me and you," Steve trilled, breaking my train of thought. I glanced up and saw him standing a few metres away from R.V., smiling. Gannen Harst was still out for the count, and although Vancha was alive, he was lying motionless, wheezing fitfully, unable to defend himself or attack.

"Yes," I agreed, standing and picking up my sword. My left hand wouldn't work and my system was maybe a minute or two away from complete shutdown. But I'd enough strength left for one last fight. First though — Vancha. I paused over him and studied at his wound. It was

seeping blood and his face was creased with pain. He tried to speak but words wouldn't form.

As I hovered uncertainly by the side of my fellow Prince, unwilling to leave him like this, Evanna crossed to his side, knelt and examined him. Her eyes were grave when she looked up. "It is not fatal," she said softly. "He will live."

"Thank you," I muttered.

"Save your thanks," Mr Tiny said. He was standing directly behind me. "She didn't tell you to cheer you up, silly boy. It was a warning. Vancha won't die for the time being, but he's out of the fight. You're alone. The final hunter. Unless you turn tail and run, it's down to you and Steve now. If Steve doesn't die, death will come within the next few minutes for *you*."

I looked over my shoulder at the small man in the yellow suit and green wellington boots. His face was bright with bloodthirsty glee. "If death comes," I said shortly, "it will be a far more welcome companion than you."

Mr Tiny chuckled, then stepped away to my left. Rising, Evanna took up position on my right. Both waited for me to move, so that they could follow. I spared Vancha one final glance — he grinned painfully at me and winked — then faced Steve.

He backed away from me casually, entering the shadows beneath the bridge. I trailed after him, sword by my side, taking deep breaths, clearing my mind, focusing on the death-struggle to come. Although this could have been Vancha's battle, a part of me had known all along that it would come down to this. Steve and I were opposite sides of a coin, linked since

childhood, first by friendship, then hatred. It was only fitting that the final confrontation should fall to the two of us.

I entered the cool darkness of the underpass. It took my eyes a few seconds to adjust. When they did, I saw Steve waiting, right eye twitching nervously. The river gurgled softly beside us, the only noise except for our panting and chattering teeth.

"There is where we settle matters, once and for all, in the dark," Steve said.

"As good a place as any," I replied.

Steve raised his left palm. I could vaguely make out the shape of the pink cross he'd carved into his flesh eighteen years before. "Remember when I did this?" he asked. "That night, I swore I'd kill you and Creepy Crepsley."

"You're halfway there," I noted dryly. "You must be delighted."

"Not really," he said. "To be honest, I miss old Creepy. The world's not the same without him. I'll miss you even more. You've been the driving force behind everything I've done since I was a child. Without you, I'm not sure I'll have much of an interest in life. If possible, I'd let you go. I enjoy our games — the hunt, the traps, the fights. I'd happily keep doing it, over and over, a new twist here, a fresh shock there."

"But life doesn't work like that," I said. "Everything has to end."

"Yes," Steve said sadly. "That's one thing I can't change." His mood passed and he regarded me with a sneer. "Here's where *you* end, Darren Shan. This is your grand finale. Have you made your peace with the vampire gods?"

"I'll do that later," I snarled, and swung my sword wide, moving forward so that on its return arc he'd be within range. But before it had completed its first arc, the tip of the sword smashed into the wall. It bounced off in a shower of sparks and a shock ran down my arm.

"Silly boy," Steve purred, mimicking Mr Tiny. He raised a knife. "No room here for swords."

Steve leapt forward and jabbed the knife at me. I pulled back and lobbed my sword at him, momentarily halting him. In that second, I drew one of the knives I'd brought from Annie's kitchen. When Steve advanced, I was ready. I caught his thrust with the hilt of my knife and turned his blade aside.

There was no room in the underpass to circle one another, so we had to jab and stab, ducking and weaving to avoid each other's blows. The conditions actually played into my favour — in the open I'd have had to be nimbler on my feet, spinning to keep up with Steve. That would have exhausted me. Here, since we were so cramped, I could stand still and direct my rapidly dwindling strength into my knife hand.

We fought silently, fast, sharp, impulsive. Steve nicked the flesh of my forearm — I nicked his. He opened shallow wounds on my stomach and chest — I repaid the compliment. He almost cut my nose off — I nearly severed his left ear.

Then Steve came at me from the left, taking advantage of my dead arm. He grabbed the material of my shirt and pulled me towards him, driving his knife hard at my belly with his

other hand. I rolled with the force of his pull, throwing myself into him. His knife cut the wall of my stomach, a deep wound, but my momentum carried me forward despite the pain. I drove him down, landing awkwardly on him as he hit the path. His right hand flew out by his side, fingers snapping open. His knife shot free and struck the river with a splash, vanishing from sight in an instant.

Steve brought his empty right hand up, to push me off. I stabbed at it with my knife and hit home, spearing him through his forearm. He screamed. I freed my knife before he could knock it from my grip, raised it to shoulder height and redirected it, so the tip was pointing at Steve's throat. His eyes shot to the gleam of the blade and his breath caught. This was it. I had him. He'd been out-fought and he knew it. One quick thrust of the knife and—

Searing pain. A white flash inside my head. I thought Gannen had recovered and struck me from behind, but he hadn't. It was an aftershock from when I blooded Darius. Vancha had warned me about this. My limbs trembled. A roaring in my ears, drowning out all other sounds. I dry-heaved and fell off Steve, almost tumbling into the river. "No!" I tried to scream. "Not now!" But I couldn't form the words. I was in the grip of immense pain, and could do nothing against it.

Time seemed to collapse. Gripped by panic, I was dimly aware of Steve crawling on top of me. He wrestled my knife from my hand. There was a sharp stabbing sensation in my stomach, followed by another. Steve crowed, "Now I have you!

Now you're gonna die!" Something blurry passed in front of my eyes, then back again. Fighting the white light inside my head, I got my eyes to focus. It was the knife. Steve had pulled it out and was waving it in my face, teasing me, sure he'd won, prolonging the moment of triumph.

But Steve had miscalculated. The pain of the stabbing brought me back from the brink of all-out confusion. The agony in my gut worked against the pain in my head, and the world began to swim back into place around me. Steve was perched on top of me, laughing. But I wasn't afraid. Unknown to himself, he was helping me. I was able to think halfway straight now, able to plan, able to act.

My right hand stole to waist of my trousers as Steve continued to mock me. I gripped the handle of a second knife. I caught a glimpse of Mr Tiny peering over Steve's shoulder. He'd seen my hand moving and knew what was coming. He was nodding, though I'm not sure if he was encouraging me or merely bobbing his head up and down with excitement.

I lay still, gathering my very last dredges of energy together, letting Steve torment me with wild promises of what was to come. I was bleeding freely from the stab wounds in my stomach. I wasn't sure if I'd be alive come the dawn, but of one thing I was certain — Steve would die before me.

"—and when I finish with your toes and fingers, I'll move on to your nose and ears!" Steve yelled. "But first I'll cut your eyelids off, so you can see everything that I'm gonna do. After that I'll—"

"Steve," I wheezed, stopping him midflow. "Want to know the secret of winning a fight like this? Less talking — more stabbing."

I lunged at him, using the muscles of my stomach to force my body up. Steve wasn't prepared for it. I knocked him backwards. As he fell, I swung my legs around, then pushed with my knees and feet, so I drove him all the way back with the full weight of my body. He hit the pavement with a grunt, for the second time within the space of a few minutes. This time he managed to hold on to his knife, but that was no use to him. I wasn't going to make the same mistake twice.

No hesitation. No pausing to pick my point. No cynical, memorable last words. I put my trust in the gods of the vampires and blindly thrust my knife forward. I brought it around and down in a savage arc, and by luck or fate drove it into the centre of Steve's left breast — clean through his shrivelled forgery of a heart!

CHAPTER TWELVE

Steve's eyes and mouth popped wide with shock. His expression was comical, but I was in no mood to laugh. There was no recovery from a strike like that. Steve was finished. But he could take me with him if I wasn't careful. So instead of celebrating, I grabbed his left hand, holding it down tight by his side so he couldn't use his knife on me.

Steve's gaze slid to the handle of the knife sticking out of his chest. "Oh," he said tonelessly. Then blood trickled from the sides of his mouth. His chest heaved up and down, the handle rising and falling with it. I wanted to pull the knife out, to end matters — he could maybe go on like this for a minute or two, the knife stopping the gush of blood from his heart — but my left hand was useless and I didn't dare free my right.

Then — applause. My head lifted, and Steve's eyes rolled back in their sockets so that he could look behind

him. Mr Tiny was clapping, bright red tears of joy dripping down his cheeks. "What passion!" he exclaimed. "What valour! What a never-say-die spirit! My money was always on you, Darren. It could have gone either way, but if I was a betting man, I'd have bet big on you. I said as much beforehand, didn't I, Evanna?"

"Yes, father," Evanna answered quietly. She was studying me sadly. Her lips moved silently, but even though she uttered no sounds, I was able to make out what she said. "To the victor, the spoils."

"Come, Darren," Mr Tiny said. "Pull out the knife and tend to your wounds. They're not immediately life-threatening, but you should have a doctor see to them. Your friends in the stadium are almost done with their foes. They'll be coming soon. They can take you to a hospital."

I shook my head. I only meant that I couldn't pull the knife out, but Mr Tiny must have thought I didn't want to kill Steve. "Don't be foolish," he snapped. "Steve is the enemy. He deserves no mercy. Finish him, then take your place as the rightful ruler of the night."

"You are the Lord of the Shadows now," Evanna said. "There is no room in your life for mercy. Do as my father bids. The sooner you accept your destiny, the easier it will be for you."

"And do you ... want me to ... kill Vancha now too?" I panted angrily.

"Not yet," Mr Tiny laughed. "That will come in its own time." His laughter faded and his expression hardened.

"Much will come in time. The vampaneze will fall, and so shall the humans. This world will be yours, Darren — rather, *ours*. Together we'll rule. Your hand at the tiller, my voice in your ear. I'll guide and advise you. Not openly — I haven't the power to directly steer you — but on the sly. I'll make suggestions, you'll heed them, and together we'll build a world of chaos and twisted beauty."

"What makes you … think I'd have anything to do … with a monster like you?" I snarled.

"He has a point, father," Evanna murmured. "We both know what lies in store for Darren. He will become a ruler of savage, unrelenting power. But he hates you. That hatred will increase over the centuries, not diminish. What makes you think you can rule with him?"

"I know more about the boy than you do," Mr Tiny said smugly. "He will accept me. He was born to." Mr Tiny squatted and looked straight down into Steve's eyes. Then he looked up into mine, his face no more than five or six centimetres away. "I have always been there for you. For both of you," he whispered. "When you competed with your friends for a ticket to the Cirque Du Freak," he said to me, "I whispered in your ear and told you when to grab for it."

My jaw dropped. I *had* heard a voice that day, but I'd thought it was only an inner voice, the voice of instinct.

"And when you," he said to Steve, "noticed something strange about Darren after your meeting with Larten Crepsley, who do you think kept you awake at night, filling your thoughts with doubt and suspicion?"

Mr Tiny pulled back half a metre. His smile had returned, and it now threatened to spread from his face and fill the tunnel. "*I* influenced Crepsley and inspired him to blood Darren. *I* urged Gannen Harst to suggest Steve try the Coffin of Fire. Both of you have enjoyed enormous slices of good fortune in life. You put it down to the luck of the vampires, or the survival instinct of the vampaneze. But it was neither. You owe your nine cat's lives — and quite a few more — to *me*."

"I don't understand," I said, confused and alarmed. "Why would you go to all that trouble? Why ruin our lives?"

"*Ruin?*" he barked. "With my help you became a Prince and Steve became a Lord. With my backing the two of you have led the creatures of the night to war, and one of you — *you*, Darren! — now stands poised to become the most powerful tyrant in the history of the world. I have *made* your lives, not ruined them!"

"But why us?" I pressed. "We were ordinary kids. Why pick on Steve and me?"

"You were never ordinary," Mr Tiny disagreed. "From birth — no, from conception you were both unique." He stood and looked at Evanna. She was staring at him uncertainly — this was news to her too. "For a long time I wondered what it would be like to father children," Mr Tiny said softly. "When, spurred on by a stubborn vampire, I finally decided to give parenthood a try, I created two offspring in my own mould, beings of magic and great power.

"Evanna and Hibernius fascinated me at first, but in time I grew tired of their limitations. Because they can see into the

107

future, they — like me — are limited in what they can do in the present. All of us have to abide by laws not of our making. I can interfere in the affairs of mankind more than my children can, but not as much as I'd wish. In many ways my hands are tied. I can influence mortals, and I do, but they're contrary creatures and short-lived. It's difficult to manipulate large groups of humans over a long period of time — especially now that there are billions of them!

"What I longed for was a mortal I could channel my will through, a being not bound by the laws of the universe, nor shackled by the confines of humanity. My ally would have to start as a human, then become a vampire or vampaneze. With my help he would lead his clan to rule over all. Together we could govern the course of the world for hundreds of years to come, and through *his* children I could control it for thousands of years — maybe even the rest of time itself."

"You're mad," I growled. "I don't care if you did help me. I won't work with you or do what you want. I'm not going to link myself to your warped cause. I doubt that Steve would have either, if he'd won."

"But you *will* join me," Mr Tiny insisted, "just as Steve would have. You must. It's in your nature. Like sides with like." He paused, then said proudly and provocatively, "Son sides with sire."

"*What?*" Evanna exploded, leaping to an understanding sooner than I did.

"I required a less powerful heir," Mr Tiny said, his gaze fixed on me. "One who'd carry my genes and mirror my

desires, but who could act freely as a mortal. To weed out any weaknesses, I created a pair, then set them against each other. The weaker would perish and be forgotten. The stronger would go on to claim the world." He stuck his arms out, the gesture both mocking and strangely heartfelt. "Come and give your father a hug, Darren — *my son!*"

CHAPTER THIRTEEN

"You're mad!" I croaked. "I have a father, a real dad. It isn't you!"

"Dermot Shan was not your father," Mr Tiny replied. "You were a cuckoo's child. Steve too. I did my work quietly, unknown to your mothers. But trust me — you're both mine."

"This is outrageous!" Evanna screeched, her body expanding, becoming more that of a wolf than human, until she filled most of the tunnel. "It is forbidden! How dare you!"

"I acted within the confines of the universe's laws!" Mr Tiny snapped. "You'd know if I had not — all would be chaos. I stretched them a bit, but I didn't break them. I am allowed to breed, and my children — if they lack my magical powers — can act the same way as any normal mortal."

"But if Darren and Steve are your sons, then *you* have created the future where one of them becomes the Lord of

the Shadows!" Evanna roared. "*You* have cast mankind into the abyss, and twisted the strands of the future to suit your own foul needs!"

"Yes," Mr Tiny chuckled, then pointed a finger at Evanna. "Do not cross me on this, daughter. I would not harm my own flesh and blood, but I could make life very unpleasant if you got on the wrong side of me."

Evanna glared at her father hatefully, then gradually resumed her regular shape and size. "This is unjust," she muttered. "The universe will punish you, perhaps not immediately, but eventually you'll pay a price for your arrogance."

"I doubt it," Mr Tiny smirked. "Mankind was heading towards an all-time boring low. Peace, prosperity, global communication, brotherly love — where's the fun in *that*? Yes, there were still plenty of wars and conflicts to enjoy, but I could see the people of the world moving ever closer together. I did my best, nudged nations along the path to battle, sowed seeds of discontent everywhere I could, even helped get a few tyrants wrongfully elected to some of the most powerful positions on Earth — I was sure those fine specimens would push the world to the brink!

"But no! No matter how tense things got, no matter how much meddling my minions did, I could see peace and understanding gradually winning through. It was time for drastic action, to take the world back to the good old days, when everyone was at everybody else's throat. I've simply restored the natural order of beautiful chaos. The universe won't punish me for that. If anything, I expect—"

"Shut up!" I screamed, surprising both Mr Tiny and Evanna. "It's bull, all of it! You're not my father! You're a monster!"

"And so are you," Mr Tiny beamed. "Or soon will be. But don't worry, son — monsters have all the fun!"

I stared at him, sickened, senses reeling, unable to take it all in. If this was true, everything in my life had been false. I was never the person I thought I was, only a pawn of Mr Tiny's, a time bomb waiting to explode. I'd been blooded simply to extend my life, so I could live longer and do more of Mr Tiny's work. My war with Steve had served only to get rid of the weaker of us, so that the stronger could emerge as a more powerful beast. I'd done nothing for the sake of the vampires or my family and friends — everything had been for Mr Tiny. And now that I'd proved myself worthy, I'd become a dictator and lay low anyone who opposed him. My wishes would count for nothing. It was my destiny.

"Fa-fa-fa..." Steve stammered, spitting blood from his mouth. With his free hand he reached out to Mr Tiny. "Father," he managed to croak. "Help ... me."

"Why?" Mr Tiny sniffed.

"I ... never ... had ... a ... Dad." Each word was a heart-churning effort, but Steve forced them out. "I ... want ... to ... know ... you. I'll ... serve ... you ... and ... love ... you."

"What on earth would I want with *love*?" Mr Tiny laughed. "Love is one of the most basic human emotions. I'm so pleased I was never cursed with it. Servitude, gratitude, fear, hatred, anger — these I like. Love ... you can take your love

to the Lake of Souls when you die. Perhaps it will provide you with some comfort there."

"But ... I'm ... your ... son," Steve cried weakly.

"You were," Mr Tiny sneered. "Now you're just a loser, and soon you'll be dead meat. I'll toss your carcass to my Little People to eat — that's how little I feel for you. This is a winner's world. Second place equals second rate. You're nothing to me. Darren's my only son now."

The pain in Steve's eyes was awful to behold. As a child, he'd been crushed when he thought I'd betrayed him. Now he'd been openly mocked and disowned by his father. It destroyed him. His heart had been full of hatred before this, but now that it was down to its last few beats, there was room only for despair.

But in Steve's anguish I found hope. Consumed by smugness, Mr Tiny had revealed too much, too soon. At the back of my brain an idea sparked into life. In a whirl I began to put various pieces together — Mr Tiny's revelation and Evanna's reaction. Evanna said Mr Tiny had created the future in which Steve or I was the Lord of the Shadows. He'd bent the laws he and she lived by, to twist things round and build a chaotic world which he and I could rule over. Evanna and Mr Tall had told me there was no escaping the Lord of the Shadows, that he was part of the world's future. But they were wrong. He was part of *Mr Tiny's* future. Des Tiny might be the most powerful individual in the universe, but he was still only an individual. What one individual could build, another could destroy.

Mr Tiny's eyes were on Steve. He was laughing at him, enjoying Steve's dying misery. Evanna's head was bowed — she'd given in and accepted this. Not me. If I'd inherited Mr Tiny's evil, destructive streak, I'd also inherited his cunning. I'd stop at nothing to deny him his vision of a ruined future.

Slowly, everso slowly, I released Steve's left hand and moved my arm away. He had a free shot at my stomach now, in the perfect position to finish the job he'd started when he stabbed me earlier. But Steve didn't notice. He was wrapped up in his sorrow. I faked a cough and plucked at his left sleeve. If Mr Tiny had seen it, he could have stopped my plan there. But he thought he'd won, that it was all over. He couldn't even imagine the vaguest possibility of a threat.

Steve's gaze flickered down. He realized his hand was free. He saw his chance to kill me. His fingers stiffened on the handle of his knife ... then relaxed. For a terrible moment I thought he'd died, but then I saw that he was still alive. What made him pause was doubt. He'd spent most of his life hating me, but now he'd been told I was his brother. I could see his brain churning. I was a victim of Des Tiny, just as he was. He'd been wrong to hate me — I'd had no choice in what I'd done. In all the world, I was the person he should be closest to, and instead I was the person he'd hurt the most.

What Steve found in those last few moments was what I thought he'd lost for ever — his humanity. He saw the error of his ways, the evil he'd committed, the mistakes he'd made. There was possible salvation in that recognition. Now that he

could see himself for what he truly was, perhaps, even at this late stage, he could repent.

But I couldn't afford humanity. Steve's salvation would be my undoing — and the world's. I needed him mad as hell, fire in his gut, filled with fury and hate. Only in that state could he find the power to maybe help me break Des Tiny's hold over the future.

"Steve," I said, forcing a wicked smile. "You were right. I *did* plot with Mr Crepsley to take your place as his assistant. We made a mug of you, and I'm glad. You're a nobody. A nothing. This is what you deserve. If Mr Crepsley was alive, he'd be laughing at you now, just like the rest of us are."

Mr Tiny howled with delight. "That's my boy!" he hooted. He thought I was getting one last dig in before Steve died. But he was wrong.

Steve's eyes refilled with hatred. The human within him vanished in an instant and he was Steve Leopard, vampire killer, again. In one fast, crazed movement he brought his left hand up and drove his knife deep into my stomach. Less than a second later he did it again, then again.

"Stop!" Mr Tiny yelled, seeing the danger too late. He lurched at us, to pull me off, but Evanna slid in front of him and blocked his way.

"No, father!" she snapped. "You cannot interfere in this!"

"Get out of my way!" he bellowed, struggling with her. "The fool's going to let Leonard kill him! We have to stop it!"

"Too late," I giggled, as Steve's blade slid in and sliced through my guts for a fifth time. Mr Tiny stopped and

blinked dumbly, at a complete loss for what may well have been the first time in his long, ungodly life. "Destiny … rejected," I said with my final whole breath. Then I grabbed Steve tight as he lunged at me with his knife again, and rolled to my right, off the edge of the path, into the river.

We went into the water together, wrapped in each other's arms, and sank quickly. Steve tried stabbing me again, but it was too much for him. He went limp and fell away from me, his dead body dropping into the dark depths of the river, disappearing from sight within seconds.

I was barely conscious, hanging sluggishly, limbs being picked at and made to sway by the current of the river. Water rushed down my throat and flooded my lungs. Part of me wanted to strike for the surface, but I fought against it, not wanting to give Mr Tiny even the slightest opportunity to revive me.

I saw faces in the water, or in my thoughts — impossible to tell the difference. Sam Grest, Gavner Purl, Arra Sails, Mr Tall, Shancus, R.V., Mr Crepsley. The dead, come to welcome me.

I stretched my arms out to them, but our fingers didn't touch. I imagined Mr Crepsley waving, and a sad expression crossed his face. Then everything faded. I stopped struggling. The world, the water, the faces faded from sight, then from memory. A roaring which was silence. A darkness which was light. A chill which burnt. One final flutter of my eyelids, barely a movement, impossibly tiring. And then, in the lonely, watery darkness of the river, as all must do when the Grim Reaper calls — I died.

INTERLUDE

✫

Timelessness. Eternal gloom. Drifting in slow, never-ending circles. Surrounded but alone. Aware of other souls, trapped like me, but unable to contact them. No sense of sight, hearing, taste, smell, touch. Only the crushing boredom of the present and painful memories of the past.

✫

I know this place. It's the Lake of Souls, a zone where spirits go when they can't leave Earth's pull. Some people's souls don't move on when they die. They remain trapped in the waters of this putrid lake, condemned to swirl silently in the depths for all eternity.

I'm sad I ended up here, but not surprised. I tried to live a good life, and I sacrificed myself at the end in an effort to save others, so in those respects I was maybe deserving of Paradise. But I was also a killer. Whatever my reasons, I took lives and created unhappiness. I don't know if some higher power has passed judgement on me, or if I'm imprisoned by my own guilt. It doesn't really matter, I guess. I'm here and there's no getting out. This is my lot. For ever.

✫

No sense of time. No days, nights, hours, minutes — not even seconds. Have I been here a week, a year, a century? Can't tell. Does the War of the Scars still rage? Have the vampires or vampaneze fallen? Has another taken my place as the Lord of the Shadows? Did I die for no reason? I don't know. I probably never will. That's part of my sentence. Part of my curse.

★

If the souls of the dead could speak, they'd scream for release. Not just release from the Lake, but from their memories. Memories gnaw away at me relentlessly. I remember so much of my past, all the times where I failed or could have done better. With nothing else to do, I'm forced to review my life, over and over. Even my most minor errors become supreme lapses of judgement. They torment me worse than Steve ever did.

I try to hide from the pain of the memories by retreating further into my past. I remember the young Darren Shan, human, happy, normal, innocent. I spend years, decades — or is it just minutes? — reliving the simple, carefree times. I piece together my entire early life. I recall even the smallest details — the colours of toy cars, homework assignments, throwaway conversations. I go through everyday chat a hundred times, until every word is correct. The longer I think about it, the deeper into those years I sink, losing myself, human again, almost able to believe that the memories are reality, and my death and the Lake of Souls nothing but an unpleasant dream.

★

But eternity can't be dodged for ever. My later memories are always hovering, picking away at the boundaries of the limited reality which I've built. Every so often I flash ahead to a face or event. Then I lose control and find myself thrust into the darker, nightmarish world of my life as a half-vampire. I relive the mistakes, the wrong choices, the bloodshed.

So many friends lost, so many enemies killed. I feel responsible for all of them. I believed in peace when I first went to Vampire Mountain. Even though Kurda Smahlt betrayed his people, I felt sorry for him. I knew he did it in an effort to avoid war. I couldn't understand why it had come to this. If only the vampires and vampaneze had sat down and talked through their differences, war could have been avoided.

When I first became a Prince, I dreamt of being a peace-monger, taking up where Kurda left off, bringing the vampaneze back into the clan. I lost those dreams somewhere during the six years I spent living within Vampire Mountain. Surviving as a vampire, learning their ways, training with weapons, sending friends out to fight and die ... It all rubbed off on me, and when I finally returned to the world beyond the mountain, I'd changed. I was a warrior, fierce, unmoved by death, intent on killing rather than talking.

I wasn't evil. Sometimes it's necessary to fight. There are occasions when you have to cast aside your nobler ideals and get your hands dirty. But you should always strive for peace, and search to find the peaceful solution to even the most bloody of conflicts. I didn't do that. I embraced the war and went along with the general opinion — that if we killed the Vampaneze Lord, all our problems would be solved and life would be hunky-dory.

We were wrong. The death of one man never solved anything. Steve was just the start. Once you set off down the road of murder, it's hard to take a detour. We couldn't

have stopped. The death of one foe wouldn't have been enough. We'd have set about annihilating the vampaneze after Steve, then humanity. We'd have established ourselves as the rulers of the world, crushing all in our path, and I'd have gone along with it. No, more than that — I'd have led, not just followed.

That guilt, not just of what I've done but of what I would have done, eats away at me like a million ravenous rats. It doesn't matter that I'm the son of Desmond Tiny, that wickedness was in my genes. I had the power to break away from the dark designs of my father. I proved that at the end, by letting myself die. But why didn't I do it sooner, before so many people were killed?

I don't know if I could have stopped the war, but I could have said, "No, I don't want any part of this." I could have argued for peace, not fought for it. If I'd failed, at least I maybe wouldn't have wound up here, weighed down by the chains of so many grisly deaths.

✳

Time passes. Faces swim in and out of my thoughts. Memories form, are forgotten, form again. I blank out large parts of my life, recover them, blank them out again. I succumb to madness and forget who I was. But the madness doesn't last. I reluctantly return to my senses.

I think about my friends a lot, especially those who were alive when I died. Did any of them perish in the stadium? If they survived that, what came next? Since Steve and I both died, what happened with the War of the Scars? Could

Mr Tiny replace us with new leaders, men with the same powers as Steve and me? Hard to see how, unless he fathered another couple of children.

Was Harkat alive now, pushing for peace between the vampires and vampaneze, like he had when he was Kurda Smahlt? Had Alice Burgess led her vampirites against the vampets and crushed them? Did Debbie mourn for me? Not knowing was an agony. I'd have sold my soul to the Devil for a few minutes in the world of the living, where I could find answers to my questions. But not even the Devil disturbed the waters of the Lake of Souls. This was the exclusive resting place of the dead and the damned.

★

Drifting, ghostly, resigned. I fixate on my death, remembering Steve's face as he stabbed me, his hatred, his fear. I count the number of seconds it took me to die, the drops of blood I spilt on the riverbank where he killed me. I feel myself topple into the water of the river a dozen times ... a hundred ... a thousand.

That water was so much more alive than the water of the Lake of Souls. Currents. Fish swam in it. Air bubbles. Cold. The water here is dead, as lifeless as the souls it contains. No fish explore its depths, no insects skim its surface. I'm not sure how I'm aware of these facts, but I am. I sense the awful emptiness of the Lake. It exists solely to hold the spirits of the miserable dead.

I long for the river. I'd meet any asking price if I could go back and experience the rush of flowing water again, the chill

as I fell in, the pain as I bled to death. Anything's better than this limbo world. Even a minute of dying is preferable to an eternity of nothingness

✱

One small measure of comfort — as bad as this is for me, it must be much worse for Steve. My guilt is nothing compared to his. I was sucked into Mr Tiny's evil games, but Steve threw himself heart and soul into them. His crimes far outweigh mine, so his suffering must be that much more.

Unless he doesn't accept his guilt. Perhaps eternity means nothing to him. Maybe he's just sore that I beat him. It could be that he doesn't worry about what he did, or realize just how much of a monster he was. He might be content here, reflecting with fondness on all that he achieved.

But I doubt it. I suspect Mr Tiny's admission destroyed a large part of Steve's mad defences. Knowing that he was my brother, and that we were both puppets in our father's hands, must have shaken him up. I think, given the time to reflect — and that's all one can do here — he'll weep for what he did. He'll see himself for what he truly was, and hate himself for it.

I shouldn't take pleasure in that. There, but for the grace of the gods ... But I still despise Steve. I can understand why he acted that way, and I'm sorry for him. But I can't forgive him. I can't stretch that far. Perhaps that's another reason why I'm here.

✱

I'm retreating from the painful memories again. Withdrawing from the vampire world, pretending it never happened. I

imagine myself as a child, living the same days over and over, refusing to go beyond the afternoon when I won a ticket to the Cirque Du Freak. I build a perfect, sealed-off, comfortable reality. I'm Darren Shan, loving son and brother, not the best behaved boy in the world, but far from the worst. I do chores for Mum and Dad, struggle with homework, watch TV, hang out with my friends. One moment I'm six or seven years old, the next ten or eleven. Continually twisting back upon myself, living the past, ignoring all that I don't want to think about. Steve's my best friend. We read comics, watch horror movies, tell jokes to each other. Annie's a child, always a child — I never think of her as a woman with a son of her own. Vampires are monsters of myth, like werewolves, zombies, mummies, not to be taken seriously.

It's my aim to become the Darren of my memories, to lose myself completely in the past. I don't want to deal with the guilt any more. I've gone mad before and recovered. I want to go mad again, but this time let madness swallow me whole.

I struggle to vanish into the past. Remembering everything, painting the details more precisely every time I revisit a moment. I start to forget about the souls, the Lake, the vampires and vampaneze. I still get occasional flashes of reality, but I clamp down on them quickly. Thinking as a child, remembering as a child, becoming a child.

I'm almost there. The madness waits, arms spread wide, welcoming me. I'll be living a lie, but it will be a peaceful, soothing lie. I long for it. I work hard to make it real. And I'm getting there. I feel myself sliding closer towards it. I

reach for the lie with the tendrils of my mind. I feel around it, explore it, start to slip inside it, when all of a sudden — a new sensation...

Pain! Heaviness. Rising. The madness is left behind. The water of the Lake closes around me. Searing pain! Thrashing, coughing, gasping. *But with what?* I have no arms to thrash, no mouth to cough, no lungs to gasp. Is this part of the madness? Am I...

And suddenly my head — an actual, real *head*! — breaks the surface. I'm breathing air. Sunlight blinds me. I spit water out. My arms come clear of the Lake. I'm surrounded, but not by the souls of the dead — by nets! People pulling on them. Coming out of the Lake. Screaming with pain and confusion — but no sounds. Body forming, incredibly heavy after all this weightless time. I land on hard, warm earth. My feet drag out of the water. Amazed, I try to stand. I make it to my knees, then fall. I hit the ground hard. Pain again, fresh and frightening. I curl up into a ball, shivering like a baby. I shut my eyes against the light and dig my fingers into the earth to reassure myself that it's real. And then I sob feebly as the incredible, bewildering, impossible realization sinks in — *I'm alive!*

PART TWO

CHAPTER FOURTEEN

The sun hammered down fiercely upon me but I couldn't stop shivering. Someone threw a blanket around me, hairy and thick. It itched like mad, but the sensation was delicious. Any sensation would have been welcome after the numbness of the Lake of Souls.

The person who'd draped the blanket over me knelt by my side and tilted my head back. I blinked water from my eyes and focused. It took a few seconds, but finally I fixed on my rescuer. It was a Little Person. At first I thought it was Harkat. I opened my mouth to shout his name happily. Then I did a double take and realized this wasn't my old friend, just one of his grey, scarred, green-eyed kind.

The Little Person examined me silently, prodding and poking. Then he stood and stepped aside, leaving me. I wrapped the blanket tighter around myself, trying to stop the shivers. After a while I worked up the strength to look

around. I was lying by the rim of the Lake of Souls. The earth around me was hard and dry, like desert. Several Little People stood nearby. A couple were hanging up nets to dry — the nets they'd fished me out with. The others simply stared off into space or at the Lake.

There was a screeching sound high overhead. Looking up, I saw a huge winged beast circling the Lake. From my previous trip here, I knew it was a dragon. My insides clenched with fear. Then I noticed a second dragon. A third. A fourth. Jaw dropping, I realized the sky was full of them, dozens, maybe hundreds. If they caught sight of me...

I started to scrabble weakly for safety, then paused and glanced at the Little People. They knew the dragons were there, but they weren't bothered by the giant flying reptiles. They might have dragged me out of the Lake to feed me to the dragons, but I didn't think so. And even if they had, in my feeble state I could do nothing about it. I couldn't flee or fight, and there was nowhere to hide. So I just lay where I was and waited for events to run their course.

For several minutes the dragons circled and the Little People stood motionless. I was still filled with a great chill, but I wasn't shivering quite as much as when I first came out of the Lake. I was gathering what small amounts of energy I could call on, to try and walk over to the Little People and quiz them about what was going on, when somebody spoke behind me.

"Sorry I'm late."

I looked over my shoulder, expecting Mr Tiny, but it was his daughter, (my half-sister!) Evanna, striding towards me.

She looked no different from how I remembered her, though there was a sparkle in her green and brown eyes which had been absent when last we met.

"Whuh!" I croaked, the only sound I was able to make.

"Easy," Evanna said, reaching me and bending to squeeze my shoulder warmly. "Don't try to speak. It will take a few hours for the effects of the Lake to wear off. I'll build a fire and cook some broth for you. That's why I wasn't here when you were fished out — I was looking for firewood." She pointed to a mound of logs and branches.

I wanted to besiege her with questions, but there was no point taxing my throat when it wasn't ready to work. So I said nothing as she picked me up and carried me to the pile of wood like a baby, then set me down and turned her attention to the kindling.

When the fire was burning nicely, Evanna took a flat circular object out from beneath the ropes she was wearing. I recognized it immediately — a collapsible pot, the same sort that Mr Crepsley had once used. She pressed it in the middle, causing it to pop outwards and assume its natural shape, then filled it with water (not from the Lake, but from a bucket) and some grass and herbs, and hung it from a stick over the flames.

The broth was weak and tasteless, but its warmth was like the fire of the gods to me. I drank deeply, one bowl, another, a third. Evanna smiled as I slurped, then sipped slowly from a bowl of her own. The dragons screeched at regular intervals overhead, the sun burnt brightly, and the scent of the smoke

was magical. I felt strangely relaxed, as if this was a lazy summer Sunday afternoon.

I was halfway through my fourth bowl before my stomach growled at me to say, "Enough!" Sighing happily, I laid the bowl down and sat, smiling lightly, thinking only of the good feelings inside. But I couldn't sit silently for ever, so eventually I raised my gaze, looked at Evanna and tested my vocal chords. "Urch," I creaked — I'd meant to say "Thanks."

"It's been a long time since you spoke," Evanna said. "Start simply. Try the alphabet. I will hunt for more wood, to sustain the fire. We won't be staying here much longer, but we may as well have warmth while we are. Practise while I am gone, and we can maybe talk when I return."

I did as the witch advised. At first I struggled to produce sounds anything like they should be, but I stuck with it and gradually my As started to sound like As, my Bs like Bs, and so on. When I'd run through the alphabet several times without making a mistake, I moved on to words, simple stuff to begin with — cat, dog, Mum, Dad, sky, me. I tried names after that, longer words, and finally sentences. It hurt to speak, and I slurred some words, but when Evanna eventually came back, clutching an armful of pitiful twigs, I was able to greet her in a gravelly but semi-normal voice. "Thanks for the broth."

"You're welcome." She threw some of the twigs on to the fire, then sat beside me. "How do you feel?"

"Rough as rust."

"Do you remember your name?"

I squinted at her oddly. "Why shouldn't I?"

"The Lake twists the minds of people," she said. "It can destroy memories. Many of the souls forget who they are. They go mad and lose track of their pasts. You were in there a long time. I feared the worst."

"I came close," I admitted, hunching up closer to the fire, recalling my attempts to go mad and escape the weight of my memories. "It was horrible. Easier to be crazy in there than sane."

"So what is it?" Evanna asked. When I blinked dumbly, she laughed. "Your name?"

"Oh." I smiled. "Darren. Darren Shan. I'm a half-vampire. I remember it all, the War of the Scars, Mr Crepsley, Steve." My features darkened. "I remember my death, and what Mr Tiny said just before it."

"Quite the one for surprises, isn't he — our father?"

She looked at me sideways to see what I'd say about that, but I couldn't think of anything — how do you respond to the news that Des Tiny is your dad, and a centuries-old witch is your half-sister? To avoid the subject, I studied the land around me. "This place looks different," I said. "It was green when I came with Harkat, lots of grass and fresh earth."

"This is further into the future," Evanna explained. "Before, you travelled a mere two hundred or so years ahead of the present. This time you have come hundreds of thousands of years, maybe more. I'm not entirely certain. This is the first time our father has ever allowed me to come here."

"Hundreds of..." My head spun.

"This is the age of dragons," Evanna said. "The age after mankind."

My breath caught in my throat, and I had to clear it twice before I could respond. "You mean humanity has died out?"

"Died out or moved on to other worlds or spheres." Evanna shrugged. "I cannot say for sure. I know only that the world belongs to dragons now. They control it as humans once did, and dinosaurs before them."

"And the War of the Scars?" I asked nervously. "Who won that?"

Evanna was silent a moment. Then she said, "We have much to speak about. Let's not rush." She pointed at the dragons high above us. "Call one of them down."

"What?" I frowned.

"Call them, the way you used to call Madam Octa. You can control dragons like you controlled your pet spider."

"How?" I asked, bewildered.

"I will show you. But first — call." She smiled. "They will not harm us. You have my word."

I wasn't too sure about that, but how cool would it be to control a dragon! Looking up, I studied the creatures in the sky, then fixed on one slightly smaller than the others. (I didn't want to bring a large one down, in case Evanna was wrong and it attacked.) I tracked it with my eyes for a few seconds, then stretched out a hand towards it and whispered, "Come to me. Come down. Come, my beauty."

The dragon executed a backwards somersault, then dropped swiftly. I thought it was going to blast us into a thousand pieces. I panicked and tried to run. Evanna hauled me back into place. "Calmly," she said. "You cannot control it if you break contact, and now that it knows we are here, it would be dangerous to let it have its own way."

I didn't want to play this game, but it was too late to back out now. With my heart beating fiercely, I fixed on the swooping dragon and spoke to it again. "Easy. Pull up. I don't want to hurt you — and I don't want you to hurt us! Just hover above us a bit and…"

The dragon pulled out of its fall and came to a halt several metres overhead. It flapped its leathery wings powerfully. I could hear nothing over the sound, and the force of the air knocked me backwards. As I struggled to right myself, the dragon came to land close beside me. It tucked its wings in, thrust its head down as though it meant to gobble me up, then stopped and just stared.

The beast was much like those I'd seen before. Its wings were a light green colour, it was about six metres long, scaled like a snake, with a bulging chest and thin tail. The scales on its stomach were a dull red and gold colour, while those on top were green with red flecks. It had two long forelegs near the front of its body, and two small hindlegs about a quarter of the way from the rear. Lots of sharp claws. A head like an alligator, long and flat, with bulging yellow eyes and small pointed ears. Its face was dark purple. It also had a long forked tongue and, if it was like the other dragons, it could blow fire.

"It's incredible," Evanna said. "This is the first time I have seen one up so close. Our father excelled himself with this creation."

"Mr Tiny made the dragons?"

Evanna nodded. "He helped human scientists create them. Actually, one of your friends was a key member of the team — Alan Morris. With our father's aid he made a breakthrough which allowed them to be cloned from a combination of dinosaur cells."

"*Alan?*" I snorted. "You're telling me Alan Morris made dragons? That's total and utter..." I stopped short. Tommy had told me Alan was a scientist, and that he'd specialized in cloning. It was hard to believe the foolish boy I'd known had grown up to become a creator of dinosaurs — but then again, it was hard to believe Steve had become the Vampaneze Lord, or myself a Vampire Prince. I suppose all influential men and women must start out as normal, unremarkable children.

"For many centuries, the rulers of this world will keep the dragons in check," Evanna said. "They'll control them. Later, when they lose their hold on power – as all rulers must – the dragons will fly free and multiply, becoming a real menace. In the end they'll outlive or outlast all the humans, vampires and vampaneze, and rule the world in their turn. I'm not sure what comes after them. I've never looked that far ahead."

"Why doesn't it kill us?" I asked, eyeing the dragon uneasily. "Is it tame?"

"Hardly!" Evanna laughed. "Normally the dragons would tear us apart. Our father masks this area from them — they can't see the Lake of Souls or anyone around it."

"This one sees us," I noted.

"Yes, but you're controlling it, so we are safe."

"The last time I was here, I was almost roasted alive by dragons," I said. "How can I control them now when I couldn't before?"

"But you could," Evanna replied. "You had the power — you just didn't know it. The dragons would have obeyed you then, as they do now."

"Why?" I frowned. "What's so special about me?"

"You're Desmond Tiny's son," Evanna reminded me. "Even though he did not pass on his magical powers to you, traces of his influence remain. That is why you were skilled at controlling animals such as spiders and wolves. But there is more to it than that."

Evanna reached out, her hand extending far beyond its natural length, and touched the dragon's head. Its skull glowed beneath the witch's touch. Its purple skin faded, then became translucent, so I could see inside to its brain. The oval, stone-like shape was instantly familiar, though it took me a few seconds to recall what it reminded me of. Then it clicked.

"The Stone of Blood!" I exclaimed. While this was much smaller than the one in the Hall of Princes, it was unmistakably the same type. The Stone of Blood had been a gift to the vampires from Mr Tiny. For seven hundred years

the members of the clan had fed their blood to it, and used it to keep track of and communicate with each other. It was an invaluable tool, but dangerous — if it had fallen into the hands of the vampaneze, they could have tracked down and killed almost every living vampire.

"Our father took the brain of a dragon into the past and gave it to the vampires," Evanna said. "He often does that — travels into the past and makes small changes which influence the present and future. Through the Stone of Blood he bound the vampires more tightly to his will. If the vampires win the War of the Scars, they will use the Stone to control the dragons, and through them the skies. I don't think the vampaneze will use it if they win.. They never trusted this gift of Desmond Tiny's — it was one of the reasons they broke away from the rest of the vampire clan. I'm not sure what their relationship with the dragons would be like. Perhaps our father will provide them with some other way of controlling the beasts — or maybe it will please him to let them be enemies."

"The Stone of Blood was supposed to be the clan's last hope," I muttered, unable to take my eyes off the dragon's glowing brain. "There was a legend — if we lost the war with the vampaneze, the Stone of Blood might some night help us rise again."

Evanna nodded and removed her hand from the dragon's head. It stopped glowing and resumed its normal appearance. The dragon didn't seem to have noticed any change. It continued staring at me, awaiting my command.

"Above all else, our father craves chaos," Evanna said. "Stability bores him. He has no interest in seeing any race rule for ever. For a time it pleased him to let humans rule this planet, since they were violent, always at war with one another. But when he saw them heading the way of peace during the latter half of the twentieth century – or thought he did; to be honest, I don't agree with his assessment – he set about overthrowing them. He will do the same with their successors.

"If the vampaneze win the War of the Scars and wipe out the vampires, he'll use the Stone in the future. He will lead humans to it and teach them to extract the blood cells and build a new army of cloned vampires. But they won't be vampires as you know them. Desmond will control the cloning process and meddle with the cells, twisting and re-shaping them. The new creatures will be more savage than the original vampires, with less developed brains, slaves to the whim of our father." Evanna smiled twistedly. "So yes, our father told the truth when he said the Stone of Blood could help the vampires rise again — but he kept a few of the less savoury facts to himself."

"Then neither side can truly win," I said. "He's just setting the victors up for a later fall."

"That has always been Desmond's way," Evanna said. "What he helps create, he later destroys. Many empires – Egyptian, Persian, British – have already learnt that to their cost."

"Egyptian?" I blinked.

"Our father is a great fan of empires," Evanna said. "Cavemen hitting each other with sticks and bones were of

very limited interest to him. He prefers to see people killing each other with more effective weapons, and in greater numbers. But for mankind to advance barbarically, it also had to advance in other ways. It had to grow socially, culturally, spiritually, technologically, medically. Only a nation which was great in all aspects could wage war greatly.

"Our father has had his hand in most of the notable architectural, technical or medical breakthroughs of mankind. He could never openly lead, but he influenced slyly. The only area where he had no real power was that of literature. Desmond is not a fictional dreamer. Reality is everything to him. He has no interest in the wonderful stories of mankind. Writers have always been alien to him — he does not read works of fiction, or take any notice of them."

"Never mind that," I grunted, not giving a hoot about Mr Tiny's choice of reading material. "Tell me more about his meddling with mankind, and time-travelling. You say Mr Tiny goes into the past to change the present and future. But what about the time paradox?" I'd seen lots of science fiction movies and TV shows. I knew all about the problems associated with the theory of time travel.

"There is no paradox," Evanna said. "The universe keeps natural order. The key events of the past cannot be changed — only the people involved."

"Huh?" I said.

"Once something important happens in the present — the universe, to give the higher force a name, decides what is important or not — it can never be changed," Evanna

explained. "But you can alter the people involved. For instance, now that it has happened, you cannot travel to the past and prevent World War Two — but you *could* go back and kill Adolf Hitler. The universe would immediately create another person to fill his shoes. That person would be born like any normal person, grow up, then do what Hitler did, with precisely the same results. The name would change, but nothing else."

"But Hitler was a monster," I said. "He murdered millions of people. Do you mean, if Mr Tiny went back and killed him, some innocent guy would take his place? All those people would still die?"

"Yes," Evanna said.

"But then that person wouldn't have chosen their fate," I frowned. "They wouldn't be responsible for their actions."

Evanna sniffed. "The universe would have to create a child with the potential for wickedness – a good man cannot be forced to do evil – but once it did, yes, that person would become a victim of destiny. It does not happen often. Our father only occasionally replaces important figures of the past. Most people have free will. But there *are* a few who don't."

"Am I one of them?" I asked quietly, fearing the answer.

"Most definitely not," Evanna smiled. "Your time is the present time, and you are an original creation. Though you were manipulated by our father since birth, the path you trod had not been laid down by anyone before you."

Evanna thought for a few seconds, then tried to explain the situation in a way which I could more easily understand.

"Although our father cannot change the events of the past, he can make minor alterations," she said. "If something happens in the present which is not to his liking, he can return to the past and create a train of events designed to lead to a solution to whatever is troubling him. That's how vampires came to be so numerous and powerful."

"Mr Tiny created vampires?" I shouted — there was a myth that he'd made us, but I'd never believed it.

"No," Evanna said. "Vampires came into being by themselves. But there were never many of them. They were weak and disorganized. Then, in the middle of the twentieth century, our father decided mankind was taking a path towards peace and unity. Disliking it, he travelled to the past and spent a couple of decades trying different approaches to undermine humanity. In the end he settled on vampires. He gave them extra strength and speed, the power to flit and share their thoughts — all the supernatural abilities which you know about. He also provided them with leaders who would knock them into shape and turn them into an army.

"As powerful as the clan became, our father ensured they couldn't be a threat to humans. Originally vampires were able to come out by day — Desmond Tiny made them prisoners of the night, and robbed them of the gift of childbirth. Carefully shackled and maintained this way, the vampires had to live separately to the world of man and remain in the shadows. Since they didn't change anything important in the human history, the universe let them exist,

and they eventually become part of the present — which is when our father was free to use them however he wished."

"And the present was my time?" I asked.

"Yes," Evanna said. "Time passes at the same rate, whether our father is in the past, present or future. So, since he spent almost twenty years stuck in the past, trying to find a way to topple humanity, it was late in the twentieth century when he returned to the present."

"And because vampires were now part of that present," I said, my brain hurting as I tried to keep up with all this mind-boggling information, "they were free to influence the future?"

"Correct," Evanna said. "But our father then saw that the clan wouldn't launch an attack on humanity if left to their own devices — they were content to stay out of the affairs of men. So he went back again — just for a few months this time — and engineered the vampaneze breakaway. By then planting the legend of the Lord of the Vampaneze, he edged them towards conflict with the vampires."

"And that led to the War of the Scars, and eventually the downfall of humanity," I growled, sick at the thought of the little man's terrible slyness.

"Well," Evanna smiled, "that was the plan."

"Do you mean—" I began to say excitedly, sensing hope in her smile.

"Hush," Evanna stopped me. "I will reveal all shortly. But now it is time for us to move on." She pointed to where the sun was setting on the horizon. "The nights are

colder in this time than in yours. We will be safer underground. Besides," she said, rising, "we have an appointment to keep."

"With who?" I asked.

She looked at me steadily. "Our father."

CHAPTER FIFTEEN

Mr Tiny was the last person in the world — in all of time! — that I wanted to see. I argued with Evanna hotly, wanting to know why I should present myself to him, or what it could achieve. I hated and feared the meddler more than ever now that I knew so much about him.

"I want to be on the opposite side of the world to wherever he is!" I cried. "Or in another universe, if possible!"

"I understand," Evanna said, "but we must go to him regardless."

"Is he forcing you to do this?" I asked. "Is he the one who ordered me fished out of the Lake? Is he making you take me to him, so that he can mess my life up all over again?"

"You will find out when you meet him," Evanna said coolly, and since I didn't really have any option but to follow her lead — she could have had me tossed back into the Lake if I disobeyed — eventually, and with much angry

muttering, I reluctantly followed after her as she set off into the arid wilderness.

As we left the warmth of the fire, the dragon flapped its wings and took to the skies. I watched it join the throng of dragons far above me, then lost track of it. When I looked back at Evanna, I saw that she was still staring up at the sky. "I wish we could have gone for a flight," she said, sounding curiously sad.

"On the dragon?" I asked.

"Yes. It has always been a wish of mine to fly on a dragon."

"I could call it back," I suggested.

She shook her head quickly. "This isn't the time for it," she said. "And there are too many of them. The others would see us on its back and attack. I don't think you would be able to control so many, not without more practice. And while I can mask us from them downhere, I couldn't up there."

As we continued to walk, I looked around and backwards, and my gaze settled on the Little People standing motionless by the Lake. "Why are that lot here?" I asked.

"This is the age in which our father fishes for the souls of the dead to create his Little People," Evanna said, without looking back or slowing. "He could take them from any time, but it's easier this way, when there is nobody to interfere. He leaves a small band of his helpers here, to fish when he gives the order." She glanced at me. "He could have rescued you much earlier. In the present, only two years have passed. He had the power to remove you from the Lake then, but he wanted to

punish you. Your sacrifice threw his plans into disarray. He hates you for that, even though you are his son. That's why he sent me forward to this point in time to help you. In this future, your soul has suffered for countless generations. He wanted you to feel the pain of near-eternal imprisonment, and perhaps even go mad from it, so that you couldn't be saved."

"Nice," I grunted sarcastically. Then my eyes narrowed. "If that's the way he feels, why rescue me at all?"

"That will soon become clear," Evanna said.

We walked a long way from the Lake. The air was turning cold around us as the sun dipped. Evanna was looking for a specific spot, pausing every few seconds to examine the ground, then moving on. Finally she found what she was searching for. She came to a halt, knelt and breathed softly on the dusty earth. There was a rumbling sound, then the ground split at our feet and the mouth of a tunnel opened up. I could only see a few metres down it, but I sensed danger.

"Don't tell me we have to go down there," I muttered.

"This is the way to our father's stronghold," she said.

"It's dark," I stalled.

"I will provide light," she promised, and I saw that both her hands were glowing softly, casting a dim white light a few metres ahead of her. She looked at me seriously. "Stay by my side down there. Don't stray."

"Will Mr Tiny get me if I do?" I asked.

"Believe it or not, there are worse monsters than our father," she said. "We will be passing some of them. If they get their hands on you, your millennia of torment in the

Lake of Souls will seem like a pleasant hour spent on a beach."

I doubted that, but the threat was strong enough to ensure I kept within a hair's breadth of the witch as she started down the tunnel. It sloped at a fairly constant thirty-degree angle. The floor and walls were smooth and made of what looked like solid rock. But there were shapes moving within the rock, twisted, inhuman, elongated shapes, all shadows, claws, teeth and tendrils. The walls bulged outwards as we passed — the *things* trapped within were reaching for us. But none could break through.

"What are they?" I croaked, sweating from fear as much as the dry heat of the tunnel.

"Creatures of universal chaos," Evanna answered. "I told you about them before — they're the monsters I spoke of. They are kin to our father, though he is not as powerful as them. They are imprisoned by a series of temporal and spatial laws — the laws of the universe which our father and I live by. If we ever break the laws, these creatures will be freed. They will turn the universe into a hell of their own making. All will fall beneath them. They'll invade every time zone and torture every mortal being ever born — for ever."

"That's why you were angry when you found out I was Mr Tiny's son," I said. "You thought he'd broken the laws."

"Yes. I was wrong, but it was a close-run thing. I doubt if even he was sure of his plan's success. When he gave birth to Hibernius and me, we knew of the laws, and we obeyed them.

If he was wrong about you — if he'd given you more power than he meant to — you could have unknowingly broken the laws and brought about the ruin of everything we know and love." She looked back at me and grinned. "I bet you never guessed you were that important to the world!"

"No," I said sickly. "And I never wanted to be."

"Don't worry," she said, her smile softening. "You took yourself out of the firing line when you let Steve kill you. You did what Hibernius and I never thought possible — you changed what seemed an inevitable future."

"You mean I prevented the coming of the Lord of the Shadows?" I asked eagerly. "That's why I let him kill me. It was the only way I could see to stop it. I didn't want to be a monster. I couldn't bear the thought of destroying the world. Mr Tiny said one of us had to be the Lord of the Shadows. But I thought, if both of us were dead..."

"You thought right," Evanna said. "Our father had edged the world to a point where there were only two futures. When you killed Steve *and* sacrificed yourself, it opened up dozens of possible futures again. I could not have done it — I would have broken the laws if I'd interfered — but as a human, you were able to."

"So what's happened since I died?" I asked. "You said two years have passed. Did the vampires defeat the vampaneze and win the War of the Scars?"

"No," Evanna said, pursing her lips. "The war still rages. But an end is within sight — an end very much not to our father's liking. Persuasive leaders are pushing for

peace, Vancha and Harkat Mulds on the side of the vampires, Gannen Harst for the vampaneze. They are debating a treaty, discussing the guidelines by which both sides can live as one. Others fight against them — there are many in both clans who do not wish for peace — but the voices of reason are winning out."

"Then it worked!" I gasped. "If the vampires and vampaneze make peace, the world will be saved!"

"Perhaps," Evanna hummed. "It's not as clear-cut as that. Under Steve, the vampaneze made contact with human political and military leaders. They promised them long lives and power in exchange for their help. They wanted to create nuclear and chemical warfare, with the aim of bringing the world and its survivors under their direct control. That could still happen."

"Then we've got to stop it!" I shouted. "We can't let—"

"Easy," Evanna hushed me. "We are trying to prevent it. That's why I am here. I cannot meddle too deeply in the affairs of mankind, but I can do more now than before, and your actions have convinced me that I *should* interfere. Hibernius and I always stayed neutral. We did not get involved in the affairs of mortals. Hibernius wished to, but I argued against it, afraid we might break the laws and free the monsters." She sighed. "I was wrong. It's necessary to take risks every now and then. Our father took a risk in his attempt to wreak havoc — and I must now take one in an attempt to secure peace."

"What are you talking about?" I frowned.

"Mankind has been evolving," she said. "It has a destiny of its own, a growth towards something wonderful, which our father is intent on ruining. He used the vampires and vampaneze to throw mankind off course, to reduce the cities of the world to rubble, to drag humans back into the dark ages, so that he could control them again. But his plan failed. The clans of the night now seek to reunite and live separately from mankind, hidden, doing no harm, as they did in the past.

"Because the vampires and vampaneze have become part of the present, our father cannot unmake them. He could return to the past and create another race to combat them, but that would be difficult and time-consuming. Time, for once, is against him. If he cannot divide the clans within the next year or so, it is unlikely that he will be able to bring about the downfall of mankind which he craved. He might — and no doubt will — plot afresh in the future, and seek some other way to break them, but for the time being the world will be safe."

Evanna paused. Her hands were directed towards her face, illuminating her features. I'd never seen her look so thoughtful. "Do you remember the story of how I was created?" she asked.

"Of course," I said. "A vampire — Corza Jarn — wanted vampires to be able to have children. He pursued Mr Tiny until he agreed to grant him his wish, and by mixing Corza Jarn's blood with a pregnant she-wolf, and using his magic on her, he fathered you and Mr Tall."

"That was not his only reason for creating us," Evanna said, "but it was an important one. I can bear a vampire or a vampaneze's children, and they in turn could have children of their own. But any children of mine will be different from their fathers. They will have some of my powers — not all — and they'll be able to live by day. Sunlight won't kill them."

She looked at me intently. "A new breed of creature, an advanced race of vampire or vampaneze. If I gave birth to such children now, it would drive the clans apart. The war-mongers of both sides would use the children to stir up new visions and violence. For instance, if I had a child by a vampire father, those vampires opposed to peace would hail the child as a saviour, and say he was sent to help them wipe out the vampaneze. Even if the wiser vampires prevailed, and talked down the troublemakers, the vampaneze would be afraid of the child and suspicious of the vampire clan's long-term plans. How could they discuss peace terms, knowing they were now inferior to vampires, for ever at risk?

"The War of the Scars promises to end because both sides see that it might go on for ever. When the Lord of the Vampaneze and the vampire hunters were active, everybody knew the war would have a destined end. Now that Steve and you are dead, it might never finish, and neither vampires nor vampaneze want that. So they're willing to talk about peace.

"But my children could change everything. With the renewed promise of victory — either for the vampires or vampaneze, depending on which I chose to be the fathers of my young — the war would continue. As my children

grew — and they'd grow quickly, since they'd be creatures of a certain amount of magic — they'd be raised on hatred and fear. In time they'd become warriors and lead their clan to victory over the other — and our father's plan would fall back into place, a little later than anticipated, but otherwise intact."

"Then you mustn't have them!" I exclaimed. "Mr Tiny can't make you, can he?"

"Not directly," she said. "He has threatened and bribed me ever since the night you and Steve died. But he does not have the power to force me to give birth."

"Then it's OK." I smiled weakly. "You won't have any children, and that will be that."

"Oh, but I will," Evanna said, and lowered her hands so that they shone on her stomach. "In fact, I'm pregnant already."

"*What?*" I exploded. "But you just said—"

"I know."

"But if you—"

"I know."

"But—"

"Darren!" she snapped. "I. Know."

"Then why do it?" I cried.

Evanna stopped to explain. As soon as she paused, the shapes in the walls began to press closer towards us, hissing and snarling, claws and tendrils extending, stretching the fabric of the rock. Evanna spotted this and strode forward again, speaking as she walked.

"I asked Desmond to free your spirit. Guilt drove you to the Lake of Souls, and would have kept you there eternally — there is no natural escape from that Lake of the damned. But rescue is possible. Souls can be fished out. Knowing that you were my half-brother, I felt honour-bound to free you."

"What about Steve?" I asked. "He was your half-brother too."

"Steve deserves his imprisonment." Her eyes were hard. "I feel pity for him, since he was to some extent a victim of our father's meddling. But Steve's evil was primarily of his own making. He chose his path and now must suffer the consequences. But you tried to do good. It wasn't fair that you should rot in the Lake of Souls, so I pleaded with our father to help." She chuckled. "Needless to say, he refused.

"He came to me a few months ago," she continued. "He realized his plans were unravelling and he saw me as his only solution. He'd spent most of the time since your death trying to convince me to have children, with no more success than I'd had trying to get him to free you. But this time he took a fresh approach. He said we could help each other. If I had a child, he'd free your soul."

"You agreed to that?" I roared. "You sold out the world just to help me?"

"Of course not," she grunted.

"But you said you were pregnant."

"I am." She looked back at me and smiled shyly. "My first thought was to reject our father's offer. But then I saw a way to use it to our advantage. There is still no guarantee

of a peaceful settlement between the vampires and vampaneze. It looks promising but is by no means certain. If talks break down, the war could continue, and that would play into our father's hands. He would have time to go back to the past and create a new leader, one who could pick up where Steve left off.

"I was thinking of this when Desmond put his suggestion to me. I recalled the way you tricked him, and wondered what you would do in my situation. Then, in a flash, I saw it.

"I accepted his proposal but told him I wasn't sure whether I wanted a vampire's child or a vampaneze's. He said it didn't matter. I asked if I could choose. He said yes. So I spent some time with Gannen Harst, then with Vancha March. When I returned to our father, I told him I had chosen and was pregnant. He was so delighted, he didn't even complain when I refused to reveal who the father was — he just quickly arranged to send me here to free you, so that we could move forward without any further distractions."

She stopped talking and rubbed her stomach with her hands. She was still smiling that strange shy smile.

"So whose is it?" I asked. I didn't see what difference it made but I was curious to know the answer.

"Both," she said. "I am having twins — one by Vancha, one by Gannen."

"A vampire child *and* a vampaneze child!" I cried, excited.

"More than that," Evanna said. "I have allowed the three blood lines to mix. Each child is one third vampire, one third vampaneze, and one third me. That's how I've tricked him.

He thought any baby of mine would divide the clans, but instead they will pull them closer together. My children, when they are ready, will breed with other vampires and vampaneze, to give birth to a new, multi-race clan. All divisions will be erased and finally forgotten.

"We're going to create peace, Darren, in spite of our father. That's what you taught me — we don't have to accept destiny, or Des Tiny. We can create our own future, all of us. We have the power to rule our lives — we just have to make the choice to use it. You chose when you sacrificed your life. Now I've chosen too — by giving life. Only time will tell what our choices lead to, but I'm sure that whatever future we help usher in, it has to be better than the one our father planned."

"Amen to that!" I muttered, then followed her silently down the tunnel, thinking of the future and all the surprises and twists it might hold. My head was buzzing with thoughts and ideas. I was having to take on board so much, so quickly, that I felt overwhelmed by it all, not sure what to make of everything. But there was one thing I was absolutely sure of — when Mr Tiny found out about Evanna's babies, he'd all but explode with anger!

Thinking of that, and the nasty little meddler's face when he heard the news, I burst out laughing. Evanna laughed too, and the laughter stayed with us for ages, following us down the tunnel like a flock of chuckling birds, acting almost like a protective spell against the banks of walled-in, ever-moving, ever-reaching monsters.

CHAPTER SIXTEEN

About an hour later the tunnel ended and we entered the home of Desmond Tiny. I'd never really thought of him having a home. I just assumed he wandered the world, always on the move, in search of bloodshed and chaos. But, now that I considered it, I realized every monster needs a den to call its own, and Mr Tiny's had to be the strangest of them all.

It was a huge — and I mean HUGE — cave, maybe a couple of miles or so wide, and stretching as far ahead as I could make out. Much of the cave was natural, stalagmites and stalactites, waterfalls, beautifully weird rock colours and formations. But much more of it was incredibly *un*natural.

There were grand old cars from what I guessed must be the 1920s or 1930s floating in the air overhead. At first I thought they were attached to the ceiling by wires, but they were in constant motion, circling, crossing paths,

even looping around like planes, and not a wire in sight.

There were mannequins all over the place, dressed in costumes from every century and continent, from a primitive loincloth to the most outrageous modern fashion accessories. Their blank eyes unsettled me — I got the feeling that they were watching me, ready to spring to life at Mr Tiny's command and leap upon me.

There were works of art and sculpture, some so famous that even an art cretin like me recognized them — the *Mona Lisa, The Thinker, The Last Supper*. Mixed in with them, displayed like art exhibits, were dozens of brains preserved in glass cases. I read a few of the labels — Beethoven, Mozart, Wagner, Mahler. (That one gave me a jump — I'd gone to a school named after Mahler!)

"Our father loves music," Evanna whispered. "Where humans collect sheet music or gramophone records—" She obviously hadn't heard about CDs yet! " —he collects brains of composers. By touching them, he can listen to all the tunes they ever composed, along with many they never completed or shared with the world."

"But where does he get them from?" I asked.

"He travels to the past when they have just died and robs their graves," she said, as though it was the most casual thing in the world. I thought about questioning the right and wrong of something like that, but there were weightier issues to deal with, so I let it slide.

"He likes art too, I take it," I said, nodding at a flowery Van Gogh.

"Immensely," Evanna said. "These are all originals of course — he doesn't bother with copies."

"Nonsense!" I snorted. "These can't be real. I've seen some of the real paintings. Mum and Dad—" I still thought of my human Dad as my real father, and always would. " —took me to see the *Mona Lisa* in the Loo once."

"The Louvre," Evanna corrected me. "That is a copy. Some of our father's Little People are created from the souls of artists. They make perfect copies of pieces he especially admires. Then he slips back to the past and swaps the copy for the original. In most cases even the actual artist cannot tell the difference."

"You're telling me the *Mona Lisa* in Paris is a fake?" I asked sceptically.

"Yes." Evanna laughed at my expression. "Our father is a selfish man. He always keeps the best for himself. What he wants, he takes — and he normally wants the best of everything. Except books." Her voice became pointed, as it had earlier when she'd been talking about his attitude towards books. "Desmond never reads works of fiction. He doesn't collect books or pay any attention to authors. Homer, Chaucer, Shakespeare, Dickens, Tolstoy, Twain — all have passed him by unmarked. He doesn't care what they have to say. He has nothing to do with the world of literature. It's as if it exists in a separate universe from his."

Once again I didn't see her point in telling me this, so I let my interest wander. I'd never been a big art fan, but even I was impressed by this display. It was the ultimate collection,

capturing a slice of pretty much all the artistic wonder and imagination mankind had ever conjured into being.

There was far too much for any one person to take in. Weapons, jewellery, toys, tools, albums of stamps, bottles of vintage wine, Fabergé eggs, grandfather clocks, suites of furniture, thrones of kings and queens. A lot of it was precious, but there were plenty of worthless items too, stuff which had simply caught Mr Tiny's fancy, such as bottle tops, oddly shaped balloons, digital watches, a collection of empty ice-cream tubs, thousands of whistles, hundreds of thousands of coins (old ones mixed in with brand new ones), and so on. The treasure cave in *Aladdin* seemed like a bargain bin in comparison.

Even though the cave was packed with all manner of wonders and oddities, it didn't feel cluttered. There was plenty of space to walk about and explore. We wound our way through the various collections and artefacts, Evanna pausing occasionally to point out a particularly interesting piece — the charred stake on which Joan Of Arc was burnt, the pistol which had been used to shoot Lincoln, the very first wheel.

"Historians would go crazy in this place," I noted. "Does Mr Tiny ever bring anybody here?"

"Almost never," Evanna said. "This is his private sanctuary. I've only been here a handful of times myself. The exceptions are those he pulls out of the Lake of Souls. He has to bring them here to turn them into Little People."

I stopped when she said that. I'd had a sudden premonition. "Evanna…" I began, but she shook her head.

"Ask no more questions," she said. "Desmond will explain the rest to you. It won't be long now."

Minutes later we reached what felt like the centre of the cave. There was a small pool of green liquid, a pile of blue robes and, standing beside them, Mr Tiny. He was staring at me sourly through the lenses of his thick glasses.

"Well, well," he drawled, hooking his thumbs behind his braces. "If it isn't the young martyr himself. Meet anyone interesting in the Lake of Souls?"

"Ignore him," Evanna said out of the side of her mouth.

Mr Tiny waddled forward and stopped a few metres shy of me. His eyes seemed to dance with fire this close up. "If I'd known what a nuisance you were going to be, I'd never have spawned you," he hissed.

"Too late now," I jeered.

"No it isn't," he said. "I could go back and erase you from the past, make it so you never lived. The universe would replace you. Somebody else would become the youngest ever Vampire Prince, hunt for the Vampaneze Lord, etc. — but *you* would never have existed. Your soul wouldn't just be destroyed — it would be unmade completely."

"Father," Evanna said warningly, "you know you aren't going to do that."

"But I could!" Mr Tiny insisted.

"Yes," she tutted, "but you won't. We have an agreement. I've upheld my end. Now it's your turn."

Mr Tiny muttered something unpleasant, then forced a fake smile. "Very well. I'm a man of my word. Let's get on

160

with it. Darren, my woebegotten boy, get rid of that blanket and hop into the pool." He nodded at the green liquid.

"Why?" I asked stiffly.

"It's time to recast you."

A few minutes earlier, I wouldn't have known what he was talking about. But Evanna's hint had prepared me for this. "You want to turn me into a Little Person, don't you?" I said.

Mr Tiny's lips twitched. He glared at Evanna, but she shrugged innocently. "A right little know-it-all, aren't you?" he huffed, disgusted that I'd ruined his big surprise.

"How does it work?" I asked.

Mr Tiny crossed to the pool and crouched beside it. "This is the soup of creation," he said, running a finger through the thick green liquid. "It will become your blood, the fuel on which your new body runs. Your bones will be stripped bare when you step in. Your flesh, brain, organs and soul will dissolve. I shall mix the lot up and build a new body out of the mess." He grinned. "Those who've been through it tell me it's a most frightfully painful procedure, the worst they've ever known."

"What makes you think I'm going to do it?" I asked tightly. "I've seen how your Little People live, mindless, speechless, unable to remember their original identities, slaves to your whims, eating the flesh of dead animals — even humans! Why should I place myself under your spell like that?"

"No deal with my daughter if you don't," Mr Tiny said simply.

I shook my head stubbornly. I knew Evanna was trying to out-fox Mr Tiny, but I didn't see why this was necessary. How could I help bring about peace between the vampires and vampaneze by going through a load of pain and becoming a Little Person? It didn't make sense.

As if reading my thoughts, Evanna said softly, "This is for *you*, Darren. It has nothing to do with what is happening in the present, or the War of the Scars. This is your only hope of escaping the pull of the Lake of Souls and going to Paradise. You can live a full life as you are, in this waste world, and return to the Lake when you die. Or you can trust us and place yourself in our father's hands."

"I trust *you*," I said to Evanna, shooting an arch look at Mr Tiny.

"Oh, my boy, if you only knew how much that hurts," Mr Tiny said miserably, then laughed. "Enough of the dawdling. You either do this or you don't. But take heed, daughter — by making the offer, I've fulfilled my end of the bargain. If the boy refuses to accept your advice, on his head be it. I'll expect you to keep your word."

Evanna looked at me questioningly, not placing any pressure on me. I thought about it at length. I hated the idea of becoming a Little Person. It wasn't so much the pain as letting Mr Tiny become my master. And what if Evanna was lying? I'd said I trusted the witch, but thinking back, I realized there was precious little reason to trust her. She'd never betrayed her father before, or worked for the good of any individual. Why start now? What if this was a twisted scheme to ensnare me,

and she was in league with Mr Tiny, or had been tricked into doing his bidding? The whole thing stank of a trap.

But what other option had I? Give Evanna the cold shoulder, refuse to enter the pool, walk away? Even assuming Mr Tiny let me leave, and the monsters in the tunnel didn't catch me, what would I have to look forward to? A life lived in a world full of dragons, followed by eternity in the Lake of Souls, wasn't my idea of a good time! In the end I decided it was better to gamble and hope for the best.

"OK," I said reluctantly. "But there's one condition."

"You're in no position to set conditions," Mr Tiny growled.

"Maybe not," I agreed, "but I'm setting one anyway. I'll only do it if you guarantee me a free memory. I don't want to wind up like Harkat, not knowing who I was, obeying your orders because I've no free will of my own. I'm not sure what you have planned for me once I become a Little Person, but if it involves serving as one of your fog-brained slaves..."

"It doesn't," Mr Tiny interrupted. "I admit I quite like the idea of having you toady to me for a few million years or so, but my daughter was very precise when it came to the terms of our agreement. You won't be able to talk but that's the only restriction."

"Why won't I be able to talk?" I frowned.

"Because I'm sick of listening to you!" Mr Tiny barked. "Besides, you won't need to speak. Most of my Little People don't. Muteness hasn't harmed any of the others, and it won't harm you."

"OK," I muttered. I didn't like it, but I could see there was no point arguing. Stepping up to the edge of the pool, I shrugged off the blanket which the Little People had draped around me shortly after I emerged from the Lake of Souls. I stared into the dark green liquid. I couldn't see my reflection in it. "What—" I started to ask.

"No time for questions!" Mr Tiny barked and nudged me hard with an elbow. I teetered on the edge of the pool a moment, arms flailing, then splashed heavily into what felt like the sizzling fires of hell.

CHAPTER SEVENTEEN

Instant agony and burning. My flesh bubbled, then boiled away. I tried to scream but my lips and tongue had already come undone. My eyes and ears melted. No sensation except pain.

The liquid stripped my flesh from my bones, then set to work on the marrow within the bones. Next it burnt through to my inner organs, then ate me up from the inside out. Inside my head my brain sizzled like a knob of butter in a heated frying pan, and melted down just as quickly. My left arm — just bone now — tore loose from my body and floated away. It was soon followed by my lower right leg. Then I came apart completely, limbs, charred organs, tiny strips of flesh, bare pieces of bone. All that stayed constant was the pain, which hadn't lessened in the slightest.

In the midst of my suffering came a moment of spiritual calm. With whatever remained of my brain, I became aware of

a separation. There was another presence in the pool with me. At first I was confused, but then I realized it was the flicker of Sam Grest's soul which I'd carried within me since drinking his blood at the time of his death. Sam had passed on to Paradise many years ago, and now this final shard of his spirit was departing this world too. In my mind's eye a face formed in the liquid, young and carefree, smiling in spite of the torment, popping a pickled onion into his mouth. Sam winked at me. A ghostly hand saluted. Then he was gone and I was finally, totally alone.

Eventually the pain ceased. I'd dissolved completely. There were no pain sensors left to transmit feelings, and no brain cells to respond to them. A weird peace descended. I'd become one with the pool. My atoms had mixed with the liquid and the two were now one. I *was* the green liquid. I could sense the hollow bones from my body drifting to the bottom of the pool, where they settled.

Some time later hands – Mr Tiny's – were dunked in the liquid. He wiggled his fingers and a shiver ran up the memory of my spine. He picked up the bones from the floor – being careful to scrape up every single piece – and dumped them on the ground of the cave. The bones were covered in molecules of the liquid – molecules of *me* – and through them I felt Mr Tiny putting the bones together, snapping them into small pieces, melting some down, bending or twisting others, creating a frame entirely different to my previous form.

Mr Tiny worked on the body for hours. When he had all the bones in place, he packed them full with organs – brain,

heart, liver, kidneys — then covered them with clammy grey flesh, which he stitched together to hold the organs and bones in place. I'm not sure where the organs and flesh came from. Perhaps he grew them himself, but I think it more likely that he harvested them from other creatures — probably dead humans.

Mr Tiny finished with the eyes. I could feel him connecting the orbs up to my brain, fingers working at lightning-fast speed, with all the precision of the world's greatest surgeon. It was an incredibly artistic undertaking, one which even Dr Frankenstein would have struggled to match.

Once he'd finished with the body, he stuck his fingers back into the liquid of the pool. The fingers were cold this time, and grew colder by the second. The liquid began to condense, becoming thicker. There was no pain. It was just strange, like I was squeezing in upon myself.

Then, when the liquid was a fraction of the size it had been, with the texture of a thick milk shake, Mr Tiny removed his hands and tubes were inserted. There was a brief pause, then suction from the tubes, and I felt myself flowing through them, out of the pool and into ... what? ... not tubes like those which had been stuck into the pool, but similar...

Of course — *veins!* Mr Tiny had told me the liquid would serve as my fuel — my blood. I was leaving the confines of the pool for the fleshy limits of my new body.

I felt myself fill the gaps, forcing my way through the network of veins and arteries, making slow but sure progress.

When the liquid hit the brain and gradually seeped into it, absorbed by the cold grey cells, my bodily senses awoke. I became aware of my heartbeat first, slower and heavier than before. A tingle ran through my hands and feet, then up my newly crafted spine. I twitched my fingers and toes. Moved an arm slightly. Shook a leg softly. The limbs didn't respond as quickly as my old limbs had, but maybe that was just because I wasn't used to them yet.

Sound came next, a harsh roaring noise at first, which gradually died away to allow normal sounds through. But the sounds weren't as sharp as before —like all the Little People, my ears had been stitched within the skin of my head. Hearing was soon followed by a dim sense of vision — but no smell or sense or taste, since — again, in common with all of Mr Tiny's creations — I'd been created without a nose.

My vision improved as more and more blood was transferred to my new brain. The world looked different through these eyes. I had a wider field of view than before, since my eyes were rounder and bigger. I could see more, but through a slightly green haze, as though staring through a filter.

The first sight I fixed on was Mr Tiny, still working on my body, monitoring the tubes, applying a few final stitches, testing my reflexes. He had the look of a loving, devoted parent.

Next I saw Evanna, keeping a close eye on her father, making sure he didn't pull any tricks. She handed him needles and string from time to time, like a nurse. Her

expression was a mixture of suspicion and pride. Evanna knew all of Mr Tiny's shortcomings, but she was still his daughter, and I could see now that despite her misgivings she loved him — in a way.

Eventually the transfer was complete. Mr Tiny removed the tubes — they'd been stuck in all over, my arms, legs, torso, head — and sealed the holes, stitching them shut. He gave me a final once-over, fixed a spot where I was leaking, did some fine-tuning at the corners of my eyes, checked my heartbeat. Then he stepped back and grunted. "Another perfect creation, even if I do say so myself."

"Sit up, Darren," Evanna said. "But slowly. Don't rush."

I did as she said. A wave of dizziness swept over me when I raised my head, but it soon passed. I pushed up gradually, pausing every time I felt dizzy or sick. Finally I was sitting upright. I was able to study my body from here, its broad hands and feet, thick limbs, dull grey skin. I noted that, like Harkat, I was neither fully male nor female, but something in between. If I could have blushed, I would have!

"Stand," Mr Tiny said, spitting on his hands and rubbing them together, using his spit to wash himself. "Walk about. Test yourself. It won't take you long to get used to your new shape. I design my Little People to go into immediate action."

With Evanna's help I stood. I weaved unsteadily on my feet, but soon found my balance. I was much stouter and heavier than before. As I'd noticed when lying down, my limbs didn't react as quickly as they once did. I had to focus hard to make my fingers curl or to edge a foot forward.

"Easy," Evanna said as I tried to turn and almost fell back into the now empty pool. She caught and held me until I was steady again. "Slowly, one bit at a time. It won't take long — just five or ten minutes." I tried to ask a question but no sound came out. "You cannot speak," Evanna reminded me. "You do not have a tongue."

I slowly raised a chunky grey arm and pointed a finger at my head. I stared at Evanna with my large green eyes, trying to transmit my question mentally. "You want to know if we can communicate telepathically," Evanna said. I nodded my neck-less head. "No. You have not been designed with that ability."

"You're a basic model," Mr Tiny chipped in. "You won't be around very long, so it would have been pointless to kit you out with a bunch of unnecessary features. You can think and move, which is all you need to do."

I spent the next several minutes getting to know my new body. There were no mirrors nearby, but I spotted a large silver tray in which I could study my reflection. Hobbling over to it, I ran a critical green eye over myself. I was maybe four and a half feet tall and three feet wide. My stitches weren't as neat as Harkat's, and my eyes weren't exactly level, but otherwise we didn't look too different. When I opened my mouth I saw that not only did I lack a tongue, but teeth too. I turned carefully and looked at Evanna, pointing to my gums.

"You will not have to eat," she said.

"You won't be alive long enough to bother with food," Mr Tiny added.

My new stomach clenched when he said that. I'd been tricked! It *had* been a trap, and I'd fallen for it! If I could have spoken, I'd have cursed myself for being such a fool.

But then, as I looked for a decent weapon to defend myself with, Evanna smiled positively. "Remember why we did this, Darren — to free your soul. We could have given you a new, full life as a Little Person, but that would have complicated matters. It's easier this way. You have to trust us."

I didn't feel very trusting, but the deed was done. And Evanna didn't look like somebody who'd been tricked, or who was gloating from having tricked me. Putting fears of betrayal and thoughts of fighting aside, I decided to stay calm and see what the pair planned next for me.

Evanna picked up the pile of blue robes which had been lying near to the pool and came over with them. "I prepared these for you earlier," she said. "Let me help you put them on." I was going to signal that I could dress myself, but Evanna flashed me a look which made me stop. Her back was to Mr Tiny, who was examining the remains of the pool. While his attention was diverted, she slipped the robes on over my head and arms. I realized there were several objects inside the robes, stitched into the lining.

Evanna locked gazes with me and a secret understanding passed between us — she was telling me to act as if the objects weren't there. She was up to something which she didn't want Mr Tiny to know about. I'd no idea what she might have hidden in the robes, but it must be important. Once the robes were on I kept my arms out by my sides and

tried not to think about the secret packages I was carrying, in case I accidentally tipped off Mr Tiny.

Evanna gave me a final once-over, then called out, "He is ready, father."

Mr Tiny waddled across. He looked me up and down, sniffed snootily, then thrust a small mask at me. "You'd better put that on," he said. "You probably won't need it, but we might as well be safe as sorry."

As I strapped on the mask, Mr Tiny bent and drew a line in the earth of the cave floor. He stepped back from it and clutched his heart-shaped watch. The timepiece began to glow, and soon his hand and face were glowing too. Moments later a doorway grew out of the line in the ground, sliding upwards to its full height. It was an open doorway. The space between the jambs was a grey sheen. I'd been through a portal like this before, when Mr Tiny had sent Harkat and me into what would have been the future (what still might be, if Evanna's plan failed).

When the doorway was complete, Mr Tiny nodded his head at it. "Time to go."

My eyes flicked to Evanna — was she coming with me? "No," she said in answer to my unasked question. "I will return to the present through a separate door. This one goes further back." She stooped so we were at the same height. "This is goodbye, Darren. I don't imagine I'll ever make the journey to Paradise — I don't think it's intended for the likes of me — so we'll probably never see each other again."

"Maybe he won't go to Paradise either," Mr Tiny sneered. "Perhaps his soul is meant for the great fires beneath."

Evanna smiled. "We don't know all the secrets of the beyond, but we've never seen any evidence of a hell. The Lake of Souls seems to be the only place where the damned end up, and if our plan works, you won't go back there. Don't worry — your soul will fly free."

"Come on," Mr Tiny snapped. "I'm bored with him. Time to kick him out of our lives, once and for all." He pushed Evanna aside, grabbed the shoulder of my robes and hauled me to the doorway. "Don't get any smart ideas back there," he growled. "You can't change the past, so don't go trying. Just do what you have to — tough luck if you can't work out what that is — and let the universe take care of the rest."

I turned my face towards him, not sure what he meant, wanting more answers. But Mr Tiny ignored me, raised a wellington-clad foot, then — without a word of farewell, as though I was a stranger who meant nothing to him — booted me clean through the door and back to a date with history.

CHAPTER EIGHTEEN

"Ladies and gentlemen, welcome to the Cirque Du Freak, home of the world's most remarkable human beings."

I had no eyelids, so I couldn't blink, but beneath my mask my jaw dropped a hundred miles. I was in the wings of a large theatre, staring out at a stage and the unmistakable figure of the dead Hibernius Tall. Except he wasn't dead. He was very much alive, and in the middle of introducing one of the fabled Cirque Du Freak performances.

"We present acts both frightening and bizarre, acts you can find nowhere else in the world. Those who are easily scared should leave now. I'm sure there are people who..."

Two beautiful women stepped up next to me and prepared to go on. They were tugging at their glittering costumes, making sure they fit right. I recognized the women — Davina and Shirley. They'd been part of the Cirque Du Freak when I first joined, but had left after a few years to get jobs in the

ordinary world. The life of a travelling performer wasn't for everyone.

"... is unique. And none are harmless," Mr Tall finished, then walked off. Davina and Shirley moved forward and I saw where they were heading — the Wolf Man's cage, which stood uncovered in the middle of the stage. As they left, a Little Person took his place by my side. His face was hidden beneath the hood of his blue robes, but his head turned in my direction. There was a moment's pause, then he reached up and pulled my hood further over my face, so that my features were hidden too.

Mr Tall appeared by our side with the speed and silence for which he was once renowned. Without a word he handed each of us a needle and lots of orange string. The other Little Person stuck the needle and string inside his robes, so I did the same, not wanting to appear out of place.

Davina and Shirley had released the Wolf Man from his cage and were walking through the audience with him, letting people stroke the hairy man-beast. I studied the theatre more closely while they paraded the Wolf Man around. This was the old abandoned cinema theatre in my home town, where Steve had murdered Shancus, and where — many years earlier — I had first crossed paths with Mr Crepsley.

I was wondering why I'd been sent back here — I had a pretty good hunch — when there was a loud explosion. The Wolf Man went wild, as he often did at the start of an act — what looked like a mad outburst was actually carefully staged. Leaping upon a screaming woman, he bit one of her hands

off. In a flash, Mr Tall had left our side and reappeared next to the Wolf Man. He pulled him off the screaming woman, subdued him, then led him back to his cage, while Davina and Shirley did their best to calm down the crowd.

Mr Tall returned to the screaming woman, picked up her severed hand and whistled loudly. That was the signal for my fellow Little Person and me to advance. We ran over to Mr Tall, careful not to reveal our faces. Mr Tall sat the woman up and whispered to her. When she was quiet he sprinkled a sparkly pink powder on to her bleeding wrist and stuck the hand against it. He nodded to my companion and me. We pulled out our needles and string and started to stitch the hand back on to the wrist.

I felt light-headed while I stitched. This was the greatest sense of déjà vu I'd ever experienced! I knew what was coming next, every second of it. I'd been sent back into my past, to a night which had been etched unforgettably into my memory. All the times I'd prayed for the chance to come back and change the course of my future. And now, in the most unexpected of circumstances, here it was.

We finished stitching and returned backstage. I wanted to stand in the shadows again and watch the show — if I remembered correctly, Alexander Ribs would come on next, followed by Rhamus Twobellies — but my fellow Little Person was having none of it. He nudged me ahead of him, to the rear of the theatre, where a young Jekkus Flang was waiting. In later years Jekkus would become an accomplished knife-thrower, and even take part in the shows. But in this time he'd

only recently joined the circus, and was in charge of preparing the interval gift trays.

Jekkus handed each of us a tray packed with items such as rubber dolls of Alexander Ribs, clippings of the Wolf Man's hair, and chocolate nuts and bolts. He also gave us price tags for each item. He didn't speak to us — this was back in the time before Harkat Mulds, when everyone thought Little People were mute, mindless robots.

When Rhamus Twobellies stomped offstage, Jekkus sent us out into the audience to sell the gifts. We moved among the crowd, letting people study our wares and buy if they wished. My fellow Little Person took charge of the rear areas of the theatre, leaving me to handle the front rows. And so, a few minutes later, as I'd come to suspect I would, I came face to face with two young boys, the only children in the entire theatre. One was a wild child, the sort of kid who stole money from his mother and collected horror comics, who dreamt of being a vampire when he grew up. The other was a quiet, but in his own way equally mischievous boy, the kind who wouldn't think twice about stealing a vampire's spider.

"How much is the glass statue?" the impossibly young and innocent Steve Leopard asked, pointing to a statue on my tray which you could eat. Shakily, fighting to keep my hand steady, I showed him the price tag. "I can't read," Steve said. "Will you tell me how much it costs?"

I noted the look of surprise on Darren's — Charna's guts! — on *my* face. Steve had guessed straightaway that there was

something strange about the Little People, but I hadn't been so sharp. The young me had no idea why Steve was lying.

I shook my head quickly and moved on, leaving Steve to explain to my younger self why he'd pretended he couldn't read. If I'd been feeling light-headed earlier, I felt positively empty-headed now. It's a remarkable, earth-shattering thing to look into the eyes of a youthful you, to see yourself as you once were, young, foolish, gullible. I don't think anyone ever remembers what they were really like as kids. Adults think they do, but they don't. Photos and videos don't capture the real you, or bring back to life the person you used to be. You have to return to the past to do that.

We finished selling our wares and headed backstage to collect fresh trays full of new items, based on the next set of performers — Truska, Hans Hands, and then, appearing like a phantom out of the shadows of the night, Mr Crepsley and his performing tarantula, Madam Octa.

I couldn't miss Mr Crepsley's act. When Jekkus wasn't looking I crept forward and watched from the wings. My heart leapt into my mouth when my old friend and mentor walked on to the stage, startling in his red cloak with his white skin, orange crop of hair and trademark scar. Seeing him again, I wanted to rush out and throw my arms around him, tell him how much I missed him and how much he'd meant to me. I wanted to say that I loved him, that he'd been a second father to me. I wanted to joke with him about his stiff manner, his stunted sense of humour, his overly precious pride. I wanted to tell him how Steve had tricked him, and

gently wind him up for being taken in by the pretence and dying for no reason. I was sure he'd see the funny side of it once he stopped steaming!

But there could be no communication between us. Even if I'd had a tongue, Mr Crepsley wouldn't have known who I was. On this night he hadn't yet met the boy named Darren Shan. I was nobody to him.

So I stood where I was and watched. One final turn from the vampire who'd altered my life in so many ways. One last performance to savour, as he put Madam Octa through her paces and thrilled the crowd. I shivered when he first spoke – I'd forgotten how deep his voice was – then hung on his every word. The minutes passed slowly, but not slowly enough for me — I wanted it to last an age.

A Little Person led a goat on stage for Madam Octa to kill. It wasn't the Little Person who'd been with me in the audience — there were more than two of us here. Madam Octa killed the goat, then performed a series of tricks with Mr Crepsley, crawled over his body and face, pulsed in and out of his mouth, played with tiny cups and saucers. In the crowd, the young Darren Shan was falling in love with the spider — he thought she was amazing. In the wings, the older Darren regarded her sadly. I used to hate Madam Octa – I could trace all my troubles back to the eight-legged beast – but not any longer. None of it was her fault. It was destiny. All along, from the first moment of my being, it had been Des Tiny.

Mr Crepsley concluded his act and left the stage. He had to pass me to get off. As he approached, I thought again

about trying to communicate with him. I wasn't able to speak, but I could write. If I grabbed him and took him aside, scribbled a message, warned him to leave immediately, to get out now...

He passed.

I did nothing.

This wasn't the way. Mr Crepsley had no reason to trust me, and explaining the situation would have taken too much time — he was illiterate, so I'd have had to get somebody to read the note for him. It might also have been dangerous. If I'd told him about the Vampaneze Lord and all the rest, he might have tried to change the course of the future, to prevent the War of the Scars. Evanna had said it was impossible to change the past, but if Mr Crepsley — prompted by my warning — somehow managed to do so, he might free those terrible monsters which even Mr Tiny was afraid of. I couldn't take that risk.

"What are you doing here?" someone snapped behind me. It was Jekkus Flang. He poked me hard with a finger and pointed to my tray. "Get out there quick!" he growled.

I did as Jekkus ordered. I wanted to follow the same route as before, so that I could study myself and Steve again, but this time the other Little Person got there before me, so I had to trudge to the rear of the theatre and do the rounds there.

At the end of the interval Gertha Teeth took to the stage, to be followed by Sive and Seersa (the Twisting Twins) and finally Evra and his snake. I retreated to the rear of the theatre, not keen on the idea of seeing Evra again. Although

the snake-boy was one of my best friends, I couldn't forget the pain I'd put him through. It would have hurt too much to watch him perform, thinking about the agony and loss he was to later endure.

While the final trio of acts brought the show to a close, I turned my attention to the objects stitched into the lining of my robes. Time to find out what Evanna had sent me back with. Reaching underneath the heavy blue cloth, I found the first of the rectangular items and ripped it loose. When I saw what it was, I broke out into a wide toothless smile.

The sly old witch! I recalled what she'd told me on the way from the Lake of Souls to Mr Tiny's cave — although the past couldn't be changed, the people involved in major events could be replaced. Sending me back to this period in time was enough to free my soul, but Evanna had gone one step further, and made sure I was able to free my old self too. Mr Tiny knew about that. He didn't like it, but he'd accepted it.

However, working on the sly, unknown to her father, Evanna had presented me with something even more precious than personal freedom — something that would drive Des Tiny absolutely cuckoo when he found out how he'd been swindled!

I pulled all the other objects out, set them in order, then checked the most recent addition. I didn't find what I expected, but as I scanned through it, I saw what Evanna had done. I was tempted to flick to the rear and read the last few words, but then decided I'd be better off not knowing.

I heard screams from within the theatre — Evra's snake must have made its first appearance of the night. I didn't have

much time left. I slipped away before Jekkus Flang sought me out and burdened me with another tray. Exiting by the back door, I sneaked around and re-entered the cinema at the front. I walked down the long corridor to where an open door led to a staircase — the way up to the balcony.

I climbed a few steps, then set Evanna's gift down and waited. I thought about what to do with the objects — the *weapons*. Give them to the boy directly? No. If I did, he might use them to try to change the future. That wasn't allowed. But there must be a way to get them to him later, so that he could use them at the right time. Evanna wouldn't have given them to me if there wasn't.

It didn't take me long to figure it out. I was happier when I knew what to do with the gift, because it also meant I knew exactly what to do with young Darren.

The show ended and the audience members poured out of the theatre, eagerly discussing the show and marvelling aloud. Since the boys had been sitting near the front, they were two of the last to leave. I waited in silence, safe in the knowledge of what was to come.

Finally, a frightened young Darren opened the door to the stairway, slipped through, closed it behind him, and stood in the darkness, breathing heavily, heart pounding, waiting for everyone to file out of the theatre. I could see him in spite of the gloom — my large green eyes were almost as strong as a half-vampire's — but he had no idea I was there.

When the last sounds had faded, the boy came sloping up the stairs. He was heading for the balcony, to keep an eye on

his friend Steve and see that he came to no harm. If he made it up there, his fate would be sealed and he'd have to live the tormented life of a half-vampire. I had the power to change that. This, in addition to freedom from the Lake of Souls, was Evanna's gift to me — and the last part of the gift as far as Mr Tiny was aware.

As young Darren drew close, I launched myself at him, picked him up before he knew what was happening, and ran with him down the stairs. I burst through the door into the light of the corridor, then dumped him roughly on the floor. His face was a mask of terror.

"D-d-d-don't kill me!" he squealed, scrabbling backwards.

In answer I tore my hood back, then ripped off my mask, revealing my round, grey, stitched together face and huge gaping maw of a mouth. I thrust my head forward, leered and spread my arms. Darren screamed, lurched to his feet and stumbled for the exit. I pounded after him, making lots of noise, scraping the wall with my fingers. He flew out of the theatre when he got to the door, rolled down the steps, then picked himself up and ran for his life.

I stood on the front door step, watching my younger self flee for safety. I was smiling softly. I'd stand guard here to be certain, but I was sure he wouldn't return. He'd run straight home, leap beneath the bed covers and shiver himself to sleep. In the morning, not having seen what Steve got up to, he'd phone to find out if his friend was OK. Not knowing who Mr Crepsley was, he'd have no reason to fear Steve, and Steve would have no reason to be suspicious of Darren. Their

friendship would resume its natural course and, although I was sure they'd talk often about their trip to the Cirque Du Freak, Darren wouldn't go back to steal the spider, and Steve would never reveal the truth about Mr Crepsley.

I retreated from the entrance and climbed the steps up to the balcony. There, I watched as Steve had his showdown with Mr Crepsley. He asked to be the vampire's assistant. Mr Crepsley tested his blood, then rejected him on the grounds that he was evil. Steve left in a rage, swearing revenge on the vampire.

Would Steve still seek out that revenge now that his main nemesis — me — had been removed from the equation? When he grew up, would his path still take him away from normal life and towards the vampaneze? Was he destined to live his life as he had the first time round, only with a different enemy instead of Darren Shan? Or would the universe replace Steve, like me, with somebody else?

I had no way of knowing. Only time would tell, and I wouldn't be around long enough to see the story through to its end. I'd had my innings, and they were just about over. It was time for me to step back, draw a line under my life, and make my final farewell.

But first — one last cunning attempt to wreck the plans of Desmond Tiny!

CHAPTER NINETEEN

The key events of the past can't be changed, but the people in it can. Evanna had told me that if she went back and killed Adolf Hitler, the universe would replace him with somebody else. The major events of World War II would unfold exactly as they were meant to, only with a different figurehead at the helm. This would obviously create a number of temporal discrepancies, but nothing the higher force of the universe couldn't set right.

While I couldn't alter the course of my history, I *could* remove myself from it. Which was what I'd done by scaring off young Darren. The events of my life would unravel the same way they had before. A child would be blooded, travel to Vampire Mountain, unmask Kurda Smahlt, become a Vampire Prince, then hunt for the Vampaneze Lord. But it wouldn't be the boy I'd frightened off tonight. Somebody else — some other child — would have to fill the shoes of Darren Shan.

I felt bad about putting another kid through the tough trials of my life, but at least I knew that in the end – in death – he would be triumphant. The person who replaced me would follow in my footsteps, kill the Vampaneze Lord and die in the battle, and out of that death peace would hopefully grow. Since the child wouldn't be responsible for his actions, his soul should go straight to Paradise when he died — the universe, I hoped, was harsh but fair.

And maybe it wouldn't even be a boy. Perhaps I'd be replaced by a girl! The new Darren Shan didn't have to be an exact replica of the old one. He or she could come from any background or country. All the child needed was a strong sense of curiosity and a slightly disobedient streak. Anyone with the nerve to sneak out late at night and go see the Cirque Du Freak had the potential to take my place as Mr Crepsley's assistant.

Since my part would change, the parts of others could change too. Maybe another girl – or boy – would fill Debbie's role, and somebody else could be Sam Grest. Perhaps Gavner Purl wouldn't be the vampire who was killed by Kurda, and even Steve could be replaced by another. Maybe Mr Crepsley wouldn't be the one to die in the Cavern of Retribution, and would live to be a vampire of ancient years and wisdom, like his mentor, Seba Nile. Many of the parts in the story – the saga – of my life might be up for grabs now that the central character had been changed.

But that was all wild speculation. What I did know for certain was that the boy I'd once been would now lead a

normal life. He'd go to school, grow up like anybody else, get a job, maybe raise a family of his own one day. All the things the original Darren Shan had missed out on, the new Darren would enjoy. I'd given him his freedom — his humanity. I could only pray to the gods of the vampires that he made the most of it.

The objects stitched into the lining of my robes were my diaries. I'd kept a diary just about as long as I could remember. I'd recorded everything in it — my trip to the Cirque Du Freak, becoming Mr Crepsley's assistant, my time in Vampire Mountain, the War of the Scars and hunt for the Vampaneze Lord, right up to that final night when I'd had my fatal last run-in with Steve. It was all there, everything important from my life, along with lots of trivial stuff too.

Evanna had brought the diary up to date. She must have taken it from the house where Debbie and Alice were based, then described all that had happened on that blood-drenched night, the showdown with Steve and my death. She'd then briefly outlined my long years of mental suffering in the Lake of Souls, followed by a more detailed account of my rescue and rebirth as a Little Person. She'd even gone beyond that, and told what happened next, my return, the way I'd scared the original Darren away, and…

I don't know what she wrote in the last few pages. I didn't read that far. I'd rather find out for myself what my final actions and thoughts are — not read about them in a book!

*   *   *

After Steve left and Mr Crepsley retired to the cellar where his coffin was stored, I went in search of Mr Tall. I found him in his van, going over the night's receipts. He used to do that regularly. I think he enjoyed the normality of the simple task. I knocked on the door and waited for him to answer.

"What do you want?" he asked suspiciously when he saw me. Mr Tall wasn't used to being surprised, certainly not by a Little Person.

I held the diaries out to him. He looked at them warily, not touching them.

"Is this a message from Desmond?" he asked. I shook my neck-less head. "Then what...?" His eyes widened. "No!" he gasped. "It can't be!" He pushed my hood back – I'd replaced it after I'd scared off the young me – and studied my features fiercely.

After a while Mr Tall's look of concern was replaced by a smile. "Is this my sister's work?" he enquired. I nodded my chunky head a fraction. "I never thought she'd get involved," he murmured. "I imagine there's more to it than just freeing your soul, but I won't press you for information — better for all concerned if I don't know."

I raised the diaries, wanting him to take them, but Mr Tall still didn't touch them. "I'm not sure I understand," he said.

I pointed to the name – Darren Shan – scrawled across the front of the top copy, then to myself. Opening it, I let him see the date and the first few lines, then flicked forward to where it described my visit to the Cirque Du Freak and what had

happened. When he'd read the part where I told about watching Steve from the balcony, I pointed up and shook my head hard.

"Oh," Mr Tall chuckled. "I see. Evanna not only saved your soul — she gave the old you his normal life back."

I smiled, pleased he finally understood. I closed the diary, tapped the cover, then offered the books to him again. This time he took them.

"Your plan is clear to me now," he said softly. "You want the world to know of this, but not yet. You are right — to reveal it now would be to risk unleashing the hounds of chaos. But if it's released later, around the time when you died, it could affect only the present and the future."

Mr Tall's hands moved very swiftly and the diaries disappeared. "I will keep them safe until the time is right," he said. "Then I will send them to … who? An author? A publisher? The person you have become?"

I nodded quickly when he said that.

"Very well," he said. "I cannot say what he will do with these — he might consider them a hoax, or not understand what you want of him — but I'll do as you request." He started to close the door, then paused. "In this time, of course, I do not know you, and now that you have removed yourself from your original timeline, I never shall. But I sense we were friends." He put out a hand and we shook. Mr Tall only very rarely shook hands. "Good luck to you, friend," he whispered. "Good luck to us all." Then he quickly broke contact and closed the door, leaving me to retire, find a nice quiet spot where I could be alone — and die.

I now know why Evanna commented on Mr Tiny not being a reader. He has nothing to do with books. He doesn't pay attention to novels or other works of fiction. If, many years from now, an adult Darren Shan comes along and publishes a series of books about vampires, Mr Tiny won't know about it. His attention will be focused elsewhere. The books will come out and be read, and even though vampires aren't avid readers, word will surely trickle back to them.

As the War of the Scars comes to a wary pause and leaders on both sides try to forge a new era of peace, my diaries will — with the luck of the vampires — hit book shops around the world. Vampires and vampaneze will be able to read my story (or have it read to them if they're illiterate). They'll discover more about Mr Tiny than they ever imagined. They'll see precisely how much of a meddler he really is, and learn of his plans for a desolate future world. Armed with that knowledge, and united by the birth of Evanna's children, I'm certain they'll band together and do all they can to stop him.

Mr Tall will send my diaries to the grown Darren Shan. I don't imagine he'll add any notes or instructions of his own — he dare not meddle with the past in that way. It's possible the adult me will dismiss the diaries, write them off as a bizarre con job, and do nothing with them. But knowing me the way I do (now *that* sounds weird!), I think, once he's read them, he'll take them at face value. I like to believe I always had an open mind.

If the adult me reads the diaries all the way to the end, and believes they're real, he'll know what to do. Rewrite them, fiddle with the names so as not to draw unwelcome attention to the real people involved, rework the facts into a story, cut out the duller entries, fictionalize it a bit, create an action-packed adventure. And then, when he's done all that — sell it! Find an agent and publisher. Pretend it's a work of fantasy. Get it published. Promote it hard. Sell it to as many countries as he can, to spread the word and increase the chances of the story capturing the attention of vampires and vampaneze.

Am I being realistic? There's a big difference between a diary and a novel. Will the human Darren Shan have the ability to draw readers in and spin a tale which keeps them hooked? Will he be able to write a series of novels strong enough to attract the attention of the children of the night? I don't know. I was pretty good at writing stories when I was younger, but there's no way of knowing what I'll be like when I grow up. Maybe I won't read any more. Maybe I won't want to or be able to write.

But I've got to hope for the best. Freed from his dark destiny, I've got to hope the young me keeps on reading and writing. If the luck of the vampires is really with me (with *us*) maybe that Darren will become a writer even before Mr Tall sends the package to him. That would be perfect, if he was already an author. He could put the story of my life out as just another of his imaginative works, then get on with writing his own stuff, and nobody — except those actually involved in the War of the Scars — would ever know the difference.

Maybe I'm just dreaming. But it *could* happen. I'm proof that stranger things have taken place. So I say: Go for it, Darren! Follow your dreams. Take your ideas and run with them. Work hard. Learn to write well. I'll be waiting for you up ahead if you do, with the weirdest, twistiest story you've ever heard. Words have the power to alter the future and change the world. I think, together, we can find the right words. I can even, now that I think about it, suggest a first line for the book, to start you out on the long and winding road, perhaps something along the lines of, "I've always been fascinated by spiders..."

CHAPTER TWENTY

I'm on the roof of the old cinema, lying on my back, studying the beautiful sky. Dawn is close. Thin clouds drift slowly across the lightening horizon. I can feel myself coming undone. It won't be much longer now.

I'm not one hundred per cent sure how Mr Tiny's resurrection process works, but I think I understand enough of it to know what's going on. Harkat was created from the remains of Kurda Smahlt. Mr Tiny took Kurda's corpse and used it to create a Little Person. He then returned Harkat to the past. Harkat and Kurda shouldn't have been able to exist simultaneously. A soul can't normally share two bodies at the same time. One should have given way for the other. As the original, Kurda had the automatic right to life, so Harkat's body should have started to unravel, as it did when Kurda was fished out of the Lake of Souls all those years later.

But it didn't. Harkat survived for several years in the same time zone as Kurda. That makes me assume that Mr Tiny has the power to protect his Little People, at least for a while, even if he sends them back to a time when their original forms are still alive.

But he didn't bother to protect *me* when he sent me back. So one of the bodies has to go — this one. But I'm not moaning. I'm OK with my brief spell as a Little Person. In fact, the shortness of this life is the whole point! It's how Evanna has freed me.

When Kurda was facing death for the second time, Mr Tiny told him that his spirit wouldn't return to the Lake — it would depart this realm. By dying now, my soul – like Kurda's – will fly immediately to Paradise. I suppose it's a bit like not passing "Go" on a Monopoly board and going straight to jail, except in this case "Go" is the Lake of Souls and "jail" is the afterlife.

I feel exceptionally light, as though I weigh almost nothing. The sensation is increasing by the moment. My body's fading away, dissolving. But not like in the green pool of liquid in Mr Tiny's cave. This is a gentle, painless dissolve, as though some great force is unstitching me, using a pair of magical knitting needles to pick my flesh and bones apart, strand by strand, knot by knot.

What will Paradise be like? I can't answer that one. I can't even hazard a guess. I imagine it's a timeless place, where the dead souls of every age mingle as one, renewing old friendships and making new acquaintances. Space

doesn't exist, not even bodies, just thoughts and imagination. But I have no proof of that. It's just what I picture it to be.

I summon what little energy I have left and raise a hand. I can see through the grey flesh now, through the muscles and bones, to the twinkle of the stars beyond. I smile and the corners of my lips continue stretching, off my face, becoming a limitless, endless smile.

My robes sag as the body beneath loses the ability to support them. Atoms rise from me like steam, thin tendrils at first, then a steady stream of shafts which are all the colours of the rainbow, my soul departing from every area of my body at once. The tendrils wrap around one another and shoot upwards, bound for the stars and realms beyond.

There's almost nothing left of me now. The robes collapse in on themselves completely. The last traces of my spirit hover above the robes and the roof. I think of my family, Debbie, Mr Crepsley, Steve, Mr Tiny, all those I've known, loved, feared and hated. My last thought, oddly, is of Madam Octa — I wonder if they have spiders in Paradise?

And now it's over. I'm finished with this world. My final few atoms rise at a speed faster than light, leaving the roof, the theatre, the town, the world, far, far behind. I'm heading for a new universe, new adventures, a new way of being. Farewell world! Goodbye Darren Shan! So long old friends and allies! This is it! The stars draw me towards them. Explosions of space and time. Breaking through the

barriers of the old reality. Coming apart, coming together, moving on. A breath on the lips of the universe. All things, all worlds, all lives. Everything at once and never. Mr Crepsley waiting. Laughter in the great beyond. I'm going … I'm … going … I'm … gone.

THE END

THE SAGA OF DARREN SHAN
MAY 8TH 1997 – MAY 19TH 2004

DARREN SHAN
LORD LOSS

BOOK ONE OF **THE DEMONATA**

When Grubbs Grady first encounters Lord Loss and his evil minions, he learns three things:

- 🌀 the world is vicious,
- 🌀 magic is possible,
- 🌀 demons are real.

He thinks that he will never again witness such a terrible night of death and darkness.

…He is wrong.

Turn over for a sneak preview…

RAT GUTS

→ Double history on a Wednesday afternoon — total nightmare! A few minutes ago, I would have said that I couldn't imagine anything worse. But when there's a knock at the door, and it opens, and I spot my Mum outside, I realise — life can always get worse.

When a parent turns up at school, unexpected, it means one of two things. Either somebody close to you has been seriously injured or died, or you're in trouble.

My immediate reaction — please don't let anybody be dead! I think of Dad, Gret, uncles, aunts, cousins. It could be any of them. Alive and kicking this morning. Now stiff and cold, tongue sticking out, a slab of dead meat just waiting to be cremated or buried. I remember Gran's funeral. The open coffin. Her shining flesh, having to kiss her forehead, the pain, the tears. Please don't let anyone be dead! Please! Please! Please! Ple—

Then I see Mum's face, white with rage, and I know she's here to punish, not comfort.

I groan, roll my eyes and mutter under my breath, "Bring on the corpses!"

→ The head's office. Me, Mum and Mr Donnellan. Mum's ranting and raving about cigarettes. I've been seen smoking behind the bike shed (the oldest cliché in the book!). She wants to know if the head's aware of this, of what the pupils in his school are getting up to.

I feel a bit sorry for Mr Donnellan. He has to sit there, looking like a schoolboy himself, shuffling his feet and saying he didn't know this was going on and he'll launch an investigation and put a quick end to it. Liar! Of course he knew. Every school has a smoking area. That's life. Teachers don't approve, but they turn a blind eye most of the time. Certain kids smoke — fact. Safer to have them smoking at school than sneaking off the grounds during breaks and at lunch.

Mum knows that too. She must! She was young once, like she's always reminding me. Kids were no different in Mum's time. If she stopped for a minute and thought back, she'd see what a bloody embarrassment she's being. I wouldn't mind her having a go at me at home, but you don't march into school and start laying down the law in the headmaster's office. She's out of order — big time.

But it's not like I can tell her, is it? I can't pipe up with, "Oi! Mother! You're disgracing us both, so shut yer trap!"

I smirk at the thought, and of course that's when Mum pauses for the briefest of moments and catches me. "What are you grinning at?" she roars, and then she's off again — I'm smoking myself into an early grave, the school's responsible, what sort of a freak show is Mr Donnellan running, la-di-la-di-la-di-bloody-la!

BAWR*ing*!

→ Her rant at school's nothing compared to the one I get at home. Screaming at the top of her lungs, blue bloody murder.

She's going to send me off to boarding school — no, military school! See how I like that, having to get up at dawn each morning and do a hundred press-ups before breakfast. How does *that* sound?

"Is breakfast a fry-up or some cereally, yoghurty crap?" is my response, and I know the second it's out of my stupid mouth that it's the wrong thing to say. This isn't the time for the famed Grubbs Grady brand of cutting-edge humour.

Cue the enraged Mum fireworks. Who do I think I am? Do I *know* how much they spend on me? What if I get kicked out of school? Then the clincher, the one Mum doesn't pull too often, which I know means there'll be hell to pay when she does: "Just wait till your father gets home!"

→ Dad's not as freaked out as Mum, but he's not happy. He tells me how disappointed he is. They've warned me so many times about the dangers of smoking, how it destroys people's lungs and gives them cancer.

"Smoking's dumb," he says. We're in the kitchen (I haven't been out of it since Mum dragged me home from school early, except to go to the toilet). "It's disgusting, antisocial and lethal. Why do it, Grubbs? I thought you had more sense."

I shrug wordlessly. What's there to say? They're being unfair. *Of course* smoking's dumb. *Of course* it gives you cancer. *Of course* I shouldn't be doing it. But my friends smoke. It's cool. You get to hang out with cool people at lunch and talk about cool things. But only if you smoke. You can't be *in* if

you're *out*. And they know that. Yet here they stand, acting all Gestapo, asking me to account for my actions.

"How long has he been smoking? That's what I want to know!" Mum's started referring to me in the third person since Dad arrived. I'm beneath direct mention.

"Yes," Dad says. "How long, Grubbs?"

"I dunno."

"Weeks? Months? Longer?"

"A few months maybe. But only a couple a day."

"If he says a couple, he means at least five or six," Mum snorts.

"No, I don't!" I shout. "I mean a couple!"

"Don't raise your voice to me!" Mum roars back.

"Easy," Dad begins, but Mum goes on as if he isn't there.

"Do you think it's clever? Filling your lungs with rubbish, killing yourself? We didn't bring you up to watch you give yourself cancer! We don't need this, certainly not at this time, not when —"

"Enough!" Dad shouts, and we both jump. Dad almost never shouts. He usually gets very quiet when he's angry. Now his face is red and he's glaring — but at both of us, not just me.

Mum coughs, as if she's ashamed of herself. She sits, brushes her hair back off her face and looks at me with wounded eyes. I hate it when she pulls a face like this. It's impossible to look at her straight or argue back.

"I want you to stop, Grubbs," Dad says, back in control now. "We're not going to punish you—" Mum starts to

object, but Dad silences her with a curt wave of his hand "—but I want your word that you'll stop. I know it won't be easy. I know your friends will give you a hard time. But this is important. Some things matter more than looking cool. Will you promise, Grubbs?" He pauses. "Of course, that's if you're *able* to quit…"

"Of course I'm able," I mutter. "I'm not addicted or anything."

"Then will you? For *your* sake — not ours?"

I shrug, trying to act like it's no big thing, like I was planning to stop anyway. "Sure, if you're going to make that much of a fuss about it," I yawn.

Dad smiles. Mum smiles. I smile.

Then Gret walks in the back door and she's smiling too — but it's an evil, big-sister-superior smile. "Have we sorted all our little problems out yet?" she asks, voice high and fake-innocent.

And I know instantly — Gret grassed me up to Mum! She found out that I was smoking and she told. The cow!

As she swishes past, beaming like an angel, I burn fiery holes in the back of her head with my eyes, and a single word echoes through my head like the sound of ungodly thunder…

Revenge!

→ I love rubbish dumps. You can find all sorts of disgusting stuff there. The perfect place to go browsing if you want to get even with your annoying traitor of a sister.

I climb over mounds of garbage and root through black bags and soggy cardboard boxes. I'm not sure exactly what I'm going to use, or in what fashion, so I wait for inspiration to strike. Then, in a small plastic bag, I find six dead rats, necks broken, just starting to rot. *Excellent!*

Look out, Gret — here I come!

→ Eating breakfast at the kitchen table. Radio turned down low. Listening to the noises upstairs. Trying not to giggle. Waiting for the outburst.

Gret's in her shower. She showers all the time, at least twice a day, before she goes to school and when she gets back. Sometimes she has one before going to bed too. I don't know why anybody would bother to keep themselves so clean. I reckon it's a form of madness.

Because she's so obsessed with showering, Mum and Dad gave her the *en suite* bedroom. They figured I wouldn't mind. And I don't. In fact, it's perfect. I wouldn't have been able to pull my trick if Gret didn't have her own shower, with its very own towel rack.

The shower goes off. Splatters, then drips, then silence. I tense with excitement. I know Gret's routines inside out. She always pulls her towel down off its rack *after* she's showered, not before. I can't hear her footsteps, but I imagine her taking the three or four steps to the towel rack. Reaching up. Pulling it down. Aaaaaaaaannnddd...

On cue — screams galore. A shocked, single scream to start. Then a volley of them, one running into another. I push

my bowl of soggy cornflakes aside and prepare myself for the biggest laugh of the year.

Mum and Dad are by the sink, discussing the day ahead. They go stiff when they hear the screams, then dash towards the stairs, which I can see from where I'm sitting.

Gret appears before they reach the stairs. Crashes out of her room, screaming, slapping bloody shreds from her arms, tearing them from her hair. She's covered in red. Towel clutched with one hand over her front — even terrified out of her wits, there's no way she's going to come down naked!

"What's wrong?" Mum shouts. "What's happening?"

"Blood!" Gret screams. "I'm covered in blood! I pulled the towel down! I..."

She stops. She's spotted me laughing. I'm doubled over. It's the funniest thing I've ever seen.

Mum turns and looks at me. Dad does too. They're speechless.

Gret picks a sticky, pink chunk out of her hair, slowly this time, and studies it. "What did you put on my towel?" she asks quietly.

"Rat guts!" I howl, pounding the table, crying with laughter. "I got... rats at the rubbish dump... chopped them up... and..." I almost get sick, I'm laughing so much.

Mum stares at me. Dad stares at me. Gret stares at me.

Then —

"You lousy son of a—!"

I don't catch the rest of the insult — Gret flies down the

stairs ahead of it. She drops her towel on the way. I don't have time to react to that before she's on me, slapping and scratching at my face.

"What's wrong, *Gretelda*?" I giggle, fending her off, calling her by the name she hates. She normally calls me Grubitsch in response, but she's too mad to think of it now.

"Scum!" she shrieks. Then she lunges at me sharply, grabs my jaw, jerks my mouth open and tries her hardest to stuff a handful of rat guts down my throat.

I stop laughing instantly — a mouthful of rotten rat guts wasn't part of the grand über-joke! "Get off!" I roar, lashing out wildly. Mum and Dad suddenly recover and shout at exactly the same time.

"Stop that!"

"Don't hit your sister!"

"She's a lunatic!" I gasp, pushing myself away from the steaming Gret, falling off my chair.

"He's an animal!" Gret sobs, picking more chunks of guts from her hair, wiping rat blood from her face. I realise she's crying — serious waterworks — and her face is as red as her long, straight hair. Not red from the blood — red from anger, shame and... *fear*?

Mum picks up the dropped towel, takes it to Gret, wraps it around her. Dad's just behind them, face as dark as death. Gret picks more strands and loops of rat guts from her hair, then howls with anguish.

"They're all over me!" she yells, then throws some of the guts at me. "You bloody little monster!"

"*You're* the one who's *bloody!*" I cackle. Gret dives for my throat.

"No more!" Dad doesn't raise his voice but his tone stops us dead.

Mum's staring at me with open disgust. Dad's shooting daggers. I sense that I'm the only one who sees the funny side of this.

"It was just a joke," I mutter defensively before the accusations fly.

"I hate you!" Gret hisses, then bursts into fresh tears and flees dramatically.

"Cal," Mum says to Dad, freezing me with an ice-cold glare. "Take Grubitsch in hand. I'm going up to try and comfort Gretelda." Mum always calls us by our given names. She's the one who picked them, and is the only person in the world who doesn't see how shudderingly awful they are.

Mum heads upstairs. Dad sighs, walks to the counter, tears off several sheets of kitchen paper and mops up some of the guts and streaks of blood from the floor. After a couple of silent minutes of this, as I lie uncertainly by my upturned chair, he turns his steely gaze on me. Lots of sharp lines around his mouth and eyes — the sign that he's *really* angry, even angrier than he was about me smoking.

"You shouldn't have done that," he says.

"It was funny," I mutter.

"No," he barks. "It wasn't."

"I didn't mean anything by it!" I cry. "She's done worse to me! She told Mum about me smoking — I know it was her!

And remember the time she melted my lead soldiers? And cut up my comics? And—"

"There are some things you should never do," Dad interrupts softly. "This was *wrong*. You invaded your sister's privacy, humiliated her, terrified her senseless. And the timing! You…" He pauses and ends with a fairly weak "…upset her greatly." He checks his watch. "Get ready for school. We'll discuss your punishment later."

I trudge upstairs miserably, unable to see what all the aggro is about. It was a great joke. I laughed for hours when I thought of it. And all that hard work — chopping the rats up, mixing in some water to keep them fresh and make them gooey, getting up early, sneaking into her bathroom while she was asleep, carefully putting the guts in place — wasted!

I pass Gret's bedroom and hear her crying pitifully. Mum's whispering softly to her. My stomach gets hard, the way it does when I know I've done something bad. I ignore it. "I don't care what they say," I grumble, kicking open the door to my room and tearing off my pyjamas. "It was a brilliant joke!"

→ Purgatory. Confined to my room after school for a month. A whole bloody *MONTH*! No TV, no computer, no comics, no books — except schoolbooks. Dad leaves my chess set in the room too — no fear my chess-mad parents would take *that* away from me! Chess is almost a religion in this house. Gret and I were reared on it. While other toddlers were being taught how to put jigsaws together, we were busy learning the ridiculous rules of chess.

I can come downstairs for meals, and bathroom visits are allowed, but otherwise I'm a prisoner. I can't even go out at the weekends.

In solitude, I call Gret every name under the moon the first night. Mum and Dad bear the brunt of my curses the next. After that I'm too miserable to blame anyone, so I sulk in moody silence and play chess against myself to pass the time.

They don't talk to me at meals. The three of them act like I'm not not there. Gret doesn't even glance at me spitefully and sneer, the way she usually does when I'm getting the doghouse treatment.

But what have I done that's so bad? OK, it was a crude joke and I knew I'd get into trouble — but their reactions are waaaaaaay over the top. If I'd done something to embarrass Gret in public, fair enough, I'd take what was coming. But this was a private joke, just between us. They shouldn't be making such a song and dance about it.

Dad's words echo back to me — "And the timing!" I think about them a lot. And Mum's, when she was having a go at me about smoking, just before Dad cut her short — "We don't need this, certainly not at this time, not when—"

What did they mean? What were they talking about? What does the timing have to do with anything?

Something stinks here — and it's not just rat guts.

THE RAILWAY CHILDREN

A classic story/A classic film

**E. Nesbit's original classic story capturing
all the excitement of childhood adventure.**

Roberta, Peter and Phyllis suddenly have to
move to the countryside with their mother.
Living by a railway line they discover the
delights of trains and the characters who work
on the railway. Their lives are packed with
incidents, some dangerous and some just fun.
Underlying these experiences is the mystery of
their father – where is he and will
he ever reappear?

MATT'S MILLION

Andrew Norriss

Now a brilliant TV series

Dear Matthew, I have great pleasure in enclosing a cheque, made out to your name, for the sum of £1,227,309.87.

Matt Collins is eleven years old, and a millionaire! Suddenly he has the money to buy anything he wants – a mansion or even a Rolls-Royce. But being rich is more difficult than he thought.

THE BORROWERS

A novelization by Sherwood Smith
Based on the screenplay by Gavin Scott and
John Kamps
Inspired by the Borrowers *books written by*
Mary Norton

'The first rule of Borrowing is that a Borrower must never be seen.'

The race is on to stop the nasty lawyer Ocious P. Potter demolishing the Lenders' home. When young Arrietty Clock, a Borrower, is 'seen' by Peter Lender, a 'human bean', they join forces to stop the lawyer's plans.

Young Peter Lender helps the Borrower family to move house, but Arrietty and her brother, Peagreen, get separated from their parents and Pete. In the old house they see Mr Potter with Aunt Mary's will, but he sees them too. Can the house be saved? And will the Borrowers escape extinction?

AQUILA

Andrew Norriss

A brilliant new television series from the BBC

It's been buried underground for seventeen-hundred years.

It's been found by two boys bunking off a Geography field trip.

They have no idea where it came from, or what it does.

But Geoff's discovered that when you sit in it these little coloured lights come on, and if you push one of the big blue ones . . .

. . . Whoosh!

THE
DEMON HEADMASTER
STRIKES AGAIN

Gillian Cross

**The villainous genius is back at his desk!
He's back, and he's very, very dangerous.**

Dinah's father is headhunted for a new job at
the Biodiversity Research Centre – and who
should be the Director, but the Demon
Headmaster . . .

This time his lust for power sees him meddling
with evolution itself. The consequences of his
evil schemes will be deadly if the SPLAT gang
doesn't act – and fast.

THE
REVENGE OF THE
DEMON HEADMASTER

Gillian Cross

'Who's always right?'
'HUNKY PARKER!!!'

Hunkymania has hit the country. Suddenly everyone is desperate to buy disgusting Hunky T-shirts, trainers like pig's trotters and pigswill yoghurt.

Only Dinah isn't mesmerized by the craze. And when she and SPLAT set out to investigate, they come face to face with their old rival, the Demon Headmaster! It's a race against time. Can they stop him carrying out the final act of his demonic plan?

THE
PRIME MINISTER'S BRAIN

Gillian Cross

Octopus-s-s-s-s!

Everyone at school is playing the new
computer game, Octopus Dare – but only
Dinah is good enough to beat it.

As it begins to take hold of her, Dinah realizes
that the Octopus is trying to control her and the
other Brains in the Junior Computer Brain of
the Year Competition.

Why is it happening, and how is the Demon
Headmaster involved? And what is the reason
for wanting to get into the Prime Minister's
Brain? Find out in this exciting and
compulsive thriller.

THE
DEMON HEADMASTER

Gillian Cross

'I can see that you are not yet accustomed to our ways,' said the Headmaster. 'I hope you are not going to be a person who won't co-operate with me.'

On the first day at her new school, Dinah realizes something is horribly wrong. The children are strangely neat and well-behaved; they even work during playtime. What makes them behave this way? The answer is fear – but what is the secret of the Headmaster's control?